"What do you say? Ought we give in to my mother's tyranny and grant her this final request?"

His tone was as detached as he could manage, although the intense emotion that his own words sent lancing to his gut almost choked him. *Her final request.* After everything else was stripped away, that was the bare fact: Dorothea was dying, fading before his very eyes, and this was the last thing he could ever do for the woman who had been his last reason for living. There was no humor to be found at her meddling, only the unfillable gap her death would leave in his heart and his soul, a space that even with her final breaths she tried so ardently to mend for him. She had seen that same kindness in Grace—could it be they would truly save each other from their miserable fates?

It was only when his chest gave a wrench Spencer realized he had been holding his breath as he waited for Grace to reply. Her long lashes shielded her from looking directly at him, but nothing could hide the tremble of her lips as she spoke the only word necessary to send his heart slamming into his ribs.

"Yes."

Author Note

I'd had the vague outline of a plot simmering
for a while before I started writing *Scandalously
Wed to the Captain*, although—as is often the way—
the initial idea developed over time in directions I
hadn't expected. One of those offshoots came after I
stumbled across the history of London's Fleet Prison
in the course of my research—it was so interesting
there was no way it wasn't featuring in the book.

First built in 1197, Fleet was notorious for its
poor conditions and often rough treatment of its
unfortunate inhabitants. To find oneself housed
within its grim walls would spell the end of a good
reputation in society, as our heroine Grace Linwood
finds when her father is imprisoned, leaving her
with no choice but to bear the shame. For a young
woman in nineteenth-century England, losing her
social standing could mean the death of future
marriage prospects and a lifetime of relying on her
family to support her; no wonder avoiding scandal
was so important.

The captain in the title, Spencer Dauntsey, is equally
compromised, but far less inclined to care. Haunted
by shadows of his past, he is a man in dire need
of help from his unexpected new wife, who soon
finds she has much to contend with... I hope you'll
enjoy getting to know Grace and Spencer, and find
the glimpse into the world of Regency crime and
punishment as interesting as I did!

JOANNA JOHNSON

Scandalously Wed to the Captain

Recycling programs
for this product may
not exist in your area.

ISBN-13: 978-1-335-63550-1

Scandalously Wed to the Captain

Printed in U.S.A.

Joanna Johnson lives in a pretty Wiltshire village with her husband and as many books as she can sneak into the house. Being part of the Harlequin Historical family is a dream come true. She has always loved writing, starting at five years old with a series about a cat imaginatively named Cat, and she keeps a notebook in every handbag—just in case. In her spare time she likes finding new places to have a cream tea, stroking scruffy dogs and trying to remember where she left her glasses.

Books by Joanna Johnson

Harlequin Historical

The Marriage Rescue

Visit the Author Profile page
at Harlequin.com for more titles.

For my husband, family and friends—thank you for all the help and support along the way.

Chapter One

Grace Linwood stared out at the flat haze of the horizon until she could no longer tell if the tang of salt on her tongue was from the sea spray or her own tears.

How long she'd stood on the rain-lashed Cobb she couldn't say; only that when Henry Earls had pushed a piece of paper into her hand he had worn a halo of January sunlight and now that same sun was setting over the sea somewhere far beyond her reach.

The cries of gulls wheeling overhead mixed with the whistle of wind in her ears, its invisible hands lifting her cloak to snap behind her as though it were alive. Tiny needles of rain pricked at her cold cheeks, at the hands that held a letter between nerveless fingers, but Grace was numb to everything but the lead weight of despair that had settled behind her breastbone.

In light of your father's recent incarceration I must rescind my offer of marriage. The unfortunate reversal in your position and fortune render me unable to continue our engagement and I am

*certain you will be good enough to release me
from any obligation towards you.*

A hot tide of tears rose up, stinging her eyes alongside the salt spray thrown into her face. If only they
would stop coming. Surely there couldn't be many
left to fall, but each time she recalled Henry's callous
words pain twisted like a knife in her guts and a fresh
stream fell to mingle with the rain.

Perhaps some part of her should have questioned
why such a man would notice *her*, pursue *her* above
all the other young ladies of Lyme Regis, who danced
and sang and flirted as brazenly as they dared, bright
eyes fixed on whichever fortunate gentleman sparked
their interest.

I was never one of their number.

Too bookish, too quiet, too plain—it had seemed a
miracle when Henry singled her out less than a year
previously, asking her to partner him in a quadrille,
and the strange thrill that had torn a gasp from her lips
at the first touch of his hand on hers was something
she would never forget. Staring out across the barren
sea, Grace felt those same lips twist into a grimace of
pain no words could hope to capture as she recalled
another unforgettable moment: how he had left her
that afternoon, turning and walking away from her
for ever without so much as a backward glance at the
woman whose heart he had just ripped from her chest.
There could surely be no better proof his interest had
only ever stretched as far as her connections and fortune, and now she had neither there was nothing left
for him to covet.

The approach of a pair of older women hurrying along behind her, heads tucked down and cloaks clutched tightly to them, almost made Grace turn. Instead, she stepped closer to the Cobb's slippery edge as she heard their voices lower into rapid whispers as they passed by her without so much as a nod, the words barely audible above the keen of the wind, but their tone of malice unmistakable.

'…surprised she dare stir out of doors…a shameful business…'

'They claim he was wrongfully accused! They'll have to give up that fine house, and with so many daughters…'

'Bankrupt, I heard. Can't imagine her young man will stay much longer, or that any other is like to make advances now.'

Grace flinched as each barbed word pricked her with their poison. It was hard enough that everything they said was true without the bleak reality of her situation thrown into her face: with no money, no good name and the shame of an incarcerated father— wrongfully or otherwise—neither Grace nor her three younger sisters could hope for any man half as eligible as Henry to so much as glance in their direction ever again, let alone allow himself to be shackled to a wife so humbled to dust.

She drew her hand across her eyes, feeling the wet tracks that streaked her cheeks, and took a deep breath like fire in her lungs.

'Enough. Enough of this now.'

Crying would do nothing. No words would bring Henry back to her arms, nor any river of tears make him change his mind. Nothing could undo Papa's mistake, his willingness to see the best in others the sorry cause of his family's disgrace. Mama's face was already drawn with worry, deep lines creasing the formerly smooth plane of her forehead below blonde curls that matched Grace's own; she wouldn't add to her mother's burden by arriving home with trembling lips and eyes made red by weeping.

The thought of Mama's tired face sent a fresh shard lancing through Grace's insides and she pressed a cold hand to the place where her unhappiness lay like a rock in her stomach.

It wasn't just my future that was tied to Henry's love of me—or lack of it.

Freed from the expense of maintaining all four daughters, Mama might have been able to scrape together enough money to allow them to remain in their home. This was now surely but a fantasy and Grace felt herself sag in mute despair.

She closed her eyes, screwing them shut against the grey creep of dusk. The roar of the waves and plaintive cries of gulls called to her, curiously melancholy and mingling with her grief. She should leave this rain-sodden place and go home to face her poor mother's disappointment, she knew, but something inside her held her fast to the spot on which she had last seen Henry, where she had realised her only chance at happiness had slipped from her grasp like sand through her fingers.

The wind had picked up, its strength increasing with the final disappearance of the sun's feeble rays. It whipped about Grace like a pack of savage wolves, plucking at the ribbons on her bonnet and flattening her skirts against the chill flesh of her legs. With her eyes still tight shut and her mind reeling with anguish, perhaps it was inevitable that a particularly strong gust caught her off guard—all Grace knew was that one moment she was standing buffeted by the harsh coastal air, the next that her cloak had swirled round to unbalance her and then the world was tilting, the wet ground sliding beneath her feet.

Far too late she realised how close she stood to the edge. Her eyes flew wide as she grasped for something to save her, anything but the sickeningly empty air that surrounded her on all sides. Henry's letter slid from her outstretched hand, fluttering away like a small white bird to drift out across the sea—but there was nothing Grace could do as she felt her balance shift to follow it, her heart leaping up into her throat in a silent cry of terror as she began, for what felt like a tortuously slow eternity, to fall.

'Watch out!'

Grace's head snapped back so abruptly her neck screamed in pain, the movement forcing a cry from her gaping mouth. The tumbling waves surged below her, spray reaching for her with freezing fingers, but they came no closer and when her senses jolted back into order she became aware of a vice-like grip encircling the top of her arm, the strength of one large hand the only thing restraining her from a drop that with a sudden wave of nausea she realised could have killed her.

Her unseen saviour jerked her back from the Cobb's edge with a rough movement that made her wince. Still reeling, she turned to face him on shaking legs, her breath coming hard in short, painful pants as she struggled to control the frenzied racing of her heart. It took a moment for her to register the identity of the man whose countenance she peered up into, who returned her look with a scowl, but when her whirling mind finally managed to place his familiar features it was with a sharp punch of shock that she recalled his name.

Captain Spencer Dauntsey?

All the fright of a split second before faded into the background as she stared up into that face with frozen disbelief, weeks and months scrolling backwards in her memory until clicking to a halt on the last day she had seen him. Because it *had* to be him: eight years might have passed since she had watched in dismay as the identical, newly fatherless Dauntsey twins swung up on to their horses and turned for the long road to York, but there could be no mistaking that dark hair or the masculine cleft in a well-shaped chin. Only Spencer's nose ever made it possible to tell which brother was which; healed badly after a break, its crooked line had always struck Grace as strangely attractive. The irregularity gave him—in her eyes at least—an advantage over William, whose pristine profile somehow hadn't made her younger heart beat faster beneath skinny ribs in quite the same way. It had been a sad day for Grace's mother when Mrs Dauntsey left Lyme Regis following the death of her husband and headed north with her sons to settle near their first posting, as well as spelling the end of Grace's wistful fancies. The pair of matriarchs had kept up a warm correspondence afterwards, trading news of the twins' military progress and other triumphs, although for the past two years Mrs Linwood's letters had been unable to find their recipient and all attempts at tracing the Dauntseys had failed. In the absence of anything else to do Mrs Linwood hoped her old friend was well, wherever she was, and her two fine sons likewise…which had been Grace's hope, too, until evidence that was *not* the case stood in front of her, glowering and showing not the faintest glimmer of recognition for the girl he had last seen as a blushing child of thirteen, now before him a grown woman of twenty-one.

'What the devil were you thinking?' Her grudging rescuer glared down at her, a pair of dark eyebrows drawn tightly together above warm brown eyes—the colour of which was presently the only pleasant thing about them, so filled were they with unconcealed ire that it made Grace blink. 'To be so foolish as to stray that close to the edge in this weather? Don't you know the sea is particularly vicious in winter?'

Grace looked up at him, still not yet able to form a suitable response to his bewildering anger.

What is he doing here? When did he arrive?

It seemed so unbelievable that she hadn't heard even as much as a whisper to suggest the Dauntseys had returned to town after such a long time. She could hardly credit it, although a half second later she realised the unpleasant truth.

It's no wonder, really. Who would have told us? Nobody wishes to associate themselves with us any longer, or stop to speak—we have no friends left to tell us news.

It was just so jarring to see a shadow from the past so unexpectedly before her. His frown only deepened as he waited for her to find her tongue and she could have cursed herself—if she'd known any curses—for allowing her wits to escape her so completely. For any other man she could have formed a response immediately, she was sure—but *he* was an altogether different prospect.

The recollection of how her cheeks used to burn whenever Spencer as much as nodded in her direction returned now to prick at Grace's insides, a memory—given her current circumstances—she had no desire whatsoever to revisit. Spencer had seemed so much more mature when he had left to escort his grieving mother halfway across the country, an almost grown lad of seventeen, so it was hardly surprising Grace hadn't had a similar effect on *him*. It was all too easy to imagine what he would have seen as he'd happened to glance at her all those years ago: a mousy child with her nose stuck in a book, far too shy to return the easy smile the Dauntsey boys had for everyone they met. There was no trace of that trademark grin now, however, and the difference less than a decade had wrought in the first man who had ever made Grace blush was startling.

She gave a small shudder of apprehension at the glint of danger in his narrowed eye, more unfriendly than she had ever seen before and shocking in its coldness. It would have been difficult to think what to say anyway, having stumbled across an acquaintance she'd never thought to see again; the fact he had morphed from a laughing youth to this granite-faced man only made her confusion worse, rising to mingle horribly with the unhappy weight Henry had forced into her chest.

Managing to at last bully her brain into working, Grace swallowed down her unease. Spencer towered above her, his powerful build barely concealed by the expensive cut of his clothes, but there was a touch of something like reluctant concern in his expression where moments before there had been only displeasure and it was enough to help her gather her courage and attempt to muster a reply.

His mama and mine were such friends. Perhaps he might look less severe if I remind him who I am.

'I'm so grateful to you for your help, sir.' She peeped up at him from below the brim of her bonnet, gauging his reaction. He stared back, silent and stony-faced, and her courage faltered a little. 'Even if you don't recollect we were once acquainted.'

For a long moment Spencer said nothing, the silence between them stretching out unbroken but for the insistent patter of Grace's rapid pulse and the relentless crash of waves breaking over the rocks that could have been her demise. The pinch of his brows tightened, but still no light flickered in the flinty eyes as they swept from the top of Grace's sodden bonnet to her ruined shoes, their chilly scrutiny sending a curious shiver through her jangled nerves. His face was as handsome as ever, but the new hardness she saw in every line somewhat tempered the admiration she had felt as a young girl. Only Henry's features were burned into her mind like a brand, a face that with a pinch of pain she remembered she would never touch again.

'You're correct, madam. I don't.' Spencer answered flatly, as though barely able to summon any interest, and Grace wondered again at the change in the individual she remembered. *That* version of Spencer would never have been so brusque, but this one evidently was and she was left with no other option but to answer his indifference.

'My name is Grace Linwood. Your mother and mine

were close friends before you left for York—do you recall?' She tried to force a smile, but her cheeks felt rigid with cold and frank discomfort. 'It's so pleasant to see you returned to town! Are your mother and brother with you?'

Grace felt a flicker of relief as the first hint of recognition sparked in Spencer's expression, although it did nothing to thaw the coolness that remained.

'Miss Linwood. I didn't recognise you.' He gave a short nod, the closest thing to a greeting she might have expected from this strange new creature. 'My mother asked I bring her here in search of a warmer winter. Her health has not been good of late.'

Determinedly ignoring the mechanical tone of Spencer's voice, Grace persevered in her quest for a convincing smile. 'My mama will be so pleased to see her! And William? Will he be joining you later?'

It hardly seemed possible, but Spencer's face managed to draw into an even tighter mask that sent dismay skittering at the back of Grace's neck. Evidently she'd made some grave error, although what she had said to make the firm jaw clench she only realised once it was far too late.

'He would find that difficult. He's been dead these past two years.'

A cold trickle of dread crawled down Grace's spine, drenching her with wordless horror that made her lips part in a silent gasp.

William? Dead?

It was unthinkable and for a sickening moment Grace wondered how Spencer could make such a tasteless joke. Surely the idea of him without his matching other half impossible? Wherever one twin went the other had always been sure to follow, their identical mouths quirked into charismatic curves and long-legged strides so eye-catching it was hardly surprising Grace's cheeks had warmed with heat she hadn't understood. There was no way in the world one could exist without the other, yet the tension in Spencer's broad shoulders was the proof he did not lie.

Whatever could have happened?

She couldn't exactly recall the contents of Mrs Dauntsey's final letter, but surely there had been no mention of the tragedy that now made Grace's blood turn cold and dismay hold her tighter in its grip. All that life, all that animation and charm and potential snuffed out so mercilessly, leaving behind only its silent mirror image that brought intense pity roaring up from the very depths of Grace's soul.

'I'm so very sorry. I had no idea. We hadn't heard—of late my mother's letters were always returned and we had no way of knowing your new address...'

Grace's words tripped over themselves, disjointed and stumbling, although she might as well have been talking to herself for all the notice Spencer took. He waited for her to tail off into mortified nothingness beneath his hard gaze before changing the subject so abruptly there was no hope of return.

'Why are you out on the Cobb in this mire?' It was almost an accusation, delivered so tersely Grace nearly flinched. 'You could have been killed if you'd fallen. I would have thought you'd know better, living here all your life.'

The sudden veer into a completely different conversation caught Grace by surprise. Shock still echoed through her mind, the shattered image of the Dauntsey twins flickering as she peered up at the rain-flecked face of the only one left, and she answered with honesty she regretted at once when she felt pain crackle within her once again.

'I came to meet with my fiancé. Or the man who was my fiancé, until a few hours ago.'

Spencer raised an eyebrow, some shadow of enquiry in its dark line. 'Was?'

Grace nodded mutely, eyes downcast and fixed now on the expensive boots planted immovably before her. The agony that had run through her like a cruel river prior to Spencer's appearance returned with a vengeance, freezing into a shard of ice that lodged itself in the pit of her stomach to merge with the ache of sympathy and awful surprise that already circled.

'He requested I break our engagement, ostensibly on account of my father's situation. You'll have heard all about that, I'm sure.'

Tears threatened to gather at the corners of Grace's eyes again at the thought of poor Papa and she blinked them away, although she was unable to stop one from slipping down to mix with the cold rain spotting her cheeks. If Spencer saw he gave no sign, instead merely shrugging one huge shoulder in a movement Grace found oddly unsettling.

Had he always been so…broad? The youth she remembered had been agile and lithe, his movements fluid like those of a dancer. The intervening years had increased the width of shoulder beneath a green coat darkened by rain, so different now but not *un*appealing, and Grace wondered distantly why she should have noticed such a trivial thing.

'We arrived only three days ago. My mother was

intending to surprise yours with a visit, but has been too ill to leave the house and was in no fit state to receive guests. If her health had allowed, I imagine they would be gossiping together as we speak. As it is, we've heard no news and I've been in no hurry to chase any.'

Grace flexed her cold fingers, her mind too full of a complex jumble of thoughts and emotions to know how to reply. Horror for William's loss chased sympathy for Spencer that touched her heart, in turn surrounded by a dull pulse of unhappiness and shame.

If Spencer doesn't know the particulars of my family's situation, it won't be long until he does.

No doubt Henry had told all their formerly mutual acquaintances of his clever dodge at once and lapped up their congratulations at his narrow escape. The whispers that already chased Grace down every street would surely only increase now with such fascinating fuel to stoke the flames of delicious scandal higher—how long until the stares turned to nudges and her name was dragged lower than ever before? Nobody would care that as the daughter of a bankrupt and supposed criminal all Grace now had to remind her of her broken dreams was a wedding gown that would never see the light of day and a heart battered by the person she had hoped would always cherish it. She was reduced to an object of ridicule, to be pitied at best and scorned at worst, and in her knowledge of just how far she had fallen her anguish was complete.

I will never give my heart away again.

Grace made the vow fiercely, almost oblivious to the handsome man who watched her sorrow in silent thought. To trust in the love of another person was to make a woman weak, to expose her to the pain, humiliation and agony of rejection that now swept over her like a flood.

She had one thing to thank Henry for, at least: exposing the naivety within her that could not distinguish real regard from false and the sad lack of her own good judgement. His cruel lesson would enable her to guard against making the same mistake twice and never again allow a man to impose on her who had no interests in mind other than his own.

I will never give my heart away again. Not as long as I live.

Spencer turned up the collar of his coat, feeling the wet material beneath cold fingertips. Ideally he would be inside now, warm before the fire in his favourite armchair and his black hair curling slightly as it dried, but the woman in front of him showed little sign of noticing the rain that was soaking them both to the skin or the howl of a bleak wind coming from over the sea, her grey eyes fixed now on the sodden ground and an expression of suffering obscuring her petite features.

Little Grace Linwood. I would never have known her.

She was almost pretty as a grown woman, Spencer noted reluctantly, or would have been if she wasn't so frail-looking. Certainly her face was very pale, although ruddy spots of high colour showed she had recently been crying—for good reason, if her fiancé had so suddenly called off their engagement. A small part of him wondered why the man, whoever he was, might have acted so; something to do with her father, she'd said, although what she could have been alluding to he could only guess. Robert Linwood had been an

amiable sort if he remembered correctly. Surely there
was no reason to suspect he might have acted poorly?

Spencer looked down at Grace, weighing up how
to proceed. In honesty, consoling an emotional young
woman was at the very bottom of a list of ways he
would choose to spend an evening. Already the whisper of the new bottle of port awaiting his return to
his rooms called to him, its voice sweet in his ear,
promising to blot out the memories Miss Linwood had
unwittingly stirred with her innocent question about
William. The glass and decanter had been his trusted
companions these two years, ever since the day his
life had fallen so spectacularly apart, and there was
nothing more able to dim the echoes of the screams
that haunted him.

However…

He clenched his jaw to fight back an irritable sigh.
Something inside him, some relic of his moral Quaker
upbringing, would not allow him to leave a lady in
such obvious distress, especially the daughter of an
old family friend. Most of his mother's genteel teach-
ings had fallen by the wayside in the past couple of
years, beaten out of him by the grief and guilt never
now more than a half thought away—but some dim
gleam of propriety remained, to mutter that to abandon an unhappy woman in the growing darkness was
not altogether acceptable.

*Plus I'd never hear the end of it if Mother learned
I left one of her beloved Miss Linwoods to her fate.*

A swift scan about them showed no carriage waiting
for her and Spencer made up his mind with only a half-
suppressed outbreath of impatience. 'We are getting
steadily wetter and wetter by the minute. The house

I've taken is only a step away and a good deal closer than your own, if I recall. You're welcome to return with me and have my carriage deliver you home. My mother would be delighted to see you, I'm sure.'

He glanced down at her. She still avoided his gaze, blind eyes turned to the flooded ground beneath her feet, and Spencer's brows twitched together in brief discomfort as a sudden glimmer of sympathy flared inside him, appearing from nowhere to surprise him before retreating just as quickly behind his usually impenetrable cynicism. Where the stray spark of weakness had crept from he hardly knew, but it was enough to unsettle him, more than a little taken aback by the uncharacteristic feeling. It was probably because she looked so small standing there, a curiously lonely figure swamped by her large blue cloak, unconsciously radiating such vulnerability that Spencer had to fight back another flicker of pity with more than a touch of alarm. He frowned again, the sense of unease beginning to rise within him that he sought to extinguish with a gruff cough.

You're walking a fine line, Spencer, a little voice at the back of his mind piped up, a shade too disapprovingly for comfort. *You don't want to invite her in and yet you've gone too far to back away now. Was that offer truly necessary?*

Perhaps not. Perhaps he could have escaped without extending a helpful hand, always a hazardous action, but surely there could be no threat to his defences from this pitiful drowned rat of a woman who peered at him through the gloom and whose answer was uttered so low he had to stoop to catch it.

'I admit I'd rather not linger in this storm for very

much longer, and to see your mother again would be a rare treat. But—' She broke off, shame stealing into her expression it took him a moment to understand. 'I'm already remarked on quite enough. I can only imagine how much more people would talk if they were to see me alone, on the arm of a strange man...'

Spencer stared at her for a moment, taking in the flare of colour that gleamed on her pale cheeks.

That's her fear? That people might think badly of her? Evidently I'm not the only one behind on current events, although how she could have failed to have heard I don't know.

Grace was clearly ignorant of the mutters Spencer now drew whenever he stepped out of doors, tales of his behaviour the first night he had returned to Lyme Regis already spreading like wildfire throughout the town. A small flicker of guilt rose to nag at him at the memory of his mother's face that evening: concern, distress and—worst of all—disappointment crossing it as he had stumbled up the front steps, still with a bottle in his hand and his knuckles bruised and swollen. He should never have allowed himself to lose control of his temper, answering some drunkard's challenge in the tavern with his fists... If he'd only been able to douse the flames that leapt inside him he might have avoided ending his evening in a pointless brawl that now everybody—barring Grace, apparently—seemed to have heard of, sealing his reputation as uncouth, ungentlemanly and almost certainly dangerous. Society gossips hadn't given a fig that he'd acted in self-defence, exaggerating and expanding the story until it had become a lurid tale Spencer barely recognised.

'If anybody were to whisper, it wouldn't necessarily

be about you. You might consider pulling your bonnet a fraction to conceal your face, however, if you'd rather avoid my scandal as well as your own.'

The complete lack of understanding in Grace's eyes was almost touching, a welcome change from the judgement he saw in those that had looked up at him since his return. 'Why would they be whispering about you?'

That wasn't a question he particularly wanted to answer. 'I'm sure my mother will tell you soon enough. In the meantime, I suggest we leave at once. Watch your step on this wet ground.'

He slipped his hand beneath her elbow, feeling at once how she stiffened and seemed to curb the instinct to flinch away. It was hardly a surprising reaction, he supposed, given her prim propriety in stark contrast to his own unconventional manners, but there was still something decidedly unpleasant about her recoil from his fingertips.

Spencer felt once again that unwelcome sensation of *something* he couldn't explain, a dangerous intruder into the usual indifference he so carefully cultivated. The opinions of young women—and the rest of society—as to his looks, conduct or any other part of him were worth less than nothing, so there was no obvious reason for her apprehension to disturb him. It should have been a relief that she didn't giggle, or simper, or slide an appraising eye towards him when she thought he wasn't looking as so many ladies of her type did, or had in York at any rate; but then there was something that set her apart, some flicker of suffering in her face that spoke to him like for like and forced him to pay attention. He wanted to disregard her and her quiet pain as he would anyone else, yet with another flare of discomfort he found he couldn't turn away so easily.

His mother was the single person he usually felt it necessary to in any way consider and for her sake alone he did his best to conceal the melancholy that dogged him day and night that her rapidly failing health only added to. The one other he had held in such high regard was cold in his tomb and with him in the silence of the grave lay Spencer's ability to see the world with anything other than a weary disgust now so deep it was etched on to his soul.

With a grim scowl of effort he pushed aside the icy creep of guilt and grief that attempted to rise up within him, driving the images that threatened to accompany it back with savage force.

Now is not the time. Later, with a glass in your hand, is when you can do battle with the past.

The wraithlike, damnably *disturbing* Miss Linwood was still standing close to him, his hand still cupping the delicate bend of her slight arm, and he nodded at her with a forthrightness he only half felt.

'You needn't worry about propriety, truly. Anyone with sense is indoors, so we shouldn't be observed.'

Grace flicked a sideways glance up at him, apparently on the verge of saying something at the edge he knew she would have heard in his tone. Instead she dropped her eyes at once from his darkly questioning look, wincing with the swift turn of her aching neck, and allowed him to guide her away from the sea that could so easily have claimed her.

Chapter Two

If anybody had told her the strange turns this day was going to take, Grace thought dazedly as she hurried to keep up with Spencer's long strides, she wouldn't have got out of bed that morning. How she found herself lurching from her solitary heartbreak to being marched along by a silent Captain Spencer Dauntsey she still couldn't say, the firm—and distracting—pressure of his hand on her arm the only real proof she wasn't trapped in some hideous dream.

The idea that she could wake from this living nightmare was so tempting—to find herself in her own bed with Papa reading in his library and a note from Henry on the post tray—but a sudden slip of her foot on the wet cobbles jolted her from her fantasy, grim reality flooding back in to replace it, and Spencer's grip was the only thing that kept her from sprawling into the gutter. At least the storm meant the streets were deserted and nobody would see the highly inappropriate sight of her scurrying along after dark on the arm of a man who would apparently set tongues wagging about her even more than they were already.

'As I said. Mind your step.' Spencer didn't slow his pace, his head bent slightly against the chill of the wind that flung icy rain into their faces. 'We're almost there.'

Grace squinted through the gloom, attempting to ignore the altogether too-absorbing sensation of the hand on her elbow that sent strange prickles down her arm and made it oddly difficult to focus on anything else. They were drawing into a crescent of magnificent houses, tall against the dark menace of the stormy sky and set around a small park of landscaped trees that bent and shook with the wind through their branches. It was too dim to see clearly, but Grace thought she saw a curtain move slightly at the downstairs window of one of the largest houses—the next moment a grand front door was flung open and candlelight spilled down a set of iron-railed steps, illuminating a gravelled path that gleamed wetly in the orange glow. Spencer ushered her towards it and before she had a moment to consult her thoughts on the matter Grace found herself standing in a bright entrance hall, her head spinning and her soaking cloak dripping on to a polished parquet floor.

She looked about her, blinking as her eyes adjusted to the warm light thrown out by numerous candles. There were candelabras set around the space, their flames dancing in the draught that accompanied Grace and Spencer into the house, and painted portraits smiled stiffly down from the walls to watch as she hesitated, unsure of what to do next. She'd been too distracted to give much thought to anything other than getting out of the rain and now she stood in the unfamiliar territory of Spencer's luxurious house she felt a thrill of some strange anxiety flutter through her nerves.

He's a stranger, really. I barely recognise the man he's become.

Dimly she heard Spencer speaking to somebody behind her, too low for her to catch the words, but it would hardly have mattered if he had been shouting in her ear for all her attention was fixed on the uncertainty circling in her stomach. Perhaps to take his offer of sanctuary had been a mistake. He only seemed to have offered under some kind of duress and it was with mounting unease she waited for her unwilling host to decide what to do with her now she had followed the lion into its den.

'May I take your cloak and bonnet, ma'am?' A maid materialised as if from nowhere, making Grace jump with her murmured question.

'Have them dried, please, Thorne.' Spencer glanced at Grace as he removed his own soaking outer things and handed them to another waiting servant. 'It will take a short while to ready the carriage. You might want to sit before the fire, warm yourself a little.'

Grace turned away from him quickly, mumbling her thanks. The heavy rain had penetrated the costly material of Spencer's coat, dampening the shirt beneath; it clung to his broad frame a little too lovingly for comfort, the soft white outlining a landscape of muscle that made Grace's pulse skip more than a fraction faster. Alarm swept through her, wrinkling her brow: Spencer's masculine physicality, so different from Henry's slim elegance, surely shouldn't even *register* with her. It was an irrelevant detail, no more to be noticed than the fact he had two eyes and a nose on his stern face.

She frowned, trying to silence the troubling thought. After Henry's thoughtless rejection and the suffering that even now churned within her like a stormy sea, any strange reaction of her unconscious to Spencer's admittedly impressive musculature should be dismissed without hesitation. It was laughable, the very notion of Spencer provoking her interest, and surely only a nostalgic shadow of the partiality she'd felt for him as a girl—she could almost have smiled at her momentary folly if the unhappiness in her chest hadn't been weighing her down like a stone. She would never allow herself to surrender to such weakness again and certainly not in favour of a man so apparently aloof as Spencer now was. Not even she, with her admittedly poor record of good judgement, would ever be quite that foolish.

Her disquieting host was running his hand through his short crop of dark hair when Grace dared look towards him again, raindrops glinting in the candlelight as he brushed them from his head. Now they were away from the grey shadows of dusk Grace could see the warm brown of his eyes more clearly, and the fine lines, which on anybody else she would have suspected were caused by smiling, that bracketed them at the outer corners. Surely this dour man could never now get enough use out of a smile to make such lines, she thought privately as she watched him straighten his cravat, his brows drawn together in the near-permanent scowl she had already realised he seemed to wear unconsciously.

'Rivers will see you through to the parlour.' Spencer gestured to the servant who bobbed a neat curtsy beside him. 'If you'll excuse me.'

He turned abruptly to leave, moving towards one of the doors leading from the hall with long strides Grace couldn't help but follow with reluctant—but uncontrol-lable—interest. Before he could reach it, however, it opened quietly on well-oiled hinges and a woman appeared on the threshold.

At first Grace struggled to place her; until with an unpleasant start she realised the gaunt figure barely able to stand was Spencer's formerly vivacious mother. The change was so alarming Grace felt all words flee from her as she took in the drastic alteration in the woman she remembered: just like her son the difference from eight years ago was staggering, as though some malicious enchantment had been cast over the Dauntsey family to curse both their bodies and their minds.

'I thought I heard you arrive home.' Mrs Dauntsey came towards Spencer slowly, although her pale face broke into a smile that took the edge off her otherwise painfully fragile appearance. Her skin was so papery every line of bone was clear beneath its thin cover and her hair had the dull tinge Grace had seen only once before, on her grandmama after she had been taken ill with the bad chest that had killed her.

Spencer swiftly reached out a steadying hand as the newcomer swayed on her feet.

'Why are you up? Doctor Sharp was quite insistent you shouldn't be walking about.'

His tone changed abruptly from the brusque manner of moments before, now edged with an undercurrent of worry, but it wasn't just the transformation of his voice that made Grace blink in sudden confusion that grew to join that already holding court in her chest.

The frown had left his brow, his features smoothing out into a look of concern that wiped the displeasure from his face and enhanced the comeliness of his already eye-catching features tenfold. He looked younger, closer to his real age of twenty-five rather than the years his scowl advanced him to, and even the brutal edge his broken nose lent to his appearance diminished with the alteration in his expression.

Grace swallowed down a small sound of dismay as she took in the drastic change in the man who mere moments before had looked as though he might take on a bear and win. Far from shrugging off her unnerving reaction to the glowering Spencer, this new display of tenderness only made it return—with a displeasing vengeance. When he wasn't looking as though all the world was his enemy Spencer's face was as handsome as it had been as a youth, and when it softened further into palpable concern it was uncomfortably similar to the countenance that had so intrigued her all those years ago.

She twisted her fingers together, startled by the unconscious response of her body. Perhaps she had caught a chill, standing out on the slippery Cobb in a growing storm? There could no other cause for her cheeks to flush so in Spencer's presence, or for her heart to flutter at the gentleness with which he supported his mother—only silly girls with romantic fancies would think anything otherwise and thanks to Henry's cruelty she would never again be one of *those*.

'Please don't fuss.' Mrs Dauntsey swatted at Spencer with a feeble hand. 'I heard you come back and wanted to be sure you were well. Whatever can you have been thinking of, going walking in such—oh!' She broke off abruptly as she caught sight of Grace

standing awkwardly in Spencer's wake. 'I didn't realise you'd brought company with you.'

Grace dipped a respectful greeting, wishing with all
her heart she hadn't left a trail of dirty rainwater on her
unwitting hostess's pristine floor. Now Mrs Dauntsey's
attention was focused fully on her she saw some faint
traces of the woman she had once known: a refined
jaw and delicate nose giving an air of sophistication
despite the waxy sheen of her skin and mauve shadows beneath eyes that glittered with sudden wonder.

Spencer nodded in Grace's direction; a little unwillingly, she saw. 'Mother, I'm sure you recall—'

'Grace Linwood!' The stiff introduction was cut off
by a gasp of delight. 'I'd know you at once, although I
can scarce believe how you've grown!'

Her reaction was far more gratifying than Spencer's
had been, Grace thought privately as she felt a glimmer of warmth touch her otherwise chilly insides. His
mother had always been such a kind woman, it was a
relief to find at least *that* much unchanged.

'Mrs Dauntsey, it's so wonderful to see you again!'

There was a split-second of alarm as the older
woman almost overbalanced in her eagerness to grasp
Grace's hands and Grace had to lunge forward quite in-
elegantly to stop her from falling. Mrs Dauntsey peered
into her face, drinking in the sight of her with happiness so genuine it almost made Grace forget the tide of
varied emotions causing chaos in her stomach.

'Little Grace, quite the grown woman—and the very
image of your dear mama! I'd thought to surprise her
with my return to town, but as I'm sure you can see I've
been a trifle too ill to pay any calls. I should have sent

a note, I know, but I'm afraid I was determined to see her shocked face when I appeared on your doorstep!'

Spencer's mother laughed, a thin peal so unlike the hearty sound she might have made eight years ago before her husband had died and her sons had whisked her away, only one of them now left to stand behind her like an unsmiling guard. Spencer's formerly stern expression was already beginning to set in once again, obscuring the openness of moments before like the sun disappearing behind a cloud. Perhaps he only allowed himself one moment of levity a day, Grace just had time to wonder briefly—with another unpleasant jolt of recognition that brooding could still be very attractive indeed—before Mrs Dauntsey laid one skeletal hand on the damp sleeve of her gown.

'My dear, you look absolutely chilled to the bone. Won't you sit with me before the fire and take some tea?' She cocked her head, the sparkle never leaving the brown gaze so like the colour of her son's. Out of the corner of her eye Grace could have sworn she saw Spencer stiffen, but there didn't appear to be any question of refusal as the older woman gestured towards the door she had appeared through with a welcoming smile. 'Do come through to my sitting room. I can't tell you how delightful it is to see you again after all this time!'

Mrs Dauntsey cast a quick glance up at Spencer, apparently trying to read something in his face, although what she could have seen in the straight set of his lips Grace could only guess. Certainly to her there was nothing to be seen but faint displeasure, almost bordering on discomfort, and it was a relief to follow the slow progress of his mother away from his disturbing presence in the direction of her warm and comfortable sitting room.

'Do sit down.'

Mrs Dauntsey waved a hand at an enormous chair drawn up to the fire. The flames cast Grace's shadow long across the carpeted floor as she sank into it, her body leaning instinctively towards the hearth as though longing for its heat. She hadn't realised how cold she had been; distress had numbed her senses, and it was only when her fingers tingled painfully she saw the blueish hue that tinged them.

There was a bell on a table next to Mrs Dauntsey's overstuffed armchair and she lifted it with a small sound of effort.

'There. Tea will be along in a moment. If I remember correctly, you always liked it sweet with plenty of milk.'

For the first time since Henry had thrust his fateful letter into her hand Grace felt a tentative upward tug at her mouth. Despite her fragility and in startling contrast to her glowering son, Spencer's mother radiated warmth, her memory of the preferences of a child oddly touching.

'That's right. I'm afraid I still use rather too much honey.'

'I'm not sure there's any such thing.'

Mrs Dauntsey settled herself against her cushions and regarded Grace keenly, apparently hungry for every detail of her face and windswept hair.

'Let me begin by apologising for my silence the past couple of years.' Her voice held soft regret, real feeling that Grace knew was sincere. 'We moved around so often after we left Dorset, even living in Scotland for a time, that inevitably some of my effects were lost between houses. Among them was my writing case, containing—as I'm sure you've guessed—not only all the correspondence from your mother, but also my little book of addresses. I thought I'd committed yours to memory, but when my letters were returned as misdirected I realised I must have been mistaken.'

When she smiled again it was like a shaft of sunlight in the darkened room. 'But now I've returned to the place I spent my happiest years and the daughter of my dearest friend sits before me. So please—tell me everything I missed!'

Grace hesitated, taking in the vivid interest on the drawn face, but at a loss as to how to reply.

Where should I start? With my jilting, or Papa's imprisonment?

To her unending horror Grace felt a prickling behind her eyes, the distress of the past few hours rising again at the question. Mrs Dauntsey's kindness threatened to make a fresh river of tears flow, her innocent enquiry a stark reminder of Papa's plight and the dizzying turn Grace's life had taken for the worse—but wasn't that the truth for her hostess, too? She'd lost a son since she had been in the north and Spencer had lost his twin; and both of them were now so altered it would have been forgivable for even intimate acquaintances to hesitate. So much had happened in the intervening years, including Grace's new distrust in the word of a handsome man.

Some clue as to the workings of her mind must have shown on her face, for the smile left Mrs Dauntsey's lips at once, her brow creasing in concern as she leaned forward to look into Grace's downturned eyes.

'Grace? Why, dearest, you look so troubled. Is something amiss?'

Her expression was so worried that Grace had to bite her tongue to stop herself from breaking down. It would have taken a heart of stone to resist the pull of that readily offered sympathy: how many times had Mrs Dauntsey soothed Grace's bumped head or grazed elbow as a child, or passed her a sweet beneath the cover of a card table? Her kindness had always been apparent, but never more than at that moment, her obvious dismay tempting Grace to confess every secret sorrow she'd ever had.

A single impatient sigh from directly behind her chair made Grace start in surprise, the sudden movement once again sending a shard of agony through her injured neck.

He followed us in here?

She winced, twisting to peer at Spencer looming above her and looking for all the world as though she was the bane of his existence. He was close enough for her to have touched the soft fabric of his rich breeches and the very idea of such a scandalous—and tempting—action jolted Grace into speech.

'Did you say something?'

Spencer folded his arms across his broad chest, the movement causing his impressive biceps to bunch beneath the scant cover of his shirt in a way so damnably *interesting* Grace felt her face flush scarlet as she hastily turned away again. A flicker of that same sensation she had felt earlier sparked into being within her and she would have given anything for a glass of cold water with which to douse the alarming embers that glowed at his sudden proximity.

When he replied it was directed over her head as though she wasn't there at all. 'I found Miss Linwood out on the Cobb in a state of acute distress. As far as I can gather she's had to call off her engagement this evening, although I haven't the pleasure of knowing why.'

Grace gritted her teeth, resentment simmering alongside her dismay as the older woman's brows knitted together further.

As if I needed more proof his good nature has gone for ever, taking with it the boy I thought so highly of.

She could still sense Spencer standing at her back, in all likelihood scowling down at her from his great height, and the knowledge of his unseen closeness stirred the fine hairs of her neck. Irritation at his meddling coursed through her, although another stream of something close to a kind of breathless apprehension mingled with it. His voice was deep and expressionless, yet it possessed an educated cadence so pleasing that even in the depths of her annoyance Grace felt herself give a small shudder when he spoke.

It has to be the loss of William. What else could change him so drastically for the worse?

From his stance behind her chair—*his* chair, in fact—Spencer couldn't see the set of his silent guest's expression, although if the stiffness of her shoulders was anything to go by it probably wasn't one of delight. Looking down at her from behind only afforded him a view of her blonde ringlets, one escaping from a cluster at the back of her head to snake at the base of her slender neck, but it was enough to make him avert his eyes in sudden discomfort. There was something so vulnerable about that nape, so delicate as it rose out of her lace-trimmed collar, that was deeply unexpected and just as deeply disturbing. It roused something in him, some glint of the weakness he had determinedly suppressed for so long it was a wonder to discover he could still feel it.

Be careful. A sense of danger nagged at the back of his mind, a clear warning against the perturbing turn this sorry business was taking. It must have been the suffering on her face that called to him, holding a mirror up to the pain that so often clouded his own features; but that was not a good enough reason to allow any assault on his restraint and it was with a frown he took in her words as she began to speak.

'Thank you, Spencer, for that succinct summary of my misfortune.'

Spencer raised an eyebrow at her frigid tone, but held his tongue. The distress written on Grace's features had been clear to see and his discomfort grew as he realised how much he disliked the memory. It might even have stirred the remnants of his long-buried compassion had he not been so resolutely steeling himself against the flash of momentary weakness the despondent Miss Linwood somehow already managed to provoke in him.

If Will was still alive, he would have her laughing already. He always knew how to make a woman smile. Then again...

Hadn't that been the very thing that had come between them, in the end?

Spencer gritted his teeth in instinctive dismay as the question arose, but nothing could stop the relentless march of his thoughts down the one path he would have given anything to avoid.

Not this again. Not now.

He could hardly even recall her face: Miss Constance Strong, the lively, captivating woman both twins had loved—to their everlasting detriment. The image of her beauty was eclipsed by other memories, of how he and the man he'd loved as a second self had argued over her, the only thing they had ever been unable to share. If only he'd let Will win, had stepped back and stopped their quarrel before it was too late—but that was a pointless wish and one that did nothing to erase the guilt that had swirled inside him like an icy storm ever since.

You can't allow yourself to walk that path again. If you hadn't been so foolish as to lose your heart to a woman you might still have a brother...not that any woman would want you now.

Alike in so many ways, all traces of the cheerful nature the twins had once shared were now gone for ever: Will's disappearing in the cold finality of death and Spencer's snuffed out like a candle beneath the unbearable weight of the shame and remorse that had haunted him since that terrible day two years before. Some pale shadow of his better self lingered for his mother's sake, a last echo of the person he had once been before tragedy had made him retreat from the world to drown his sorrows in drink, but even that phantom would fade as soon as her sickness overcame her. When that happened, his transformation into a mere husk of a man would be complete.

His mother's voice jolted him from his maudlin train of thought. 'Is that true? You've had to call off your engagement?'

Even from behind Spencer saw the way Grace's

throat contracted in a dry swallow, the slight curve of her cheek visible to him tight with strain. If she was battling the urge to break down and air her soul, she was putting up a good fight, he thought with a gleam of grudging respect, but nothing could overcome the kind probing of his mother and he at last heard a shuddering sigh escape her that lifted the intriguingly slight shoulders beneath her gown.

'I...'

Grace stopped at once as the sitting-room door opened and a maid bearing a tea tray appeared, lapsing into tense silence she didn't break even when the servant retreated once again.

In the ensuing quiet Spencer stepped smartly round Grace's chair to stand closer to the hearth and table laid out before it. A quick glance in her direction now gave him his first uninterrupted view of her face since she had sat down and he clenched his jaw in sudden horror at the jolt that leapt within him at the sight.

Her lips trembled in obvious emotion and her hands were clasped together tightly on her knees, one finger rubbing at her knuckles in absent-minded distress. She looked so plainly unhappy, so heartbreakingly tiny in his enveloping chair nestled among the cushions like a lost creature in need of a protective arm. The shocking urge to offer that arm was suddenly overwhelming, coming apparently from nowhere, and Spencer shoved it back from the forefront of his mind.

What are you thinking of?

He bent his head lower above the tray, ostensibly stirring the tea leaves while his mind flooded with confusion and the shrill peals of alarm bells rang in his ears.

What is the meaning of this?

It was years since he had resolved to separate himself from the world and all the people in it—both for their sake and his own. Nothing good had come from his weakness for Constance's charms, her laugh still occasionally punctuating the nightmares that plagued his fitful sleep. Only the death of one he loved and a lifetime of regret had been his reward for believing he might find happiness with another, far too high a price to pay again.

It was easier to turn oneself to unfeeling granite; to care about others was to wear one's heart outside the body and the world was cruel enough to crush it beneath its boots if given half a chance. If there was something in Grace's tender vulnerability and guileless face that touched the last shred of humanity he had left, he would fight it every step of the way—anything rather than risk another mistake, another soul-destroying loss; another scar to add to the collection borne by more than just his skin.

He roused himself with a brisk roll of his shoulders. The ridiculous thoughts that insisted on trying to worm their way into his already whirling mind would be dismissed. Grace would soon be gone from his house, taking her disconcerting effect on him with her, and then he needn't see her or her accursedly moving sadness again if he chose. It was almost amusing he'd let himself get so carried away by such folly.

How foolish to fear something that was never a danger in the first place.

Reassured at last by his own sensible thinking, Spencer risked a swift look up at Grace as he handed her a cup, which she took in one shaking hand.

'You were saying?' Mrs Dauntsey prompted gently.

'Oh. Yes.' Grace took a small sip of her tea. It was far too hot to drink yet, Spencer knew, but the attempt at normality seemed to give her the courage to go on.

She sighed again, her eyes suddenly sparkling with unshed tears that made Spencer's brows contract in a brief frown of discomfort. Grace took a deep breath before continuing, but the quaver in her voice was painfully obvious. 'My fiancé ended our engagement only this afternoon and now I find myself in a position—oh, *such* a position—I just don't know what will become of us all now!'

The tears she had tried in vain to conceal now spilled down her cheeks and she covered her face with her hand in a mixture of shame and distress that pricked Spencer in the soft underbelly of his determined indifference. Her dismay at breaking down was clear, but she couldn't seem to control the storm of weeping that held her in its merciless grasp—it was an uncomfortable relief to Spencer when his mother hurriedly set aside her cup and took the younger woman's hand in her own, helping Grace to stem the tide of misery that shook her slender frame.

'Oh, my dearest girl! Please don't cry so. Whatever do you mean, you don't know what will become of you all? What can have happened?'

Grace brushed the wetness from her face with the backs of her fingers. She hesitated, a shadow of reluctance crossing her countenance, but the entreaty in Mrs Dauntsey's face forced her to speak. 'Spencer said you hadn't heard of the misfortune that has befallen my family.'

Spencer watched as his mother nodded warily, her

glance flickering towards him briefly in a look he had no need to puzzle over. Disappointment and unhappiness gleamed in it, a clear indication of Mrs Dauntsey's thoughts. 'That's correct. I haven't been able to stir outside since we arrived and I'm afraid an...*indiscretion* of Spencer's means we've had no visitors to bring us news.'

Another flit of guilt pinched Spencer beneath his ribs at his mother's delicate phrasing of a distinctly *in*-delicate event. As a Quaker she disapproved strongly of his drinking and as his mother she despaired to see its effect on her only surviving son. His very public fight had made him notorious in a society where once he might have been welcomed with open arms, his fortune and face usually a guarantee of entry into the upper echelons. Now his actions would rob his poor mother of respectable company—for who would choose to spend time with a family whose sole heir was so evidently running wild? The inconvenient truth of his only having acted in self-defence wouldn't be allowed to get in the way of a good story, the rumours about him too salacious to be tempered by facts.

Spencer tracked the fascinating movement of Grace's throat as she swallowed down another sigh, bobbing her head in a hopeless nod. 'I see. Well. Poor Papa has been taken to Fleet Prison in London. He is completely innocent of all charges, of course, but he is accused of making fraudulent investments, running up debts and any number of financial indiscretions actually performed by his dishonest business partners. He has been declared bankrupt in his absence.'

Mrs Dauntsey's lips parted in frank disbelief. 'That cannot be so! Surely nobody could be so stupid as to believe your father capable of such actions?' She pressed a hand to her thin chest, clearly shocked to the core. 'Such a thing is impossible. Your father was always such a gentleman! Where are the real perpetrators, who allow him to be exposed to these lies?'

'They have fled, cowards that they are. Without their testimony there is nobody to take the blame but Papa, even though the first he knew of this whole affair was when the bailiffs came knocking at our door.'

Grace looked down at her hands, fingers clenched into fists and knuckles shining white through pale skin. 'As I'm sure you can imagine, our standing in society is now lower than dirt. I had hoped my fiancé would help us in our plight, but now...' Her lips trembled again and she folded them into a tight line of unhappiness that made Spencer's own twitch in unconscious reply. 'We have no prospects, no fortune, and with four daughters to support Mama faces the likelihood of having to give up our home.' She finished on a dry sob and clenched her jaw shut so firmly Spencer saw the tendons of her neck flex painfully.

There was a silence.

Standing before the fireplace, Spencer felt the warmth of the flames creeping up his back, although nothing could chase away the chilly dread that flared within his gut. It was a feeling close to sympathy that circled inside him, startlingly insistent and refusing to be dismissed. The sight of Grace's tears spoke to something in him, some aggravating weakness that he had thought his studied apathy for the world had killed off—but there it was, the desire to wipe away her tears, and the suffering in her look called to his own in a language he understood only too well.

The quiet stretched on for several moments, only the movement of Grace absently stirring her tea breaking the illusion all three were carved from stone. It almost made him jump when his mother cleared her throat and spoke with businesslike directness.

'Well. As I see it, there's an obvious solution; at least in part.'

Mrs Dauntsey glanced towards Spencer and he cocked his head in wordless query.

What scheme has she come up with?

Unease began to filter into his mind and he felt his eyes narrow in suspicion.

If his mother saw his cautious reaction, she gave no clue. 'I will, of course, employ you as my companion.' She fixed Grace with a forthright gaze, oblivious to Spencer's start of alarm. 'You can come to live here and I will meet all your expenses. With only the three younger girls to support, I'm sure your excellent mama will more than rise to the challenge.'

Watching with disbelieving eyes, Spencer saw Grace's mouth drop open, all words stolen from her by utter surprise.

'You cannot be serious?'

'As the grave. It would be a joy to have you about the house and renew the friendship between our families. If you came to live here, it would surely ease some of the financial strain, and Spencer wouldn't feel obliged to waste his time attempting small talk to entertain his aged mother. After all—' Mrs Dauntsey shot him another look that made his insides twist '—your dear mother and sisters are likely to be the only company I'll have to enjoy, given the circumstances.'

Spencer sucked in a sharp breath of dismay, covered by an abrupt turn away from both women and towards the hearth.

The *very last* thing he wanted was for Grace to take up residence in his home, her disconcerting effect on him already becoming an irritation he could have done without. It was bad enough he had felt that damned glimmer of *something* for her already, without the dangers of having to see her admittedly not *un*pretty face across his breakfast table every morning. If only there was something he could say, something he could do to dissuade his mother from this plan—but one quick glance backwards pricked at his conscience. His already tainted reputation would have long-reaching effects, the rumours of his temper unlikely to be forgotten. Perhaps there might be some small glint of merit in her scheme—although mingled with the threat of unseen complications for himself.

'But I could be getting ahead of myself. You might be hoping your fiancé will return to you?'

The shake of Grace's head was the most vehement movement Spencer had seen her make yet. 'Henry would never seek my hand again. I wish I'd known before what I now see so clearly: he never wanted anything from me other than my wealth and connections. As soon as I had neither his interest vanished at once. He never—he never truly loved me.' She gave a small sigh, a wretched thing that nipped at Spencer uncomfortably. 'The details of our separation will be forgotten soon enough, I am sure. The only thing I wish to remember with any clarity is never to venture my heart in such a way ever again. The risk to one's soul is too great.'

It was as though she had read his mind, Spencer recognised with a frown of surprise as Grace took another sip from her cup. It was the same conclusion he had come to as he sat within the belly of a storm-tossed ship returning to England, bandages staunching the flow of his blood and pain from more than just his wounds making him want to cry out in agony. Constance had been the first woman to capture his heart and his actions because of it had cost him dearly—he would not be caught out twice. How the pale young lady who had claimed his chair had managed to so exactly articulate his own feelings he didn't know—only that it was almightily unnerving.

'My only hesitation in accepting your kind offer would be my reputation.' A rosy blush spread across Grace's cheeks as she continued, the colour illuminating the delicate lines of her cheekbones and jaw that Spencer suddenly realised—with another pang of dismay—were very fine indeed. 'I couldn't bring disgrace upon this house and allow you to be connected to our shame.'

Mrs Dauntsey waved a dismissive hand, although Spencer could have sworn he saw a glint of irony in her eye.

It wouldn't be only Grace who made this house notorious. Isn't that what you're thinking, Mother?

She'd been too frail to leave the house and hear the whispers about him first-hand, but she was no fool. Anybody who had ever walked among the judgement of the *ton* knew how they could drag a man down with their words, destroying his good name in the blink of an eye if they thought him undeserving.

'I couldn't care three straws about that. Society busybodies will always find something to talk about.

I don't see what anybody else's opinion has to do with it—and that's my final word!'

She sat back in her chair and closed her eyes briefly. Her chest rose and fell a little more quickly than usual, Spencer saw in swift alarm—she was tiring rapidly, and very soon she would be worn out completely.

She needs to rest. This has been too much excitement.

Whatever his thoughts on the matter, now was not the time for further discussion. His mother's colour had already ebbed a little and her breaths bordered on laboured as she smiled across at Grace apologetically.

'I tire so easily these days. I ought to be taking to my chamber now.' She paused for a moment to regain her breath. 'But before I do, may we shake on our arrangement? If you are agreeable, of course?'

Spencer concealed his uneasiness behind one large hand, rubbing the dark bristles of his chin. Grace appeared to be hesitating, obviously turning the words over in her mind—but then she extended her hand and his mother took it firmly.

'I can't thank you enough, Mrs Dauntsey.' Grace's voice shook, but this time the tremor seemed of awed relief rather than bleak emotion. 'You will never know how grateful I am for your help.'

'It's time you called me Dorothea and I only wish I could do more. Please assure your mother of that and tell her I long to see her and your sisters soon.' Mrs Dauntsey's eyes were warm, but an edge of pain had crept into her tone and Spencer stepped towards her.

'If you ladies are quite finished, I shall escort you to your rooms, Mother.' He fixed her with a look that brooked no refusal. 'Miss Linwood, the carriage will be waiting for you now. If you are willing, I shall send it again to collect you tomorrow evening.'

'Thank you.' Grace averted her eyes from his, the trace of a blush flickering a little stronger under his intense watch. There was none of the warmth with which she had addressed his mother, he noticed.

But who do you have to blame for that?

He sketched a short bow, attempting to block out the unwelcome question. 'I hope you will excuse us. Rivers will see you out. Goodnight, Miss Linwood.'

Easing his mother to her feet, Spencer helped her from the room. Pausing on the threshold, he turned back briefly, intending to say something more—but all words escaped him as he saw the dazed relief that had flooded Grace's face and the sudden beauty of her wonderstruck smile sent him striding mutely away before she could turn to see his grim discomfort at the sight.

Chapter Three

Spencer strode through the house to his library with his jaw clenched on rising bad temper, trying with each footstep to outpace the thoughts that pursued him. The same old nightmare, the one he dreaded more than any other, had visited him as he slept the previous night and the combination of waking bathed in sweat and the tiredness that resulted from it did not improve his mood. It wasn't just the lack of sleep that tore at him, however, or the usual sickening guilt that made him reach for the nearest bottle. Ever since Grace's arrival two weeks before he'd found it increasingly difficult to find an escape from the troubling reaction her presence provoked in him and it was becoming more vexing by the day.

It wasn't as though he had any real basis for complaint, some irritable part of him recognised. The difference in his mother was striking, even after such a short time, and the change in her would have cheered anybody to see it. She still tired easily and the slow sinking of her features into her drawn face hadn't ceased, but there was a gleam in her eye Spencer hadn't seen for months and it was plain Grace's company was the cause. The regular visits from Mrs Linwood and her three younger daughters had helped, too, no doubt, but it was Grace who was always busily arranging a warm shawl about Dorothea's shoulders or making suggestions to the cook that might tempt her to take more than a mouthful. He would have to admit having Grace come to live with them, comfortably installed in her own private rooms, was the best thing that could have happened for his mother—especially given his own behaviour had played a large part in her isolation.

No. He couldn't complain. And yet…

She's handsome when she smiles.

The unwelcome thought flashed through Spencer's mind yet again and he scowled to himself in a combination of frustration and alarm. *Not this nonsense again. Is there no escaping it?*

It was irritatingly true that Grace's countenance grew in appeal the longer one looked at her. At first sight her fair skin had seemed colourless to him, her pale hair and eyes frankly a little bland, but closer inspection showed an almost pearlescent quality to her complexion and, when the shadows of sadness cleared, her eyes sparkled with an intelligence that would surely interest any sensible man. Even the fragility of her slight frame took on a new elegance after reluctant study, her movements measured and step quiet as she moved through his house.

But it was that smile—that *damned* smile—that made the biggest difference. It gave life to her face and animation to her features, highlighting the graceful contours of her pronounced cheekbones as though a candle flickered behind them. Only a simpleton could ever think she was plain after seeing that curve of her lips and the tiny dimple that appeared in one soft cheek—

No!

Spencer brought his fist down hard on his thigh as he walked, the furrow between his brows growing deeper by the second.

This will not do!

He shook his head fiercely against the unwanted barrage of images that bombarded him. Dwelling on a woman's beauty was for other men, men who hadn't caused such terrible destruction with their misplaced affections. It was for them to stare and pine and write poems praising their lady's limitless charms: all things he could no longer entertain since his catastrophic entanglement with Constance had caused such devastation. Love and death walked side by side in his mind now. Guilt ran like an icy river beneath both, linking them together with its cold fingers, and no amount of time would thaw the frost that formed around his heart. Grace might have attracted his attention for some absurd reason, but she would never be allowed to be anything more to him than a reluctantly hosted guest. The consequences were too stark and the risk of unimaginable pain could have made a weaker man shudder.

Not that she would want to be anything more. That idiot Henry Earls has cured her of any such notions once and for all, I fancy.

With a fresh wave of aggravation Spencer wrenched his focus away to remember the decanter waiting for him beside his favourite reading chair, which would provide some relief, hopefully, from the disloyal workings of his mind. Whether drink had become his closest friend or worst enemy was becoming difficult to tell these days, he thought darkly; but it was the only thing that helped silence the demons that plagued him, and with the added complication of Grace moving warily about his home his mind felt more troubled than ever.

The library door stood slightly ajar when he reached it and pushed through with an impatient hand. Perhaps it shouldn't have been quite so surprising, then, to find someone already in the room, although Spencer's thoughts were too occupied to consider the possibility until his heart gave a sudden lurch at the sight that met his eyes.

Grace sat curled in the very armchair he had been aiming for, her legs tucked beneath her and eyes intent on a dog-eared book Spencer recognised at once. It was one of a pair Mr Dauntsey had given his sons eight years before on the last birthday they would spend with him, the name of one twin inscribed in each in their father's slanting hand. Spencer's copy lay safely in his untidy desk, so it had to be William's that Grace held in slender fingers, poring over the contents with her delicate profile thrown into sharp relief by the window behind her head. It was a pose Spencer suddenly remembered vividly from when Grace was a girl, too shy to speak much in his presence, but she was far more confident now, an intelligent and accomplished young woman, and the knowledge kindled something within the broad spread of his chest.

Pull yourself together, man. So she reads—what of it? She always was a bluestocking.

She hadn't noticed him standing uncertainly in the doorway. Engrossed in her book, Spencer was at perfect liberty to take in the blonde tendrils that gleamed softly in the winter sunlight as they tumbled about cheeks it would surely be a fine thing to touch… It was an unacceptable urge, but one that roared up with a power that shocked him, strong enough to cause the faintest flicker of something long hidden deep within him to attempt to spark into life.

Spencer took a breath to centre himself, alarmed by the unwanted direction of his thoughts.

You shouldn't think like that. Have you no control?

It was bad enough to feel such things in private—to do so in Grace's presence was even worse. She'd be horrified if she suspected how his mind wandered, he was sure; aside from a polite greeting each morning she barely spoke to him, apparently unwilling to spend much time in his company. Any accord they might have enjoyed as children had long since dissipated, chased away by the brusque new identity the loss of Will had forced Spencer, in his guilt and boundless grief, to adopt.

He ought to say something, probably, and stop lingering in doorways, but it was strangely difficult to think what that something should be—especially when Grace flipped to the front page to read where Will's name would live on for ever in faded ink. Her brows twitched together, the sudden sorrow there only enhancing the fine lines of her face, and that look flew straight to the most vulnerable part of Spencer's soul. How much had his mother told her of his twin's too-early demise? Not even Dorothea knew the whole story, of course, or that Constance had even existed—his shame would never allow it—and the nightmares that stalked him whenever he slept would ensure he never forgot. No doubt Grace would flee from him if she ever knew the truth—but wouldn't he deserve that, for the damage his stupid actions had done?

He cleared his throat, although his voice, when he managed to force out the words, still sounded a trifle strangled.

'I hadn't thought you'd be in here.'

Grace started, closing the book with a guilty snap.

'I didn't hear you come in.' She unfurled herself hurriedly and slipped off the chair, although she didn't relinquish the book as she stood before him, looking for all the world as though she wished she was anywhere else.

Spencer frowned, horribly aware of an awkward silence descending on the room. Perhaps once he would have been able to fill it with banal small talk, but now all he could think of was how strangely *pleasing* the tilt of Grace's chin was as she looked up at him, tapering to a gentle point he had no way of knowing she hated.

That was yet *another* thought he shouldn't be allowing and it was a relief when Grace was the one to break the rising tension between them.

'I was just looking through this anthology of poems. Some of them are really quite beautiful.' She paused, apparently weighing up her next words. Spencer realised his jaw had tightened as he willed her not to speak them, but his wordless entreaty was in vain as she continued, a shadow of sympathy in her grey eyes he suddenly couldn't bear. 'I saw William's name written in the cover, along with a dedication from your father. I don't think I ever told you how sorry I was for the loss of Mr Dauntsey, or for Will. You must miss them so fiercely. How have you fared these past years?'

The muscles in Spencer's throat contracted like a vice.

Of all the questions she could have asked. How have I fared?

Of course he missed his father. The senior Captain Dauntsey had been a warm, compassionate man devoted to his wife and sons and his passing had plunged them all into mourning so deep Spencer had privately known his mother would never truly recover, even after eight long years. There was no guilt, though—Richard Dauntsey had died of a weak heart in his own bed, surrounded by his family in his final moments. William had perished in a foreign land, bleeding in the mud and never knowing how much Spencer regretted the final angry words between them. There could be no comparison and Spencer knew his reply would be harsh before he even opened his mouth.

'That isn't something I wish to discuss.' He saw how Grace blinked at the coldness of his tone and felt an immediate—and uncomfortable—twinge of remorse, but he *couldn't* bring himself to let her draw him in. There was already something about Grace that called to him, some reflection of his own suffering he saw in her stormy gaze. The imprisonment of her father, the loss of her reputation and finally her fiancé: it was no wonder she so often wore a cloak of sadness valiantly concealed beneath a stiff smile. Her stoicism was admirable—and that admiration was growing more dangerous by the minute.

'You have enough troubles of your own, surely, to want to know more of mine. Your time would be better spent thinking of yours than questioning others.'

As soon as the words slipped out Spencer knew

they'd been cruel. The sympathy in Grace's face slowly merged into a look of such quiet unhappiness Spencer felt a kick of powerful regret, so swift it was like a blow to the gut.

Damn you and your barbed tongue. That was unkind.

Grace's reply was soft, yet so steady it stirred the ashes of Spencer's worrying admiration even more. 'My troubles are never far from my mind, I assure you. There's scarcely a moment Papa is not in my thoughts, but I know he wouldn't want me to surrender to despair.'

He shouldn't have rubbed salt in her wounds, Spencer knew, reminding her how all her hopes for the future had turned to dust and what she was now reduced to. The proof was in the way her pretty lips twitched as though fighting the urge to turn down at the corners, all caused by his thoughtless remark born of fear she might see through his defensive façade to the damaged man within.

Internally he muttered something unfit for the ears of a lady, in equal parts dismayed by Grace's sorrow and his part in causing it, as well as how much he wished to take away her pain.

Make the effort, man. She's been the best medicine for Mother you ever could have wished for and that matters more than any feelings of your own.

He swallowed, a forced convulsion of his tight throat that made it no easier to find the right words.

'That was unfair. I shouldn't have spoken so hastily, or with so little care. I apologise.'

Grace gazed at Spencer for a long moment, not entirely sure how to respond.

Her heart still raced at his unexpected entrance to

the library, interrupting her solitude with the presence she still wasn't quite sure how to interpret. During the two weeks she had spent under Spencer's roof his transformation from open warmth to icy cold had turned Grace's ordered world on its head, and she had frequently found herself at a loss for words at some of his behaviour. His chaotic approach to life coupled with the unfortunate galloping of her pulse every time she found herself in the same room meant she did her best to avoid him, but on some occasions he was *un*avoidable—as he was now, standing in front of her and looking so sincere she felt her heart shudder over a missed beat in the most unsettling manner possible.

Her reaction to his scrutiny was one she resolutely *did not want*, too similar to the flash of heat Henry had always managed to send thrilling through her with the touch of his hand. It seemed Spencer was able to achieve that same sensation without even making contact with her skin, a realisation that made Grace's insides twist in keen dismay.

But you needn't worry. You're on your guard now and no such vulnerability will be allowed to take hold of you ever again.

If the rich darkness of Spencer's eyes was something Grace had noticed, she would disregard it at once. Henry's had been just as fine, although sapphire where Spencer's were the colour of sweet cocoa… Either way, girlish weakness for such a trivial thing was something Grace would *not* entertain, especially when those eyes were set in the face of a man surely capable of wreaking untold damage on any woman foolish enough to fall for him. She should be congratulating herself on her own good sense in realising it, Grace thought determinedly—but Spencer still watched her with an expression she had never seen before, standing close enough for her to just catch the clean scent of his shaving soap, and despite her resolve she would have to admit it was pleasing.

He had never before looked at her with anything warmer than faint disapproval at her continued presence in his house and she couldn't help the dangerous pleasure that shivered through her insides at the new lack of censure in his gaze. It was replaced by a ghost of real remorse, as honest as it was surprising and adding fuel to the new colour that simmered in Grace's cheeks. With his face no longer darkened by the grim shadows that usually cloaked it he looked so much younger, more *human* somehow, far removed from the sullen man she was still unable to fully understand and more like the lad she used to think she knew...

Grace attempted a small smile, desperately trying to make it seem natural and not the rigid thing she feared was spreading over her face. 'Think nothing of it. We all say things we regret from time to time.'

The only response was a curt nod, although Grace thought she caught a glint of faint relief. It vanished again almost instantaneously and she determined there and then she wouldn't waste a single moment trying to decipher what it meant. There were far more important things for her to be doing than dwelling on the inner workings of a man's mind—even if the man in question was more attractive than was strictly fair, a direct challenge to her vow never to be imposed on again.

'I ought to return to your mother. I managed to persuade her to stay abed a little longer this morning and

I'd like to check she hasn't escaped while my back was turned.'

One corner of Spencer's mouth twitched as if in wry amusement, a movement he checked at once—but still it captured Grace's attention.

'You certainly have a difficult task trying to keep my mother restrained. She does so love to be busy.'

'I'd noticed. I've sewn more shifts for parish orphans in these past two weeks than I have in twenty years together. She's quite the force of nature, even when unwell.'

This time the reply was the flicker of one dark eyebrow and when Spencer met her eye a look passed between them to stir the hair at the nape of her neck. It was close to understanding, as though a fine thread of commonality bridged the gap that held them so far apart, and it made Grace blink in confusion.

'You needn't tell me that. Sometimes I think it's sheer strength of will that's kept her going through all her troubles.'

Grace nodded, trying to ignore the little voice that piped up inside her to ask the obvious question: *Troubles that you've only added to, Spencer?*

Dorothea had already told her why nobody visited Nevin Place, in equal parts frustrated and worried by her son's ill-judged behaviour. The decanter Grace had spied waiting for him next to the very armchair she had just been sitting in only reinforced the truth of his mother's fears: that he spent much of his time alone, stubbornly refusing to explain his reasons for needing to seek oblivion so ardently it had cost him his reputation. It was no wonder the rumours about him swirled, when he stalked through life looking so grim-faced and a smattering of bruises still on the fists that roused such comment.

There was still a glimmer of the unnamed *something* in Spencer's look as Grace held out the book in her hand for him to take, suddenly aware how much she wanted to be free of the attention of those sharp eyes. Surely to spend too much time in Spencer's disturbing company was a mistake, his powerful presence whispering to her with a sweet voice Henry had robbed her of the ability to enjoy.

'Will you take this? I found it on the table and I'm not sure on which shelf it belongs.'

Spencer reached out for the book she proffered, his large hand taking the weight, and in so doing brushed Grace's fingers with his own, sending a shockwave streaking the length of her arm to blaze beneath her ribs.

A gasp fell from Grace's lips before she could bite it back, her breath suddenly scalding at the unexpected feeling on his skin against hers. It was the quickest of touches, so brief it shouldn't even have registered, yet the nerves in her fingertips sang in unwelcome chorus, her heartbeat leaping to beat in time with the rhythm Spencer's warmth conducted.

She could have sworn he felt a similar jolt of surprise, no doubt born of the discomfort her company already seemed to inspire. Surely *he* hadn't felt a pang of disconcerting pleasure at the feel of soft skin against his more rugged fingers, an echo of the shameful feeling that coursed in Grace's veins. Only Henry had ever made her feel anything remotely similar; and even then not as vividly as the spark Spencer sent scurrying down her spine, nor half so effortlessly. Spencer looked down at her uncertainly, his gaze moving from her eyes to lips still parted in wonder, and whatever he saw in her flushed face made him step a smart pace backwards.

'Thank you. I'll see it's returned to its proper place.'

Grace nodded, her mouth suddenly dry and mind accursedly blank. It was precisely the kind of situation she'd been so determined to avoid and when she dipped a hurried curtsy and left the library it was with far more speed than might have been necessary.

Grace's heart still hammered as she cautiously opened Dorothea's bedchamber door and quietly stepped inside. Mrs Dauntsey lay fast asleep against the richly embroidered pillows of a daybed beneath a large window, her chest rising and falling with an effort it pained Grace to see. The pretty room with its plush carpet and expensive French furniture was not as warm as it should have been, considering the January chill outside, and she moved noiselessly to stoke up the embers that gleamed in the grate.

Another layer draped over Dorothea would be a good idea, too. It made her joints ache all the more if she was not kept snug, even though she protested about being swaddled like an infant, and despite the chaos holding a carnival inside her chest Grace found a small smile at the thought of her friend's determination not to surrender to her illness. It would claim her eventually, of course, but that was a bleak possibility Grace wasn't willing to stare dead in the face.

A fine woollen blanket lay folded at the end of the daybed and Grace drew it up to cover Dorothea's sleeping form, tucking it round her with careful fingers. The more the patient slept now the more energy she'd have later, perhaps even able to be helped downstairs to stand at the garden door and take some of the crisp winter air. The doctor wouldn't approve, Grace thought wryly as she smoothed the blanket into place, but he might never know the illicit activities of two conspiring women. She and Dorothea made a formidable team, their prior connection only having deepened over the past weeks to a relationship that brought both tremendous comfort. When Mrs Linwood came to drink tea even more peals of laughter could be heard from the formerly silent chamber as events from years past were revisited, renewing bonds and adding a layer to old friendships to make them afresh.

Quite unlike my dealings with another old acquaintance, who shall remain nameless.

At the unwelcome thought of Spencer Grace's hands grew clumsy, her mind too occupied to pay much attention to her movements. Her skin still tingled where masculine fingers had brushed her own, only featherlight and accidental yet dangerously effective in making her cheeks flare with heat. It was every bit as uncomfortable a fact as it had been the moment it happened, mere minutes ago downstairs, and Grace had yet to find a way to banish the thought back to the darkest pit of her mind where it belonged.

'Have I done something to offend you, Grace? I'm not sure I deserve such manhandling!'

There was a gleam of amusement in Dorothea's eye as Grace jumped, freezing in the act of vigorously arranging the blanket. Evidently her focus had wandered too far for her to be gentle and she dropped the tasselled hem with guilty haste.

'Sorry. My mind was…on other things.'

'Don't apologise. Of all people, I know what it's like to have a lot to think about.'

Dorothea tried to ease herself up to sit back against the cushions behind her, accepting Grace's supporting hand with a pained smile. 'Did I sleep for long enough, do you think? I hope you weren't bored while I was so rudely inattentive. What pleasant thing did you find to occupy you?'

Grace wasn't entirely sure if spending time with Spencer counted as a 'pleasant thing'; two conflicting opinions wrestling each other for supremacy. It seemed safest to offer a bland smile of her own, although Grace felt her heart rate skip a fraction faster.

'I thought I'd sit in the library and read a while, until I was chanced upon by Spencer. We talked for a short while before I came to check on you.'

'Ah. And how is my son today?' With a grunt of effort Dorothea pulled a lumpy pillow from beneath her. 'He came to my rooms soon after breakfast, but I doubt I shall see him again until supper.'

Grace hesitated. The unerringly honest part of her ought to win out, but to tell Dorothea her son had made a beeline for the library decanter as she left seemed unwise. She knew how much her staunchly Quaker friend hated having strong drink in the house, although Spencer was far too stubborn to be ruled by anybody but himself. 'He—he seemed well enough. After a fashion.'

'Hmm.' Dorothea eyed her narrowly, but then merely sighed. 'You always were faultlessly polite, even as a little girl. I'm aware Spencer isn't the easiest of companions these days and it worries me relentlessly.'

'I know. I know you have much to bear, but do try not to distress yourself. It does you no good.'

Something of an understatement, Grace conceded as she watched her friend's laboured breaths.

To lose the husband she'd adored, followed by a son just six years later, was a devastating blow—only compounded by her remaining boy turning into somebody she barely knew. Her failing health was the final piece of a tragic puzzle, so sad it hardly seemed possible.

'You're right, of course. Only…' Another sigh came from the skeletal figure beneath the blanket. 'The change in him, Grace. Of course he grieved when his father passed, but since we lost William he's been a man I simply don't recognise. You must have seen that he takes no pleasure in anything, not even pursuits he used to feel passion for. There was a time when he sketched every day, you know, and showed great promise; he hasn't so much as picked up a pencil these past two years, as if the very spark of inspiration has been snuffed out like a candle.'

A sudden cough racked her frail body and she pressed her hand to her heaving chest until the spell passed, leaving her cheeks ruddy and breath coming hard.

'As time has gone by I find myself grieving less for William. I will be seeing him and my dear Richard again very soon, I am sure of it, and then I need never feel sorrow for them ever again. It is Spencer who now pains my heart the most when I think how he will be left alone with his secrets and the suffering he thinks I do not see in his face. He would never tell me exactly what happened the day Will died, but I am no fool.' She wheezed for a moment, papery eyelids closed. 'The idea of what he will become when I am gone—it haunts me.'

Bony fingers found Grace's arm, grasping at the sleeve of her gown in a twitch of distress, and she immediately covered them with her own. Her heart swelled with pity and powerful sorrow—Dorothea looked so small in her grief and fear, and the sight pained Grace more than she could say.

'If I'd as much as suspected what damage it would do for my boys to go off to war, I would never have allowed them to enlist. You know my faith prohibits all kinds of violence, but I agreed with Richard on his deathbed I would let the twins carry on the military tradition of his family. If they had only stayed in England, Grace... I curse the day they left for Belgium, and I hate the very name of the Battle of Quatre Bras with a passion I feel in my bones.'

A tear slipped down one sunken cheek and Dorothea cuffed it away, although not before the glitter of it sent ice piercing Grace's insides. For the family she had known since childhood to be ripped so cruelly apart seemed the worst of injustices and from the tumult of her emotions a new thought arose to make Grace wonder...

Had Spencer *seen* his brother die, cut down in front of him in some battlefield across the sea? Wouldn't that go some way to explaining why he seemed so closed off, so strangely emotionless? She could only imagine with a powerful shudder what kind of effect such an experience might have on a man's soul. It was a startling possibility, yet one that seemed so blindingly obvious, and Grace felt a suddenly overwhelming rush of compassion for the man who had previously inspired such wariness and confusion.

'None of what has befallen your family is your fault. I hope you know that, despite your regrets.'

Dorothea shrugged a thin shoulder beneath expensive linen. 'Regrets are one thing I have no shortage of. The reason I sleep so little every night is out of worry for my only remaining son. If only there was something I could do, some way I could rest easily, knowing he won't be left so alone when I am gone—and yet I fear nothing can turn him from the path he has chosen.'

Grace nodded gravely, the truth in Dorothea's words plain. 'I can only imagine how such thoughts must trouble you. I wish there was something I could do to ease your cares.'

Her sad gaze was fixed on the white hand that held her arm, lost in the world of compassion that gripped her—so she entirely missed the slow movement of her friend's eyes in her direction and the look of dawning contemplation that crept in to brighten them.

'Do you truly mean that?'

'Why, yes.' Grace forced her lips into a small smile despite the sorrow growing ever heavier in her chest. The image of Spencer's grim face crowded out all other thoughts, the most obvious reason for his tightly drawn expression suddenly clear to her in terrible understanding.

He has suffered so much and with his mother so ill surely there can only be more heartache to come for him. I wish for his sake, and for the friendship we might once have had, that things could be different.

'Believe me—if there was any way I could help you

or Spencer with the unhappiness that plagues you, all you would have to do is ask.'

'*Any* way? Any way *at all*?' Dorothea reached for a glass of water standing beside her bed, turning away so for a moment Grace couldn't see her face. 'Even if it were in a way you never would have dreamed? Even if it seemed the most unlikely thing imaginable?'

'Even then, to repay your kindness and ease your cares, I give you my word.'

Chapter Four

The weeks passed slowly at Nevin Place, dragging out until January gave way to February and the weather turned from merely cold to biting. Time continued its unstoppable march, but the month shown on Grace's calendar wasn't the only thing that seemed to progress.

The stares that accompanied her had increased since Henry's rejection and her residence at Spencer's vast home, she saw now as she drew her cloak closer about her body and wished her bonnet covered more of her face. Each time she left the safety of the imposing house to visit her family she had to run the gauntlet of whispers that followed her, and now her situation was common knowledge and her link with the scandalous Captain was known the mutters had only grown worse.

Grace Linwood. Daughter of a criminal, wife of nobody and companion to a woman with a reprobate for an heir. No wonder society hasn't rushed to reclaim me.

It didn't matter that poor Papa was innocent, Henry a selfish rogue or Spencer not a common brawler. The gossip attached to Grace's name was too fascinating for any dull truth to temper it and, when combined with Spencer's own notoriety, she could only grit her teeth and plough onwards as another set of eyes turned towards her in undisguised curiosity she hadn't yet learned to ignore.

'Why, Grace! What a surprise to see you here!'

She looked up sharply at a voice to the side of her and felt the horrid sensation of her heart sinking into her boots as she saw the man it belonged to: Henry's younger brother, George Earls—one of the most spoiled, spiteful and disagreeable men she had ever had the misfortune to meet. Even in the first blissful flush of love for Henry Grace had seen how his brother was rotten to the core, a difference between them she had thought so stark.

Perhaps I should have known then the apple doesn't fall far from the tree. It would have saved me such pain if I'd seen how alike they truly are.

The sight of George and the memories he conjured squeezed the breath from Grace's lungs to replace it with ice and for a moment she stood frozen before the man's horrible smirk.

'Good evening, George.' Grace forced her lips to move, feeling a sudden rush of blood in her ears as dismay leapt inside her. Entertaining himself at the expense of others was George's favourite pastime and surely there could be no better provider of a moment's cruel sport than the woman his brother had helped to shame.

'A very good evening to you, I'm sure. Won't you stop and talk a while?'

Nausea writhed in Grace's stomach and her throat felt tight as she glanced about her, searching for a route of escape. Dusk was setting in the chilly street, stealing over the shops and houses like mist, but there were still far too many people around for her to risk an undignified retreat. She'd be exposed to yet more ridicule if she turned and ran, her hair flying and skirts flaring in the breeze, and to call for help would only bring more attention she could have done without.

She squared her shoulders, bringing her chin up to look George in the eye. 'I'd rather not. I don't think there's anything we have to say to each other.'

George sighed in mock disappointment. 'Oh? But we haven't spoken for so long! I was sorry you didn't attend the Campbells' winter ball. I realise you weren't invited, but I'm sure you would have enjoyed seeing Henry again and to meet his delightful new friend Miss Scott. Such an accomplished woman, with a perfectly flawless reputation and at *least* three thousand a year.'

Grace felt her face stiffen as George's mouth shaped into a smug curve she would have given anything to wipe away. Instead there was nothing she could do but stand with her breathing fast and shallow and her mind reeling, finally grinding to a halt on the crux of George's cruel words.

Henry has a new object already.

She'd known he wouldn't pine for her, his attentions as false as the compliments that had flowed so easily from dishonest lips, yet it was with a searing dart of pain Grace realised how swiftly she was forgotten. The speed at which Henry's gaze had switched to another only underlined the truth: that she was worthless without her good name and fortune, apparently the only things able to catch the eye of an eligible man. With neither now at her disposal all she had to rely on were her own charms…evidently so sorely lacking they amounted to little more than nothing. It wasn't the loss of Henry's lacklustre affections that hurt so much as the knowledge of how easily she was replaced, supplanted by another as though she had never existed at all.

As if I needed more proof of his indifference—or my own lack of value.

George must have seen how his words hit their mark and, attempting to engage Grace's averted eyes beneath the brim of her bonnet, his attention only shifted when she became aware of a silent presence at her shoulder, a sudden apparition that changed the atmosphere at once.

Spencer stood behind her like a pillar of rock, his face impassive and yet one swift glance enough to tell him all he needed to know. Grace's heart gave a curious leap as she saw his familiar jaw tighten as he took in her tense posture, her brow pinched and cheeks flushed; she swallowed as another of those complex looks passed between them just as that day in the library, when the touch of his hand had struck sparks in her stomach.

'Good evening, Grace. I hope you found your mother and sisters well.'

It wasn't really a question, so Grace had no need to do anything other than nod as powerful relief rushed in to relieve some of the rigidity of her frame. It seemed a strange thing for Spencer's unexpected appearance to trigger *relief,* of all things, but in that one quick look he seemed to understand her distress and not for the first time came reluctantly to her rescue.

'If you're returning to Nevin Place now, I'd be pleased to escort you.'

His expression wasn't *quite* one of pleasure, but

Grace could have sworn she saw a glimmer of assurance pass through it before vanishing. It hardly seemed possible and yet there it was: the tiniest gleam of the kind boy he had once been, although determinedly suppressed as though something of which he was ashamed. Despite her dismay Grace's pulse flitted a fraction faster at the sight, but George still stood before her with his features *so* like Henry's and that was all it took for her to shy away from her disloyal reaction with a jolt of alarm.

Spencer looked at George for a moment, his face hard and expressionless as stone. His dark eyes wandered slowly from the top of George's ostentatious hat to his boots, taking in every detail with unhurried, ice-cold judgement that made the other man's grin fade gradually, before turning his back entirely and holding out his arm.

'The sun's setting. We should return home before the evening chill grows worse.'

Grace's eyes flicked from Spencer's face to the proffered arm to his face again, surprise and gratitude growing to wash away the horrid churn of emotion George had prompted. Spencer had cut him dead, not even bothering to introduce himself as though the other man was a minor inconvenience so irrelevant he was beneath Spencer's notice. It was inconceivably rude, of course, and yet Grace felt the strangest hint of admiration as she slipped her hand into the crook of Spencer's elbow and allowed herself to be borne away without so much as a backward glance at George's now heated face.

Admiration wasn't the only thing Grace felt steal over her as Spencer guided her down the darkening street, almost scurrying to keep up with his much-longer strides. The warmth of his body seeped through her thin glove to kindle in her fingers, her hand pressed to an unyielding bicep she realised with a fresh sweep of discomfort felt just as firm as it looked. Her unpleasant encounter with George had stirred feelings she'd never wanted to revisit, proving she was correct in her promise to hold herself apart for ever, but she was still a woman of flesh and blood. Surely no young lady would be *completely* immune to the sculpted muscle of a strong arm, especially when its owner had just saved her from such a hideous situation.

'Thank you. That was Henry's brother, someone I never wanted to meet again. I don't know what I would have done if you hadn't come to rescue me.'

Spencer inclined his head, although his eyes stayed fixed on the street ahead.

'I see charm must run in the family.'

Grace felt her cheeks flush a little at his tone. Evidently he thought little of her judgement—and on this occasion, wasn't he correct? She disliked the idea of him thinking her foolish, she realised with an unsettling recognition that she struggled to understand.

'George took great pleasure in informing me that his brother has already found a new lady to pursue, one of spotless reputation and impressive fortune. I think he thought the revelation would wound me.'

They walked on for a short while in silence, Grace all too aware of the tumult of feelings cartwheeling through her mind. Distress at seeing George, embarrassment at his humiliation of her, topped off with that insistent pulse of *something forbidden* each time Spencer's arm flexed around her hand, irritating and unwanted yet refusing to be ignored. Out of the corner of her eye she saw how frequently faces turned towards them, unabashed interest flitting between her and the man who walked beside her so sternly. It was something of a novelty for people to stare at somebody other than herself, but of course Spencer's reputation preceded him and low mutters followed their progress that Grace didn't have to hear to understand.

How much more will George now strive to drag that reputation through the mud after Spencer slighted him? Grace wondered with sudden regret.

Gratitude for Spencer's uncannily timely appearance still glowed, but tinged now with worry and the faintest wish Spencer had been able to summon up even the slightest of basic manners. His utter contempt for George, no doubt as a result of seeing Grace's face frozen into a mask of dismay, had been so obvious it would only compound the rumours that already stalked him: that Captain Dauntsey was barely a gentleman, entirely lacking in charm and ready to be rude with little provocation. George would be only too keen to spread the story, she knew with certainty, and with it the further damning of Spencer's good name.

'It must have been painful for you to know that.' Spencer broke the quiet between them, distracting Grace from her concern. 'To think of him with another.'

'Yes.' Grace's voice was small. Pain did indeed still flicker within her, but not born of jealousy. It was the effortless way she had been disregarded that stung, bolstering her knowledge of just how far she had fallen and what she had lost.

'You must have cared for him.'

'I did.' She nodded, although Spencer didn't look down to see it. They were almost at Nevin Place, just in time to close the door on the first frost of nightfall. 'He was the first man who made me feel desired— even if it was all an act. I don't know if any woman would forget her first love, especially when her noto- riety makes it so unlikely she will ever have another.'

Or her own sensible thinking, Grace finished pri- vately. *I won't make that mistake again.*

They drew into the close of imposing houses with quiet steps, the only other sound those of a couple be- hind them. As the elderly man and wife moved to pass by they stared at Spencer with disapproval so clear Grace risked a swift glance up at his face, although what she saw there she couldn't quite tell.

It was no wonder Dorothea worried for him, Grace mused sadly. There was so much going on behind that blank façade, so much suffering he must be keeping inside. It was on the tip of her tongue to ask him *why* he felt he must live a life of such determined loneli- ness, so set on fulfilling the rumours of his unfriend- liness as he had that very evening, when a pounding of feet on the pavement in front of them signalled the approach of Thorne, her face pale and eyes stretched wide with wordless horror it took both only a split sec- ond to understand.

As soon as he entered Dorothea's bedchamber, Spencer knew.

A sheen of sweat across his mother's brow gleamed dimly in the firelight, the reflection of the flames flick- ering in the dulled curve of her eyes. They turned to- wards him as he approached, crinkled slightly at the corners as she tried to smile, but the sparkle had left them and in a moment of pure, crystal realisation Spencer knew he would never see it again.

Dorothea's fingers found his hand, snaking into his palm with shocking coldness. 'I think the time draws near.'

No. It can't be. Not yet.

Time seemed to have slowed, each second stretching into an eternity as he looked at her, his throat too dry for any words and his chest squeezed in breathless agony as though held in an unrelenting iron grip.

'Is Grace with you? Come forward. I would like to see you both clearly.'

He only dimly heard the swish of Grace's skirts as she moved to kneel at the other side of the bed, reaching immediately to take hold of Dorothea's other hand. Her face contained a complex mix of powerful gentleness and such sweet sorrow it would have taken Spencer's breath away, had his lungs not already burned within the prison of his ribs.

It was the strangest of comforts to know he was not alone, that it wasn't just he who heard Dorothea's rattling breaths or saw how her chest rose and fell with visible effort. Grace was with him in the terrible silence that he was unable to fill, radiating compassion he actually *felt* deep inside him as well as saw, but he pushed that consolation aside in confusion as he shook his head. There had never been a time when his weakness for Grace's disturbing presence was less appropriate and the touch of agitation helped him find his tongue.

'Don't speak like that. Doctor Sharp told me only yesterday how pleased he was with your progress. I've sent for him. He will be here within a half hour.'

A short, painful sound escaped Dorothea's dry lips that it took Spencer a moment to realise was a laugh. 'Spencer, you have never been a fool. Don't start now.' She squeezed his fingers gently. 'I think we all knew there would never be any way back for me.'

The urge to deny her words rose within Spencer like a boiling tide, tempting him to argue despite the truth he knew he was powerless to change. She was right. Of course, she always was, damn it. His mother was dying, her time on earth growing shorter by the moment, and there was nothing he could do to stop her from slipping away to join William and his father and leave him alone in the silent house that would feel so empty without her.

Dorothea's dim eyes met his and it was as though she could read his thoughts as easily as the pages of a book.

'I wish I didn't have to leave you. I'd do anything to spare you the sorrow I can see already in your face.'

He almost flinched away from the pain in her voice. 'Think nothing of me. Is there anything I can bring to you? Anything I can do that might make you more comfortable while we wait for the doctor?'

Even as he spoke Spencer knew his questions were pointless, the steady chill of dread growing ever colder in his gut. Out of the corner of his eye he could just make out the vaguest blur of Grace's slender figure kneeling breathlessly a few steps away, one hand never leaving Dorothea's and the other softly stroking the thin hair back from his mother's forehead in a movement so tender it brought a lump to his throat. If there was anything they could do to ease her passing, he knew with sudden certainty, Grace would help him

without a moment's hesitation. Her affection for Dorothea was plain for anybody to see, and Spencer knew
it was only with great determination that her obvious
emotion was held in check.

'There's only one thing I would ask of you. Just one
thing, if I thought I dared.' Mrs Dauntsey's mouth attempted to curve into a hesitant smile and Spencer felt
his own lips twist in a wordless grimace as he bent
closer to hear the low-spoken words. 'I fear it would
not please you, however, and I would so hate for us to
quarrel at this pass.'

Redoubling his grip on her hand, Spencer gritted his
teeth. Grace's careful fingers still smoothed the lank
curls, her cool touch no doubt blissful against burning
skin, and Spencer felt the muscles of his jaw tighten
with sudden force.

*If nothing else, I will always be grateful for Grace's
kindness during this terrible night. How many people
would know how to tend a dying woman with such instinctive care?*

It was only more proof of the good heart he already
knew lay beneath her quiet surface, but fresh admiration flared inside him and would not be repressed.
There was nobody else he would have chosen to be
with him in that moment and the knowledge rocked
him to his foundation.

'Surely you know you can ask anything of me. Name
it. Whatever you wish for, name it, and I swear it will
be done.'

A beat of silence descended that none of the three
people in the warm, candlelit room broke with anything other than the sound of slow, laboured breathing.

'Are you quite certain you ought to make that promise before you hear my request?'

Spencer nodded gravely, too full of a wild tumult of feelings to think any further than granting his mother the final favour she would ever ask. 'Completely. If it is in my power, I will do whatever you ask.'

'Even if it means putting aside your own wishes? Taking a path for my sake you would not have chosen for yourself?'

'Even then.'

Dorothea sighed, the tiniest sound so bizarrely like relief it made Spencer's frown deepen further.

'And you, Grace?' The dim gaze shifted to look to the other side. 'You said once if there was anything you could do to help me all I would have to do is ask. Is that still true?'

Grace's voice came as a thin thread, the anguish in it forcing a shard of glass between Spencer's ribs.

'Yes. Anything.'

'Your word is still mine to use as I believe best?'

'Always.'

His mother's cracked lips stretched into another painful smile.

'Then I have a request to make of you, Grace. A task I'd charge you with, if you would accept it.'

Out of the corner of his eye he saw Grace's resolute nod, absolute determination in every line of her delicate profile. 'I'll accept, Dorothea. Whatever it is, whatever you ask of me, I swear now I will do anything to ease your mind.'

'Very well.' Dorothea's eyes fluttered closed, for all the world as though steeling herself to take a leap of faith into the unknown. There was another moment of perfect quiet. Then:

'Spencer—I wish for you to marry Grace. Here, tonight, in my rooms. I ask you be a good husband to her as she has been a friend to me in my last weeks, making my life so much sweeter. Grace, in return I ask you would guide Spencer from the darkness he has chosen and back into the light, towards the life both of you ought to be living.'

A sharp intake of breath came from opposite him and Spencer's head snapped up to look at the woman who sounded as though she struggled to breathe. Her eyes flashed wide and one hand leapt up to press against her chest as though she could scarcely comprehend what she had heard, just as he himself was filled with horrified confusion, and he turned back to his mother with a hundred questions roaring up within him. He stared at her for a long moment, hardly trusting himself to reply.

'You want me to—*what*?'

'You heard me perfectly well. It is my senses that grow dim, not yours.' Dorothea swallowed painfully, eyes still firmly shut. 'It is my dearest wish you marry Grace, Spencer, for the good of both of you. I don't know what happened on the day Will passed, but you have never been the same since. I would die with a smile on my lips if I knew for certain you wouldn't spend the rest of your years alone with your grief and regrets.'

She broke off, evidently tired by the effort of speaking. Spencer sensed Grace's frozen form now standing immovably beside the bed, one hand still twined around Dorothea's, but the other clutched at the bodice of her gown. She must have leapt to her feet in shock—hardly surprising, given the turn of events neither one of them could have predicted.

He didn't raise his head to look at her directly; with a flicker of shame he realised he didn't dare. What expression of dismay, disgust, abject horror would be etched on to the pallor of her face? Surely she was as shocked by his mother's request as he was, the very idea of marrying him one she might have laughed at had the notion not been so jarring. *She* would never entertain the idea, he was certain, and besides, he baulked at the suggestion of allowing her—or anyone—into the silent misery his life had become two years before, the mention of Will's name only adding to the roiling swirl of emotion Spencer was not sure he could endure. He'd entertained the idea of marriage only once before and it had led to a catastrophe that woke him each night to bathe him in cooling sweat.

It was absurd, impossible—

And yet we swore we would grant any request. How could we have been so foolish?

Still refusing to lock eyes with the woman who stood mere feet away, her tense frame close enough for him to caress with wondering fingertips should he stretch out one arm, he took a breath. The strange desires Grace roused in him were exactly what made her more dangerous than any other woman, her gentle nature and determined spirit an intoxicating combination that called to the last vestiges of vulnerability suffering had yet to rip from him.

'It never crossed my mind to marry.' He could barely utter the words, so tightly had his jaw frozen in dismay, choking him with every syllable.

'I know. You thought to live alone with only a bottle for company, slowly drinking yourself into an early grave.' There was an edge to Dorothea's thin voice. 'I can't allow it.'

Damn it all. Spencer swore beneath his breath and ran a hand distractedly through the riot of his hair. Had he truly been so transparent? If his mother possessed a crystal ball, it wouldn't have surprised him—her summation of his plans for the future was uncannily accurate.

He forced himself at last to turn to Grace in desperation.

'Surely you have some opinion of all this? How can you stand so quietly?'

Grace blinked at him, her eyes wide with unspoken bewilderment. No doubt a hundred thoughts ran through her sharp mind, he thought in reluctant admiration, but apparently none of them had made it as far as her mouth, for she said nothing before his mother nodded in Grace's direction with firm finality.

'Grace is an intelligent woman who will appreciate the merits of such a marriage. She will be well provided for. I do not intend to be cruel, dear Grace, when I say it is unlikely your circumstances will allow you to receive such an offer again.' Dorothea spoke as gently as her dry throat would allow and Spencer saw Grace swallow painfully. 'Take the chance in front of you, honour the promise you made me and see if between the two of you there might be some happiness to be found in life after all.'

The suggestion of any kind of *happiness* resulting from his mother's scheme was so unlikely Spencer had to fight the urge to bark a grim laugh. That allowing

Grace Linwood to share his house, his life—his bed, he thought with a sudden pang of that unnamed *something* she so often managed to make glimmer within him—could bring any improvement to his future was unthinkable. They had nothing in common, aside from the desire to spend as little time in each other's company as possible—what kind of a basis was *that* for a marriage? If the sculpted curves of her cheekbones and jaw brought forward thoughts he hadn't expected to ever have again it should mean nothing; surely no good could come of indulging them, history sure to repeat itself should he allow it the chance. And Grace herself—hadn't she as good as told him she never intended to wed another after Henry had disappointed her so cruelly?

No woman forgets her first love. Those were the words she had spoken only this evening.

Despite the horror and bewildering agony of their current circumstances Spencer couldn't suppress a sudden pinch of something uncomfortably close to jealousy at the memory, a sharp dig he could have done without. For a man so unworthy as Henry to be permitted a space in Grace's heart was surely unfair when there might be *other* men more deserving, but that wasn't something on which he should dwell, instead needing to consider the shocking proposal laid out before him.

Apparently, however, his mother hadn't finished. 'Grace has made my final weeks so much more comfortable. Would you repay her by allowing her to remain a costly worry to her mama and left with no real prospects of anything more? When you had the means to save her?'

Spencer rubbed his forehead with a rough hand.

She makes a good point on that score, at least.

The company of a lively young woman had brought such obvious respite to the darkness of his mother's final weeks, meeting a need Spencer had been powerless to fill himself. Laughter had been heard coming from her formerly lonely chambers and nothing could have been more pleasing to him than the new brightness he had seen in the clouded eyes that matched the colour of his own.

And her actions tonight? Helping to comfort a woman in her last hours?

Another thrill of that appreciation crackled through his veins as he thought of the gentle sorrow on Grace's countenance that very night, as she had stroked damp curls with such care it had made it difficult for him to breathe.

Surely she deserves your help now. More so than anybody.

'You are the only one left.' Dorothea's voice was barely a murmur now. 'My only son, the last of the Dauntseys. Don't let our family fade because of the secrets I know you keep inside.'

The muscles of Spencer's throat squeezed tighter, but he could find no words to reply.

She was right. The image of his father's dying smile flashed before him, followed closely behind by the last memory he had of Will: stretched out on the muddy ground, eyes wide and staring and his red uniform shredded to blood-drenched ribbons. Soon those final pictures would be joined by one of his mother, lying still and white and leaving him entirely alone.

Grace's low entreaty interrupted the dizzying train of his thoughts. 'But, Dorothea, consider. Even if we *were* to marry—' She broke off for a moment. Spencer caught the swiftest of glances in his direction, a flick of storm-cloud grey that somehow managed to quicken the already racing pulse of his heart. 'We cannot do it here. There must be banns, an arrangement made for a church service...'

'Not so.' Despite the tightly drawn set of her features Dorothea managed to look quietly triumphant. 'I took the liberty of procuring a marriage certificate for just such an occasion. If you are married in the Quaker faith, we can perform the ceremony right here in my chamber. All you require is witnesses and it can be done this very night.'

Both watching faces slackened in surprise, neither able to immediately find a reply.

'You've had this planned for some time.' Spencer raised a wry eyebrow in something close to unwilling admiration. 'Everything neatly taken care of.'

He turned his head to Grace, taking in the stiff arrangement of her limbs and the dusky hint of colour that flared across her cheeks. She was dignified in her silence, only the rapid flit of her pulse at the base of her slender neck a clue as to the whirling of her clever mind. Spencer watched her for a moment and then surrendered to his fate.

'It would appear we have been outmanoeuvred.'

'It certainly seems that way.' Her reply was little more than a whisper, yet she didn't flinch away. Instead she moved closer, standing so near to the edge of the bed on which he sat Spencer could see the delicate pattern on her dress in perfect detail and how the knuckles of the hand that gripped the other stood out like white pebbles beneath the skin.

He stood abruptly, tracking the upward movement of her eyes as he towered above her. She barely came up to his shoulder, but there was a determined angle to the set of her jaw that made him wonder, with a surprising lack of displeasure, if he might finally have met his match.

'What do you say? Ought we give in to my mother's tyranny and grant her this final request?' His tone was as detached as he could manage, although the intense emotion that his own words sent lancing through to his gut almost choked him.

Her final request.

After everything else was stripped away, that was the bare fact: Dorothea was dying, fading before his very eyes, and this was the last thing he could ever do for the woman who had been his last reason for living. There was no humour to be found at her meddling, only the unfillable gap her death would leave in his heart and his soul, a space that even with her final breaths she tried so ardently to mend for him. She had seen that same kindness in Grace—could it be they would truly save each other from their miserable fates?

It was only when his chest gave a wrench that Spencer realised he had been holding his breath as he waited for Grace to reply. Her long lashes shielded her from looking directly at him, but nothing could hide the tremble of her lips as she spoke the only word necessary to send his heart slamming into his ribs.

'Yes.'

All the air seemed to have been sucked out of the room by that one syllable, murmured so quietly Spencer could scarce believe he had heard her correctly.

For a measureless time nobody spoke. Time ceased

to mean anything to Spencer as he stood still and felt his entire world shift beneath the power of one whispered word. All his thoughts for the future, all his plans to give himself up to the darkness that writhed inside him: destroyed by the woman who now looked him straight in the eye with a steadfast courage that dared him to test his own mettle. There was uncertainty in the shifting tide of her expression, a touch of vulnerability that pinched Spencer somewhere beneath the armour of his indifference, but Grace's head was up and her jaw was set, and she watched him with the bravery of a frightened person who had decided that to jump from a ledge was better than to fall.

He stared back, for the first time allowing himself to drink her in as much as he wished. There was no trace of the smile that had lodged itself immovably at the forefront of his brain, nor the dimple mined in the flawless porcelain of her cheek. Instead she was solemn, the dull tinge of grief starting to steal the light from her stormy gaze, and it was with a searing bolt of wonder Spencer realised it would fall to him, her *husband,* to dry her tears. It was an unspeakably odd notion and one that hit him like a physical blow: Grace would be his *wife*, bound to him for the rest of their time on earth, and the same realisation shone out of her face with an apprehension he could almost have tasted.

A knock at the door broke the wordless tension between them, shattering the moment of shared feeling like glass dropped on a cold stone floor.

Both tense figures turned to watch as Dr Sharp stepped into the room, carrying his medical case, but his face grave as though he knew it was useless baggage.

'Doctor. Thank you for coming.' Spencer moved

to clasp his shoulder, pleased as he extended his hand to note it was perfectly steady despite the chaos that reigned in his stomach. 'Your timing is impeccable, sir. I'd like to invite you to witness my wedding.'

The doctor's mouth dropped open in a perfect circle of naked surprise which in any other circumstances might have been amusing.

'A wedding? Here? Now?' His gaze flipped from Spencer to Grace to the scant shape of Dorothea lying milk-white beneath her luxurious covers and his bushy brows rose in astonishment.

'Captain Dauntsey, surely this is neither the time nor the place!'

A tut of impatience from the bed drew every eye in the room. 'An old woman's last request, Dr Sharp. There will never be the opportunity for a better time or a better place.'

The doctor's look of shock persisted as Spencer hunted for the marriage certificate in Dorothea's desk, although by the time a pen was thrust into his hand the old gentleman seemed more dazed than disapproving. In all likelihood he had no desire to argue with the obviously rapidly failing Dauntsey matriarch, although her eyes remained closed until Spencer stood before Grace at the foot of the great oak bed and prepared to recite the words he had never thought would pass his lips.

I should probably take her hand. Isn't that the usual way for these things?

He glanced down at her delicate fingers, as white as though she wore gloves; they twisted together in a repetitive movement that betrayed whatever agitation Grace was trying to hide. The enticing thought of how her delicate hand might feel within his sent a shiver of unease thrilling through him and Spencer resolutely clasped his own in front of him in reflexive discomfort.

Perhaps not. I can't imagine such a thing would be wise—or welcome.

Silence stretched out like a blanket of silk, nobody moving or even blinking in a moment so tense it was almost tangible until Spencer cleared his throat and began to speak.

'In the presence of God and these our friends, I take thee, Grace Elizabeth Linwood, to be my wife, promising with divine assistance to be unto thee a loving and faithful husband as long as we both shall live.'

She followed the movement of his lips, entirely focused on the strange vows Spencer realised she might never have heard before. In another life he might have attempted to ease her obvious anxiety with a small smile, but that was the man he had been before, when his mother was more than a mere husk about to be swallowed by the unforgiving jaws of death.

Such thoughts were pointless, he reminded himself grimly as Grace took a deep breath and with a tremor in her voice began to repeat the same promises that would bind them.

What is there to be said? She doesn't wish to marry me and I can't pretend I desire a wife either—I won't insult her by starting our marriage on a lie.

He heard his mother's soft intake of breath, a gentle sigh of something like release as Grace forced the words past unwilling lips. Each movement of her mouth drew Spencer's eye like a moth to a flame, their lush rose hue like petals made to be kissed. The whole world seemed to have shrunk to focus on that mouth, shaping the sounds that drew her ever closer to a fate neither of them could have foreseen.

It was over before Spencer could really believe it. Even after taking up his pen and signing his life into Grace's keeping he could only stare down at his scrawled signature in numb disbelief.

It's done. It's done, and there's no going back from it now—even if she wishes I was another man entirely.

Grace's elegant mark glittered in the firelight, ink still wet on the thick parchment. Doctor Sharp signed in silence, a deep furrow of misgiving pitting his brow, and Dorothea's name was little more than a scratch of the pen, a shapeless smudge made with great effort by her weak and trembling hand.

I am hers and she is mine. Now—what the hell am I to do with her?

The question repeated itself over and again, echoing through his mind empty of all thoughts but the unanswered whisper he couldn't seem to face. He had fulfilled Dorothea's final wish, had granted her that last request, but what did this mean for him now? And for the woman who had become, against their united better judgement, his lawfully wedded wife?

Nothing was able to displace the roar of confusion or the pounding of his heart in his ears, obliterating all other sound until finally, after what felt like half an eternity, he heard Grace murmur his name.

She was looking down at his mother, standing so still and pale beside the bed she might have been a marble statue. He followed her gaze to the woman he had loved for twenty years and more, who now lay in perfect, untouchable serenity with the sweetest smile of relief upon her lifeless lips.

Chapter Five

Not a word had passed between them for almost an hour, Grace's glance up at the clock on the mantel showed. The gilt hands crept closer and closer to reading two o'clock in the morning, and the terrible silence that surrounded the figures sitting on either side of the cold hearth was punctuated only by the sound of heavy footfalls from overhead. The local midwife, Mrs Lake, had answered Spencer's midnight summons at once, and she and her daughter would see Dorothea was properly laid out with dignity. They attended her now, washing and dressing her with the respect a lifetime of kindness deserved, although the knowledge of why she was no longer able to do such things for herself made Grace want to curl into a ball of anguish.

Instead she looked towards Spencer, sitting so still and quiet he might have been sculpted from ice. His jaw was set so tightly Grace could see the straining muscle of his neck, the only outward sign of whatever horrors reeled through his mind.

'Spencer.'

He appeared not to hear her at first, so delayed was

his reaction to her low murmur. When he finally lifted his head Grace felt a terrible stab of pity pierce her as his eyes met hers and she saw how they burned with unspeakable pain, alight yet absent as though looking right through her.

The suffering in that one glance spoke to something inside her Grace had barely known existed. It was as though a key had been turned to unlock the floodgates of her sympathy for this strange and unfriendly man who was now her husband and partner in whatever the future might hold, and the urge to comfort him welled up with rapid and bewildering force. It came as though from nowhere, surprising her with its intensity, but she had to force it back as cold rationality tempered the sudden spark. He wasn't the boy she'd known any longer and she might have just made the biggest mistake of her life in making him her husband. Surely now her notoriety would only increase, clandestinely wedded to a dangerous man in the middle of a freezing night.

Doubtless I am the last person whose pity he would want. Forced into marrying me by his mother's dying wish—how he must resent it.

A chill flickered up the length of Grace's spine that had nothing to do with the lack of a fire. The enormity of what she had done only just began to unfurl before her, previously too distracted by Dorothea's condition to truly consider her position. Now a sickening mixture of grief and panic churned within her, swooping in the pit of her stomach in a nauseating flutter as she took in the blank stare of the man she was now tied to for life.

The swirling combination of too many emotions made Grace's head swim and she closed her eyes for a moment to steady herself. Whatever else she might feel, whatever confusion and worry for the future, her main concern should be the present, attempting to console Spencer despite what she feared would be his strenuous objections. He might not have been her first choice of a match, but Dorothea had been right—what other offers would the daughter of a criminal receive? Poor Papa had been devastated to have ruined her chances, she knew with a flurry of unhappiness at the thought of his pain. Was he even now losing sleep in his cell, fretting about the future his actions had bought his eldest daughter? To reject Spencer's hand would have been to sign herself into eternal spinsterhood, remaining a heavy burden on the family that could no longer afford to keep her. It would be a difficult decision to explain, but Grace was at least assured her mama and sisters would come to see its necessity and help her through the worst.

You'll have to learn to get along now, she thought dimly, aware of Spencer's gaze upon her, but not yet able to speak further. *You have no other choice.*

She got to her feet. The muscles of her legs complained painfully, but Grace ignored their protest as she stepped to Spencer's side. He watched her with the wary eyes of a wounded animal, but even so Grace felt him flinch a little as though in surprise when she knelt beside his chair and resolutely, before she had the chance to take fright and change her mind, folded her small hand over one huge, scarred fist.

The reaction of her body to the feel of his rough skin beneath her own was instant. A streak of flame fled straight to her chest and settled there, hot against the cage of her ribs that rose and fell in breaths all of a sudden unsteady in their shuddering rhythm. His

hand was as cold as her own, but the heat that flickered in every nerve felt as though it lit her from the
inside and it was with great difficulty Grace managed
to check the urge to pull away as though he stung her
with his touch.

Alarm shrilled within her as she looked up into her
husband's face and saw the deeply etched suffering
covering his features like a shroud. Her nerves still
sang at the contact between them, disobeying her strict-
est orders to remain indifferent to Spencer's proximity
or the contours of his fist. The very idea of allowing her
aggravating reaction to him to surface at such a time—
or *any* time, especially after her encounter with George
had renewed her determination to control it—made the
fire in her lungs burn all the brighter, although this
time with dismay at her weakness.

*Control yourself. You know better than to behave
like a foolish, moonstruck girl.*

She reached up to smooth a blonde tendril behind
her ear, all the while trying to douse the flames that
leapt within at her nearness to the man who managed
to provoke such a response in her disloyal body. He
hadn't even taken her hand when they wed, instead
standing to attention at the foot of the great bed like the
proud soldier he had once been. He would be dismayed
at the notion a mere touch of his hand could affect her
so; if they were to live together and attempt to fulfil
Dorothea's plea for their salvation, she would have to
try harder to curb the weakness so uncomfortably like
that she had felt for him as a young girl.

Now she knelt beside him she found herself at a loss
for words. What could one say to comfort a person in
such bleak circumstances? Surely nothing could take

away the pain she saw in every line of Spencer's countenance, despite his attempts to conceal it, or soothe the agitation of his mind.

'You've been sitting here for a long time without as much as a single word.' She heard herself falter a little beneath the unwavering granite stare that fixed her, but summoned her courage and continued. 'I'll ring for the servants to bring tea and make up the fire. Perhaps it might give you some comfort if you were to talk…?'

The slow shake of Spencer's head reduced the rest of Grace's sentence to a tailed-off murmur. It was a jerky movement, similar to that of a puppet on a string, but its meaning was plain.

'No tea.' His voice was flat, devoid of the emotion Grace was certain she saw hidden in the rigid set of his face. 'And I have no need of comfort. I knew perfectly well this would come to pass eventually. I was quite prepared.'

Such an obvious lie, she thought in private dismay. The smallest of glances at him showed his broad frame held unnaturally stiffly and the usual gruff tone of his address increased tenfold by stubbornly repressed emotion. Why was he so set on concealing it? Surely it was dangerous to keep such a boiling tide inside.

'A fire, then, at the very least. It's getting colder in here. Let me call for Thorne.'

Again her request was met with that decided shake of the head.

'I sent the servants to their beds some hours ago. If you feel a chill, I can make a fire myself.'

He paused for a moment, his eyes fixed on the small hand sitting above his own. Grace could have sworn she felt it burn warmer beneath his intense gaze, but the thought was wiped from her mind by a piercing arrow of shock as Spencer slowly brought his other palm up from his lap to cover her fingers.

'I should thank you. In her final moments I believe your kindness made my mother truly happy and for that you will always have my gratitude. Not everybody would have done as you did.'

Grace swallowed, aware of every tiny movement of Spencer's skin against hers as he cradled her hand with gentleness his huge one should not have been able to manage. They were scarred hands, not the usual manicured set of most gentlemen, but honest, capable and strong, just as she suspected Spencer might have been, but for the tragedies that had so changed his life.

His unexpected thanks touched her, that faint gleam of simple human gratitude warming her despite the ice in her heart.

There's such feeling there, deep down in his soul.

She saw it glimmer, the smallest chink in the armour he wore, and for the first time wondered if there might be the chance of *some* accord between them.

At least, I hope so. The rest of our lives will seem like a prison sentence if not.

He stood abruptly and Grace straightened likewise to stand before him. She had to tilt her head back to look into his face, so much taller was he, and for a moment they regarded each other in taut silence.

Spencer's eyes roamed her face as though searching for something, although quite what Grace could only wonder. All she knew was that her heart hammered at a speed that frightened her at how closely he stood, near enough that they could have easily fallen into an embrace—*if he thought of you in that way.*

Which overwhelming evidence says he doesn't, never has and never will.

That was the truth she should cling to, remind herself of whenever she felt weakness rise within her again, and it was enough to help her stand her ground until she finally moved aside to allow him to pass her and kneel before the cold hearth. Perhaps it was a distraction of sorts, some way of exorcising whatever demons leapt within him; so she said nothing as he settled on the floor and drew towards him kindling and a tinderbox.

Three quiet taps at the door caught Grace's attention.

Opening it, she found Mrs Lake and her daughter hovering in the hallway, wearing mirrored expressions of respectful sympathy that made Grace's breath claw at her throat.

'We've finished laying out the late Mrs Dauntsey, ma'am.' The midwife spoke gently, many years of experience softening her voice. 'Everything was done quite properly, as befitting such a lady.'

Deep inside her chest something twisted sharply and Grace almost winced in pain.

The late Mrs Dauntsey. 'Late' being the worst of words.

A glance back into the room showed Spencer's head turned resolutely in the direction of the empty hearth, the sharp lines of his fine profile laid bare for Grace's guilty appreciation. She hurriedly stepped out into the hall, shutting the sitting-room door smartly behind her as though it could contain the wayward thoughts that stalked her.

'Captain Dauntsey is, understandably, indisposed

at present. I shall send a servant to call on you very
first thing in the morning with your payment, if you
are agreeable?'

'Of course, ma'am. We wouldn't expect the poor
Captain to be troubling himself with anything tonight.'

Nothing else was said as the three figures moved
through the shadowy house. Evidently in the chaos and
confusion of this dreadful night nobody had thought to
light the candles, so it was by moonlight Grace stood
on the imposing front doorstep and felt the winter darkness turn her skin to gooseflesh that she rubbed at with
cold hands.

'Thank you for coming, especially so late and under
such…*sad* circumstances.' There was a tremor lurking beneath each word Grace forced through taut lips
and she was obliged to grit her teeth against a sob that
would have burst from her mouth. 'We are so grateful
for your tender care. Mrs Dauntsey will be very much
missed by all who knew her.'

Another sob rose up—another one to catch before
it could break free.

Not yet.

She swallowed down the swell of her emotion, unhappiness bitter as bile in her throat.

*If you surrender control now, you will be lost. The
privacy of your rooms is the place for your grief to
unleash its storm.*

Spencer heard the door open and shut again as Grace
returned to the sitting room, but didn't pause in his
task, steadily stacking kindling into the fireplace with
a kind of grim focus.

He worked methodically, first putting down one

layer and then another on top in a neat criss-cross pattern that would allow air to pass between them. A few small logs placed on top would be enough to let the fire take hold, he thought absently, once a spark was allowed to skitter across them. His father had taught him and Will how to start a good blaze when they were small boys and now Spencer was the only one left it was up to him to keep the family knowledge going.

It was a thought so blindingly agonising for a moment Spencer could scarcely breathe. He closed his eyes, fighting the growing ache that bloomed inside him like a dark flower. It unfurled its tendrils, snaking outwards to curl around his heart and squeeze it in a thorny grip so tightly it hurt.

Except you're not the only one left, are you? Thanks to Mother's scheming at the last.

The whispered thought cut into his pain, reverberating inside his mind like an echo in an empty room.

You're not alone. You have Grace now—your wife.

She had looked so hesitant as her little hand had reached out to touch his own, so sweetly unsure it had taken everything within him not to grasp hold of her slender fingers and pull her closer. How would she have reacted if he had done just that? he wondered, for one blessed moment able to consider something other than his grief. Would she have ripped herself free of his grip, horrified he had misunderstood the intention behind her unexpected gesture?

The answer was obvious.

Of course she would. She'd be mortified if she suspected your weakness. Any kindness she showed you was just that, simple kindness, of the sort a woman like Grace would give to anybody in need of it. You'd be a fool to think any different and an even bigger fool to desire anything more, especially since she as good as told you her heart still yearns for that simpering wastrel Earls.

If there was a quality to Grace that spoke to something inside him, her tenderness and kind nature a soothing balm for his troubled soul, he *must* fight against it. To accept her compassion could all too easily lead to the weakening of his defences, built up by guilt and grief into a fortress he had thought impenetrable. If his experience with Constance had taught him nothing else it was that his affections only brought pain—to others as well as himself. A woman like Grace would never look at him with anything warmer than pity, and besides: Henry had broken her heart like cheap china, the uncomfortably enviable first love no other man would ever eclipse.

It was only when he realised he hadn't heard Grace's footsteps move across the room that Spencer finally looked up from the hearth, still holding the tinderbox between numb fingers.

She was watching him, standing just inside the doorway dimly lit by the feeble light of dying candles set about the room. Their soft orange glow threw shadows across her face, but even in the gloom Spencer could make out the luminous pallor of her skin and the world of compassion contained in the grey beauty of her eyes. They fixed on him unwaveringly, radiating concern only tempered by an air of uncertainty betrayed by the pinch of her eyebrows. Her close scrutiny stirred the fine hairs at the back of his neck; for a brief, unstoppable moment his mind reeled back to revisit the memory of Grace's corresponding nape, so delicate it had stolen words from his lips and set him on a course more uncomfortable than any he had ever known.

He must have looked up more sharply than she had been expecting, catching her before she could swiftly turn her head away and pretend she hadn't been studying him.

'I told the midwives we would send a servant with their payment in the morning.'

Spencer nodded, although the roulette wheel of his mind slowed to stop on one particular word: *we*. They were a pair now, he realised with a dawning sense of dread and wonder. It was the strangest feeling to think it was *Grace*, of all people, to whom he was now bound by one familiar word.

There were dark smudges beneath her eyes, tiredness making her look older than her years, and with a flicker of wonder Spencer saw again how she had matured from the girl he had known into an elegant woman, still far too young to look so haunted, both by grief and fear of a future she had not foreseen.

It was an effort to rise to his feet and turn towards her. 'It's late and you look tired. You ought to go to bed.'

For a moment she merely stared at him, pale and delicate in the growing warmth of his fledgling fire. Her mouth opened as though to reply, but then her eyes slid away from his and she nipped at her lower lip. When she spoke it was in a low murmur he couldn't quite catch.

'What was that?'

Grace's discomfort was almost palpable in its intensity. 'I said I'm not sure which chamber to sleep in. I would of course have gone to my own, but now...after tonight…' She delivered the final words in a rush, as though determined to get through them before she lost her nerve. 'If I am to stay here, there can be no doubt as to our situation. Perhaps, given our new arrangement, we ought to share.'

Spencer felt the muscles of his face freeze as a cold wave of surprise crashed over him like an icy sea against rocks. *Share a bedchamber?* She wanted to share a bedchamber—and presumably his bed?

It was such an obvious question for her to ask, he realised belatedly as he stared at her burning face; sensible, even. Even in the half-light the crimson sheen of her cheeks was plain to see and Spencer felt himself swallow as a sudden picture of how she might look laying against his rich pillows leapt within him before he could stop it.

'I confess I had given *that* no thought whatsoever.' She mustn't see his discomfort—indeed, it was *vital* Grace have no inkling of the whirl of feelings that swirled inside him at the thought of her curled beneath his covers, a warm shape so painfully tempting he felt his mouth dry at the very thought.

Calm yourself.

Of course they would have to reach some kind of arrangement. Regardless of his feelings on the matter, or whatever misgivings Grace might have, they would have to find their way through the uncharted darkness of matrimony together—in all its forms.

'It would be the most fitting thing.' Still Grace didn't meet his eye, instead staring fixedly down at the patch of sitting-room carpet between her neat little slippers. 'There could be even more rumours if we are seen to be living together but not quite as man and wife, especially as our wedding was so unconventional. We of all people know how society likes to whisper.'

The automatic temptation to reply with some barbed retort was strong, but Spencer held his tongue. His own disregard for the thoughts of others meant he cared little for his own sake about what talk already swirled, or might begin to, but for Grace it could spell further humiliation worse than any she had experienced before. To be the daughter of a suspected criminal was one thing; the suspicion she might be living unwed with a man as notorious as himself was quite another and so it was with a supressed sense of extreme misgiving Spencer inclined his head.

'Very well. Feel free to move into my rooms as soon as you please.'

There was a decanter and glasses set out on a table not far from the fireplace and Spencer turned to it with relief. It was becoming too much: the death of his mother, his new identity as an unwilling husband, the knowledge his life would never be the same again… It weighed on him like a rock on his chest and suddenly all he wanted was to be alone with his grief and the confusion that churned inside him, turning upside down every secret vow he had made in the solitude of his suffering. How he was to proceed with not *just* a wife, but the dangerous entity that was Grace, was a puzzle he had no hope of solving while she stood across from him, watching his every move as though he was a wild animal she didn't yet know if she could trust.

He poured himself a generous measure of port, drank it down without tasting it and poured out another. 'I doubt I shall sleep tonight. You will not be disturbed.'

Grace said nothing for a long moment, her eyes finally rising from the floor to read whatever she could in the blankness of his expression. There mustn't have been much to see, for with only a small nod of her head she turned away from him, one hand on the smooth brass of the door handle that stood between her and escape.

Just before she disappeared from his sight she turned back, a complicated mixture of compassion and worry mingling to enhance the porcelain loveliness of her face that made Spencer's jaw tighten with unconscious admiration. 'Is there truly nothing more you'd like to say? After everything that's happened here tonight?' She gestured around the room, glancing in particular dismay at the glass he held in one cold hand.

Spencer looked at her, held her gaze for what felt like far too long. She didn't falter, gazing back at him with that vivid concern that made him want to allow a growl of grief and confusion to erupt from his lips, regardless of the consequences.

Instead he turned away, staring into the fire with blind eyes that saw nothing of what lay before them.

'You'll learn I'm not one for talking these days. Goodnight, Grace.'

Chapter Six

It didn't take long for Grace to realise her new husband was as good as his word.

Barely a single sentence had passed between them since the night Dorothea died: a week of scarcely broken silence. She'd held on to the slim hope the funeral might prompt Spencer to unburden himself, but he had returned from that sorry event—as usual barred to women, for fear their distasteful *emotion* might not be publicly contained—with his lips pressed into a tight line and disappeared back into his study from which the only sound that came was the gentle splash of liquid against fine crystal. That was where he slept, if the fitful armchair doze he lapsed into occasionally could be termed sleep, leaving Grace to wait breathlessly upstairs for a footstep outside their bedchamber door that never came. Mama had hinted delicately at what that footstep might lead to on Grace's first visit home after her hasty marriage, when she and her daughters had stared at the new Mrs Dauntsey with wide eyes and mute disbelief; but for now Grace had been spared whatever subtleties her mother had been trying, with ladylike vagueness, to express.

The servants had noticed Spencer's absence from the great feather bed—Grace had overheard them whispering and knew it was only a matter of time before fresh rumours began to spread. Older couples might sleep apart, after years of matrimony and the necessary heirs had been obtained, but for a pair of young newlyweds... It cast doubt over their arrangement, blurring boundaries that should have been crisp. He would *have* to share with her eventually if they were to avoid yet more gossip as to the legitimacy of their unconventional marriage, already raising eyebrows for its secrecy and speed. Spencer didn't care about that, of course, but the idea of being subject to more assaults on her reputation gave Grace a second reason for increasing concern.

On the morning of the seventh day that she awoke alone in the grand expanse of Spencer's bed, Grace lay back against the smooth linen of unrumpled sheets and stared up at the embroidered canopy while she decided how to proceed.

Currently the only other person in the calm green-papered bedchamber was the maid laying out Grace's clothes for the day ahead. A black bombazine dress was complemented by a string of jet beads and a cameo brooch to be pinned to the bodice, finished by a pair of queen's silk slippers—all in the sombre tones of deep mourning, which with a sigh Grace recalled she'd be enveloped in for months. It wasn't that she begrudged Dorothea such a mark of respect; more that it seemed so at odds with the vibrant personality of the woman whose passing it marked, for whom a dress of the brightest silks would have surely been more appropriate. All the gloom of mourning did was remind Grace of her grief, a connection that couldn't have escaped Spencer's keen eye, either.

Perhaps that was why he seems so intent on avoiding me, Grace mused as the maid helped her into her dreary gown.

She must seem like a spectre haunting the rooms of his house, her dark presence tangible proof of a nightmare come true, but he couldn't hide away from her for ever.

Grace caught sight of herself in the long mirror affixed to one wall of what *should* have been her marital chamber and gave a wry nod at the determination she saw in the face reflected back at her. Dorothea had as good as given her a binding task before she died: to guide her straying son back to the right course. And by heaven, Grace meant to keep her word as well as she could, despite her own hesitations—whether Spencer liked it or not.

He was exactly where she had known he would be when she was ready to go in search of her errant husband, although Grace felt her breath halt in her throat at the sight that greeted her as she quietly opened the study door and peeped inside. The room was dim, the servants obviously not having dared enter to open the heavy curtains despite the wintery sunshine battling earnestly to stream inside—so it was in semi-darkness Grace saw Spencer asleep in his chair, even while unconscious his face never free of the permanent scowl he wore like a second skin.

With those sharp, dark eyes of his closed Grace found herself in the novel position of being able to stare as long as she liked and she felt heat climb her neck as she took in the powerful breadth of his chest that rose and fell with uneasy breaths, fitful as though sleep brought no relief from whatever dark thoughts stalked his waking mind. It wasn't just the movement of his chest that drew her gaze like an arrow, however; he had evidently loosened his cravat at some point during the night and a few buttons of his white shirt had come unfastened in careless disregard of any kind of propriety. The overall result, when combined with the tousled mess of his hair, was one of such indecent abandon Grace felt her heart rate pick up speed. She shouldn't be looking, her innate sense of decorum instructed prissily, yet something about the line of his sculpted collarbone giving way to a teasing glimpse of toned chest transfixed her attention so stubbornly she could barely tear herself away. What would that chest feel like beneath her fingertips, she wondered, the hair there gently curling to mirror the soft waves on his head…?

Grace's brows drew together in a brief frown as a prickle of conscience nagged at her.

That's not what you're here for. You came to try to help him, not lurk in doorways.

Still, she had to admit it would have taken a woman of stone to remain unmoved by the scandalously uninhibited sight of her reluctant new husband and Grace was as human as any other.

Spencer lounged against the cushions with legs outstretched and one wrist hanging over the arm of the chair, fingers twitching slightly as Grace stepped carefully past him. On the floor directly beneath his hand lay an empty glass, rolled on to its side amid a congealing stain she had no need to inspect any closer.

At the first shaft of blinding sunshine that burst into the room Spencer flung up a hand to shield his face, drawing in a harsh breath as Grace seized another curtain and yanked it back to allow yet more light to flood in. He groaned something Grace was quite grateful she didn't catch as he peered round the room to locate his tormentor with eyes narrowed against the sudden brightness. They grew narrower still when he saw his wife standing before one floor-to-ceiling window, beckoning reassuringly to Rivers who now hesitated on the threshold.

'Good morning, Spencer. Did you sleep well?' Grace allowed no time for him to reply before gesturing to Spencer's untidy desk. 'Set the tray down there, please. Thank you.' The poor maid did as she was asked, laying her burden down while shooting nervous glances at the glowering figure in the chair, before scuttling from the room as quickly as good manners would allow.

Grace turned the smile on Spencer, resisting the impulse to wilt slightly beneath his unforgiving stare. 'I'll pour, shall I?' She moved over to the desk with as much authority as she could muster, the very image of a well-bred lady hosting an honoured guest.

'Grace.'

Staunchly ignoring the hoarse voice at her back, Grace busied herself with the cups. 'Will you take sugar this morning?'

'I don't want—'

'Perhaps just a little.'

'I said I don't—'

'Now, do be careful. It's very hot—'

'Grace!' The words burst forth in infuriation, although Spencer was left with no choice but to grasp the drink fairly shoved under his nose. 'For pity's sake, woman—what are you about? What do you mean by bursting in here, ripping my curtains to shreds and then harassing me with a teapot?'

'Coffee.'

'What?' He peered up at her with exasperated eyes, more than a little bloodshot. Grace had to battle not to allow her own gaze to stray from his face, slipping down to survey that hard sliver of chest that peeked so temptingly from his unbuttoned collar.

'It's coffee in this pot, not tea. And I'm not *harassing* you, I'm trying to help you.'

The firm jaw clenched visibly, defining the already chiselled contours of his tired face. 'For the last time. I don't require any *help.*'

'No?' She raised an eyebrow with more confidence than she felt. 'When was the last time you quit this room during daylight? Or did anything other than sit in here, in the darkness, nursing your sorrows with the contents of a bottle?'

For one long, tense moment Grace wondered if she might have pushed too far, too soon. It *had* only been a week. Perhaps she should have left him to cope in his own way a little longer? But then the spilled glass in its sticky puddle caught her eye and she softened her voice in gentle persuasion.

'Please, Spencer. I promised Dorothea I would help you, if I can—will you not let me? If you would just talk to me, share with me your grief, perhaps together we can find a better way through this terrible time.'

Spencer shot Grace a look that she didn't enjoy. 'Any fears you may have for me are misplaced, I assure you. There's nothing I can't overcome if left to my own devices, the loss of my mother included.'

It was on the tip of Grace's tongue to argue with him that wasn't the very reason Dorothea had herded them down this sorry path *because* of Spencer's self-destructive way of coping? His mother had been sadly accurate in her prediction of the downward spiral that would follow her passing. Sitting all night in a lonely room with a rapidly emptying decanter, stubbornly withdrawing from the world, was the very future Dorothea had feared would claim her son.

'You say that, but I can't help but feel your *own devices* are not the best course. Why, you must be freezing when you wake in here with no fire and it can't be comfortable to sleep in that chair either.'

Spencer had taken a swig of coffee, but he swallowed it down quickly with a sharp look. 'Would you *rather* I slept upstairs? In my bedchamber? With you?' Something passed across his handsome features Grace didn't understand; a lightning-fast flicker of *something* that flitted by and was gone before he could control it. 'Surely you can't be eager for *that*?'

She avoided his gaze, staring down into her coffee cup in pink-cheeked agitation.

Careful, now.

The idea of Spencer stretched out beside her on expensive sheets made heat pool low down in her insides, a distinctly unladylike reaction and in direct defiance of her determination to remain unmoved.

'I don't like the idea of you languishing down here every night, but equally I want to put an end to the whispering among the servants that could so easily travel further afield.' In the very corner of her field of vision Grace could just make out how closely he watched her, dark eyes never leaving her flushed face. 'You *know* how people already mutter when I leave the house; only yesterday I heard them again when returning from visiting Mama. What do you think they'll say when it becomes known I live with a man I call my husband, but who sleeps apart in an entirely different part of the house? It's an oddity for two people our age so recently wed and sure to provoke more speculation than I care to allow.'

Spencer huffed out a humourless laugh. 'So it's on account of your reputation you object to my behaviour? Because of what people who barely know you might have to say?' Another flash of some unrecognisable thought crossed his face—this time so startlingly close to a shadow of disappointment Grace felt herself blink in confusion. Surely he didn't care whether she worried for him, or wanted him beneath her bedclothes? He had made it perfectly clear he wanted none of her fussing, yet that flit of an indescribable expression nagged at something in the back of Grace's mind.

'My reputation is already more damaged than I ever would have thought possible, both by my poor father's mistakes and Henry's rejection.' An image of Papa's dear face drifted in front of her mind's eye for a moment, pale and wan in a draughty cell, and Grace forced herself to turn from it with a sudden wrench of her insides. It was a thought she had to fight back all too often and always managed to make her throat tighten around a lump of searing unhappiness at his undeserved fate. He should be in his own home, surrounded by his family and enjoying the quiet, refined life the Linwoods had always led, but her father remained in the Fleet and Grace had no choice but to watch the changing tide of her husband's unreadable expression.

'I don't think it's unreasonable not to want it tarnished further by you—a man who already generates quite enough talk as things stand, given your past actions. Can it truly be a wonder to you that I'd like to avoid further comment on my person and my life?'

She spoke more sharply than she'd intended, caught off guard by the perplexing look on his face that posed questions she didn't know how to answer. It was hardly surprising that Spencer's frown deepened at her tone with a flicker of real displeasure that made Grace shrink a little.

'My actions are nobody's business but my own. If anybody objects to how I conduct myself, let them say so in person.'

Grace clenched her hands into fists at Spencer's obstinate words.

He's impossible!

Could he not see how mortifying this conversation was for her? Was he blind to the indignity of having to beg for him to share her bed? She tried to force herself to remain calm, but a mixture of worry and anger began to build in her chest.

'*I* object and *I* am saying so in person. Do you not see how it looks for us to be living alone together, a married couple in some respects and yet with no real evidence of our connection in others? Surely you can understand why society might question the legitimacy—'

'Hang *society*.' Spencer got to his feet, towering above Grace with his impressive height that even in her current state of high emotion she couldn't help but admire. 'What has society done for you, other than treat you with contempt? I care nothing for their whispers and neither should you.'

A current of something like electricity prickled beneath Grace's skin as she looked up at her stubborn husband, only an arm's length away yet as untouchable as if in another world. With a start of horror she felt how her body wanted to curve towards him, to close the gap between them that was not only physical, and again felt hopeless confusion as to how he could affect her so effortlessly, even against her strongest resolve.

'Perhaps you're right. Perhaps I shouldn't care. But I don't *want* to shut myself away, to ignore the world and turn my back as you do.'

Spencer's eyes narrowed and Grace swallowed hard at their sudden coldness. Any hint of the appreciation she thought she'd glimpsed so fleetingly the night Dorothea died was entirely absent as he looked at her, the darkness that so often haunted his face covering it like a grim mask.

'Do you truly think you understand how I see the world? That you have any grasp on why I have to be the way I am?'

Her heart skittered inside her like a trapped animal as she took in the hard set of his jaw, but Grace managed to hold her ground and return his unwavering stare with one of her own.

'No. How can I, when you won't talk to me about anything? We're married now, bound together for the rest of our lives. Can't you at least try to let me in? I know you must have good reasons, but there might be some way to work through them if you would only share your pain.'

She saw how his brows twitched into a frown and realised with a pinch of dismay just how much she wanted to touch the crease with gentle fingertips, that harsh handsomeness managing once again to find the last traces of weakness in her and invade without mercy. Once she started tracing the contours of that face she might not be able to stop, running her fingers over the crooked nose and lips tense with whatever emotions he thought it necessary to conceal. He always seemed so alone, so solitary even when she was near him, and the thought Dorothea's fears were coming true just about broke her heart.

'There isn't.' Spencer broke the intense connection of their eyes to run a hand through tousled hair. 'Sometimes turning his back is the only thing a man can do.'

He set his coffee cup on the desk and walked away from her, ill-mannered as ever, but this time Grace could have sworn she sensed something else as he made for the door. With his cravat gone and his shirt collar open he looked more like a pirate than a gentleman and Grace had to force back the dangerous image of him careless and confident out on the high seas. It was too appealing by half.

'I've business with my lawyers in town. Don't wait for me to dine later. I've no fixed idea of when I shall return.'

Spencer barely heard one word in ten that his lawyers spoke during their meeting, so fixed were his thoughts on the image of Grace's earnest face as it had looked minutes before he left the house. That eagerness had faded to quiet unhappiness at his brusque refusal, the expression he realised with a prickle of discomfort he had given her reason to wear on more than one occasion. Perhaps she shouldn't have pressed him, but her intentions were—*as always, you ungrateful wretch*—good, and another spike of unease in the region where other men might keep their conscience told him his reaction had been ill-judged.

'…and so with your approval, Captain Dauntsey, we'll meet again tomorrow to finalise these papers.'

The two men seated across from Spencer on the other side of an impressive desk stood to shake his hand and he rose likewise, feeling a niggling ache in his back as he moved. Sleeping in that old chair in his study did him no favours, as the grumble in his muscles attested, but the alternative…

'Thank you, Mr Hallam; Mr Slade. I'll return tomorrow morning.'

He gave each a curt bow and withdrew from the fusty chambers, the sound of pens scratching on paper and the low hum of clerks' conversations hardly registering in a mind too full of Grace to notice much else. The growing feeling of dissatisfaction with his behaviour formed the backdrop of his uncomfortable thoughts, muttering that to dismiss Grace's pleas was not the action of a good husband.

Not that I should care about that, he reminded himself grimly as he reached the front door and stepped out into the chill of the busy street.

It was a fact getting more and more difficult to remember each time he recalled the tenderness with which she had cared for his mother in her last hours, only more proof of the goodness that he so wanted to believe in... But the darkness inside him knew that was impossible, still so aware of his failings as both a brother and a man and the risks in exposing one's heart. Constance had once held his in one hand and Will's in the other—and the quarrel between them had resulted in nothing but death and guilt so deep it choked him each night. William might not be there this time to compete, but the memory of the last time Spencer had been captivated by a woman was enough to make the idea painful beyond belief.

Sleeping in that overstuffed chair was supposed to help him hide the nightmares that made him thrash and beat back the unfortunate temptations that sang to him so sweetly, although apparently he could have saved himself the twinge of a bad back for all the good his self-imposed exile had done him. All he had gained from it was tiredness, irritability and another opportunity to make a fool of himself before Grace, his temper spilling out before he could force it into retreat.

Sharing a bed with her was a thought so tantalising it almost made him groan and he stopped any such thing with a swift clench of his jaw as he walked past gleaming shopfronts and the people stopping to admire them. Of course it wasn't her actual *request* that had made his temper flare—it was the idea upper-class society dictated he do it and that Grace felt the need to bow to its rules.

What was it she'd said? *My actions tarnished her reputation?* He couldn't help the sound that escaped him, a cross between a grunt and a growl that said more about his state of mind than any words.

Ridiculous that she should care what people who

scarcely know her think. Surely anybody even slightly acquainted with Grace would see her kindness, her patience, her willingness to help others…

Far too late Spencer tried to slam the brakes on that runaway train of thought, but it wouldn't be halted as the long list of his wife's virtues unfurled before him.

Sweet-tempered. Clever. Determined. Calm.

He lengthened his stride as though to outrun the roll call of Grace's qualities, although nothing could stop the thought that he ought to at least *try* to understand her point of view. Society and all its shallowness meant nothing to him any more, it was true, and he couldn't imagine ever again caring one jot what people might say of him; but Grace didn't feel the same, and it seemed even more unfair that she should pay the price for his disregard. He had meant it when he said she shouldn't care about their whispers, but perhaps that was easy for him to say, when he had no intention of being part of a world he'd thought so little of for the past two years.

'Flowers for your sweetheart, sir?'

A piping voice at his elbow made Spencer turn. Standing close to him was a small girl, perhaps only about eight years old, but made to look younger still by huge eyes set in a thin face. Her clothes had clearly seen better days and she shivered slightly beneath the scant cover of a threadbare shawl as she gazed up at him nervously; it took a moment for Spencer to realise he ought to remove the intimidating scowl he wore so unthinkingly on his handsome features.

The little girl held out the basket of posies she carried with an uncertain smile.

'Only thruppence, sir. They'll make your home smell like spring.'

There was indeed a lovely scent coming from the little bunches of sweet violets tied with twine, although it wasn't their fragrance that made him hesitate.

Flowers for my sweetheart?

The girl's chirrup hit a nerve, uncomfortably close to the thoughts he had been trying to outpace. Grace was not his *sweetheart,* for heaven's sake—although his innards gave a twist at the admittedly interesting idea—but a glimmer of how pleasantly surprised she might be by such a gesture would not allow him to turn away. Mightn't it help make up for his rudeness to her that morning? A flicker of guilt sparked somewhere in his gut, reminding him of the unhappiness that had crossed her pale face. It was a dangerous feeling, no doubt, and yet the knowledge he had behaved badly towards his gentle new wife left a bad taste in his mouth he found he wanted to wash away with disquieting vigour.

Resigned to his own intolerable weakness, with a sigh Spencer reached into his pocket for a couple of shillings and held them out to the child, who stared at them for a moment with eyes like saucers.

'I'll have two bunches. Then take these coins and get out of the cold.'

The little girl hesitated, two clusters of violets between small fingers, but not reaching for the coins. 'Those are shillings, sir. I only said thruppence.'

Spencer inclined his head, appreciating the child's honesty, but seeing how she shivered beneath her thin shawl.

'I know you did. It's bitter cold today, however.

Find yourself a hot-chestnut seller and then somewhere warm to eat them.'

The little girl blinked at the coins in her palm as though she couldn't believe her luck and pressed the violets into Spencer's hand with quiet awe.

'Your wife's a lucky lady, sir, to have such a kind husband.'

Spencer huffed out a dry laugh, his memory spinning back to think of his irritation with Grace that morning that now made him prickle with shame. 'I'm not so sure. She has much to contend with.'

His new little friend settled her basket on her arm again and peeped up at him with innocent consideration that somehow reminded him of Grace's complete lack of guile. 'I don't know about that, sir. My ma always says a kind husband is one of life's greatest treasures. She says that's why she married my pa.'

The words rang in Spencer's ears as he watched the little mite scurry away with delighted haste, making his insides knot once again. It was true he had not been as kind to Grace as he should have, he had to admit. All his new bride had been trying to do that morning was tell him of her worries and attempt to help him with his own, and he had brushed her aside with brusqueness she did not deserve.

You should try harder. She deserves that much, at least.

He wouldn't be telling her what happened that day two years ago, across the heaving sea. That sorry tale would die with him, his shame and guilt no doubt lingering throughout the rest of his life. But there was something else he could do to make amends for his mistake that morning, the first stirring of an idea, and he strode towards a nearby shop, posy in hand, with a sudden sense of purpose that almost made him want to smile—and grimace in equal measure at this new and dangerous folly.

It was past eleven o'clock when Grace dimly heard a door open and close again, the creak and click muffled by her luxurious pillow. In all likelihood it was the butler doing his rounds before locking up, she thought distantly, pleasantly warm and drifting somewhere between waking and sleep, so it was with a start of sharp alarm she suddenly sat bolt upright in bed, eyes wide as a shadowy figure stumbled into the bedchamber lit by the shuddering light of the lone candle it carried.

'Spencer? What are you *doing*?'

Half hissed, half whispered, her words came out more prudishly than she had intended, but that was the least of Grace's worries as she felt her heartbeat begin to skitter. She was in nothing but her nightgown, she realised with a start of virtuous alarm, watching as he set the candle down—a little unsteadily—and sat heavily on the ottoman at the end of the bed.

'I would have thought that was obvious.' Spencer's voice was low, his words slightly blurred at the edges with what Grace suddenly suspected was one too many glasses of something. 'I'm coming to bed.'

Grace's eyes flew wide as she watched him wrestle to pull off his long leather boots. His movements were imprecise, slower than usual, and she swallowed down a sudden powerful sense of regret she had ever suggested such a thing. What was he expecting? Would he want to—to—? She couldn't finish that train of thought, a frightening combination of dread and, to her everlasting shame, tentative anticipation beginning to run through her veins. Her maidenly sensibilities baulked at such a notion, of course, but something hidden away much deeper, in some feral part of her she had never even known existed, slowly lifted its head to wonder if sharing Spencer's bed and all it entailed might not be so unthinkable... Perhaps maybe even the answer to the secret desires that murmured to her, creeping in beneath the shutters she had so firmly fastened around her heart?

Her pulse, already quickened by his entrance to the room, picked up even more, bounding so hard she wouldn't have been surprised if he could hear it—but he merely squinted at her through the semi-darkness and shook his head at the rigid set of her face.

'No call to look like a frightened rabbit.' His voice was curt, although Grace thought she detected a note of blunt reassurance that caused a sudden flurry of goosebumps to rise on her skin. 'I'm not here to impose on you. I like a woman to lie with me out of desire, not duty.'

A flustered denial sprang to her tongue, but it died in her mouth as Spencer moved round to the side of the bed with uneven steps and unceremoniously sat down mere inches from where Grace leaned, propped up against snowy pillows.

She looked away hurriedly as he began to loosen his cravat, the beat of blood in her ears increasing to a thunderous roar. Was he truly going to undress in front of her? It was unbelievable, unthinkable—and so horrifyingly exciting Grace was lost in a world of self-reproach so vigorous she didn't notice the small package Spencer drew from his pocket until it landed in her lap with a soft thud.

Blessedly distracted from her own worrying thoughts, Grace blinked at Spencer in unfeigned surprise. 'What's this?'

He didn't answer straight away, instead taking a moment to recline against the pillows with his long legs stretched out on the pristine covers. His shoulder was almost touching hers, close enough for Grace to feel the steady warmth of his skin through the shirt he still—thankfully—wore.

'I bought it for you today. Given your dissatisfaction with me earlier I thought it might please you.'

He brought both hands up to rest behind his head and watched as Grace cautiously, as though wary it might be some kind of trick, opened the little box.

For a moment she simply stared down at the delicate wedding band inside with nothing running through her mind aside from pure wonder. In the dim candlelight the gold gleamed like buried treasure, smooth and perfect against black velvet, and when she reached for it with hesitant fingers its coldness contrasted jarringly with the sudden burst of heat that swirled within her chest.

A wedding ring. He's bought me a wedding ring?

No other words came to her and she could only blink at the unexpected treasure in her hand with mute wonder.

'As I understand it, women place a lot of importance on this kind of thing,' Spencer muttered, folding his arms across his chest. 'Given what you said this morning, I thought it might please you to have *proof* of your new status.'

Grace nodded slowly, still unable to fully comprehend what was happening. The ring was beautiful, en-
graved with a pattern created with great skill, but it
was what the golden surprise could possibly represent
that gave her such wordless pause. Spencer had listened
to her fears after all, taken heed of them despite his
apparent disregard, and then found a way to ease her
worries more thoughtfully than she ever would have
thought him capable. It was such a sweet gesture, even
if the delivery was brusque and determinedly unsenti-
mental. Could it be the ice he had so resolutely built up
between them might be thawing at last, even a little?

'It's beautiful. Thank you.'

If it was possible for a man to sound simultaneously
terse yet satisfied, Spencer managed it. 'I hope it isn't
too big. I told the jeweller you had slender fingers.'
He turned fully towards her, propped on one elbow to
bring himself level with where Grace sat with her legs
curled beneath her. 'Let me see if it fits.'

The touch of his fingers against her palm as he took
the ring sent a thrill of pure feeling through Grace's
body and she gave an involuntary shudder at the primi-
tive sensation. There was something almost animalistic
about the uncontrollable way she reacted to even the
smallest touch, and when he took her left hand in his
own and gently slipped the band on her third finger, it
was all Grace could do not to gasp aloud. The warmth
of his skin was intoxicating—she felt as though she
burned with a fever when he softly moved her finger
back and forth to watch the gold gleam in the candlelight, the dancing flame seeming a pitiful thing in comparison to the blaze Grace was sure must be scorching
her from within.

He didn't release her hand. Instead Grace felt all the air leave her lungs as he inspected it, holding it inside his much larger grasp as carefully as one might cradle a child. What he was searching for as he gazed down at it Grace couldn't say, but eventually the taut silence between them was fragmented by Spencer's sigh.

'I fear I've drunk too much again, Grace. I never intend to and yet...'

She blinked, the spell between them broken by the pain in his voice and the concern that rushed up within her to meet it.

'Why don't you stop?' She spoke softly, eyes finding his in the gloom and seeing the sudden agony barely contained. Spencer's hand still held her own, her nerves still tingling with shameful delight, but she drove the maelstrom of her thoughts back with new vigour. Spencer seemed on the cusp of opening up to her, of sharing with her what nightmares caused him to behave as he did—nothing should distract her. 'Surely you can see it does you no good?'

'You wouldn't understand. I have my reasons.'

It was so tempting to ask the question she already knew the answer to—*Because of whatever happened when Will died, you mean?*—but she stopped herself just in time. 'I'm sure I would, if you would only tell me.'

It was a gamble—he could so easily decide she'd gone too far. If she pushed too hard, made him feel she was prying, he might slam shut the drawbridge on his feelings once again. She waited in the short silence with bated breath; but he merely shook his head slowly.

'All I'll say is this: it helps me forget and it helps to numb my pain.' He looked away for a moment; but

Grace frowned to herself in the semi-darkness, the single candle barely shedding any light as it burned lower, before her eyes flew wide, glittering like stars in the dying glow.

Surely not. Surely he couldn't mean—?

'A simpleton to have—let *me* go? Is that what you're saying?'

She could hardly believe it; her breath, already coming hard in a heady mixture of shock and confusion, sped up a fraction more. What could be his meaning? Surely not the delicious suspicion that began to wend its way through her nerves as she waited for his reply—

But Spencer's eyes had closed and he gave no answer besides the easy breathing of a man finally claimed by restful sleep.

just a moment, and then when his eyes met hers again Grace saw something in them that made it suddenly difficult to think. 'Even if it does sometimes cause me to make mistakes I might regret when I'm sober. Would you allow me to make one now, Grace?'

Grace had thought Spencer a passionate man, quick to anger and with a glint in his eye that told of dark thoughts and even darker deeds, so it was a surprise his lips were so gentle when they came down on her own, a soft brush of skin against skin that stole every breath from her scorching body and then wanted more.

He asked permission?

The unlikely thought skipped through her blank mind like a pebble across a still pool.

So he has at least some manners left?

But then all such things were swept away by the movement of Spencer's mouth against hers and all she could do was allow her eyes to drift closed as she surrendered to mindless sensation she had never known could be so intense.

There was no power on earth that could have torn Grace away from Spencer's touch as he held her against him, the pattern of her breathing slowing to match the steady rhythm of the man who *so* gently, more than she ever would have thought him capable of, reached up to cup her cheek in one rough hand. He stroked the soft skin of her face in a tiny movement of his thumb that sent a shower of sparks glittering through Grace's every nerve, igniting her to burn with a flame she had never felt before. He didn't break away for even a moment, keeping his lips firmly slanted across hers with tender yet insistent pressure that ebbed and flowed with the skilful dance of his kiss.

A blistering conflagration blazed across Grace's skin, hidden beneath the thin cover of her prim nightgown. Some far-off part of her consciousness barked a sharp rebuke at her shocking lack of decorum, but she didn't seem able to break away from the delightful feeling of his mouth on hers, or resist the too-powerful temptation to shyly move her hand up the formidable shape of his arm, to feel the strange contours of sinew and muscle so unknown to her innocent understanding. The warmth of his body surrounded her, heating her blood past boiling point as she traced the hills and valleys of his bicep and heard the growl torn from Spencer's throat at the feel of her wandering fingers. It hardly seemed real, more like a dream Grace had been powerless to stop as she lay alone in the bed Spencer now shared with her, and the sudden truth of their embrace reared up to drag Grace from her feverish bliss.

He's been drinking and he said himself he might regret his actions once he's sober. I ought to stop this— now.

With more reluctance than she ever could have imagined Grace moved a hand to Spencer's chest, allowing herself the briefest of moments to appreciate the solid breadth she felt beneath her palm before pushing him away. He withdrew slowly, his eyes seeking hers with a questioning look that made her want to abandon her sensible restraint and wind her arms around his neck once more, but she forced herself to sit up and smooth down her rumpled nightgown with shaking hands.

'I've offended you.' Spencer's voice was low, the regret in it fleeing to Grace's chest to touch her racing heart. 'Catching you up like some blundering oaf…'

Grace shook her head, privately dismayed crease between Spencer's brows.

He thought I didn't like it?

If his thinking was too hazy to realise she pulled away out of horror, it was definitely a sig had done the right thing—even if the desire to re to his arms gnawed at her insides with a hunger wouldn't be satisfied by anything other than the of his lips on hers once more.

'It isn't that. I'm just not sure it's a good idea to this when you've had too much to drink. The last thi I want is for you to wake tomorrow and feel distres for what the port made you do tonight.'

The husband that caused her so much confusior was quiet for a moment before he nodded thoughtfully, turning to lie flat on his back and stare upwards at the canopy above them.

'Thinking of my well-being again. I don't look forward to the day you realise I don't deserve your kindness.'

Any argument Grace could have made was stolen by the troubled look in his eye, an uneasy gleam that dulled gradually until all that was left was flat darkness.

'You're a good woman, Grace. Earls must be feebleminded to have—to have let go…'

He tailed off, his voice fading into an indistinct murmur that she couldn't quite catch as he relaxed further into the downy mattress, tension leaving his limbs.

'To have what? Feeble-minded to have let what go?'

Again the voice from the pillows, even more muffled than before. 'Foolish. A simpleton. Entirely…entirely undeserving.'

Chapter Seven

It was the unpleasant sensation of pins and needles in his left arm that woke Spencer from the deepest sleep he had enjoyed in months.

No nightmares had plagued him, no river of sweat slicked the tight muscles of his back and he surfaced gradually without the racing heart and bursting lungs that so often hauled him panting into wakefulness.

With his eyes closed against the light that tried to sneak between heavy curtains, he wondered absently *why* his arm was so numb. An exploratory wriggle of the offending limb was met with no success, instead feeling as though something lay across it that pinned it to the mattress with a warm, soft weight… That warmth spread across the whole front of his body, combined with something else, a clean-scented *something* just close enough to gently tickle his nose—

Spencer froze as he opened one eye to see confirmation of his suspicions. An unruly jumble of blonde curls obscured almost all of his vision and that agreeable feeling of softness and warmth radiated from the woman curled up against his chest, facing away from him with her breath coming slow and steady in the depths of sleep. His left arm lay beneath her and his right draped loosely across her waist in a position dangerously close to an embrace; their bodies seemed to fit together seamlessly, as though they had been created as two halves of a whole, each made complete by the presence of the other.

What? How?

Spencer's mind raced as he tried to make sense of the entirely un-sensible turn of events. What had brought him to this, trapped in his own bed by one arm beneath his sleeping wife, whose delightfully tempting frame now lay in his grasp? It was one of his most secret dreams come to life, his guiltiest desires made real, but now it was actually happening all he could think of was how to extricate himself as quickly as possible.

He remembered now, with a sudden thrill of dread, the series of steps that had resulted in his current predicament. A few glasses too many after returning home from the lawyers' office; coming to sleep in their marital chamber; fairly flinging the wedding ring at her, and then…

If he hadn't been so desperate not to wake his sleeping bride Spencer would have covered his face with his hand. Instead all he could do was groan in quiet regret as he remembered—hazily, through the heady fog of port—Grace's gasp as he had leaned down to kiss her and the feel of her soft lips moving against his own.

You kissed her, you fool. See what trouble your drinking has got you into now?

It was supposed to help him stem the tide of his worries, not add to them a layer of confusion he could have done without. Having disgraced himself and no doubt mortified Grace with his advances he had then gone the extra mile of drawing her to him as they slept, fitting her against him as though they were married for love and not two people thrown together by chance and circumstance. If she awoke to find herself in his hold, the secret, warm lines of her figure agonisingly obvious to him beneath the thin material of her nightgown, would she not be horrified beyond measure?

The thought was not one on which Spencer wished to dwell. Somehow freeing himself from his delicate dilemma was the only thing he allowed himself to think about as he gently slid his right hand beneath Grace's waist in an awkward attempt to roll her off his arm. Unfortunately the movement only served to highlight even further the feminine geography of her body, the undulation of waist to hip so tantalising he didn't dare allow himself to acknowledge it. The fuzzy memory of that kiss was already more prominent in his mind than was strictly comfortable, the sensation of Grace's hand tracing the muscle of his arm and her eyelids fluttering closed only adding to the whirl of feeling Spencer tried manfully to dismiss as he gritted his teeth in concentration.

She made a little noise as he carefully, inch by painstaking inch, withdrew his arm; a sound halfway between a sigh and a sweet murmur of protest that shot through Spencer's defences like an arrow. The sudden terrifyingly strong urge to abandon his better judgement and return to cradle Grace once more burst upon him, but he steadfastly ignored it, sliding warily across the bed until he reached the edge and stepped to freedom.

Smoothly done. Of course it would have been bet-

*ter if you hadn't had to slip away like a thief in the
first place.*

Shoving the unwanted truth aside, Spencer glanced
back at the mound beneath the bedcovers. The back of
a flaxen head was all he could see and he silently con-
gratulated himself on his escape before moving across
to his armoire. Sleeping in one's clothes wasn't particularly dignified, he had to admit—yesterday's shirt and
breeches would need to be exchanged for fresh—and
the call of a hot bath purred seductively. That would
have to wait, of course, until Grace had vacated their
rooms; her stumbling upon him bathing would be the
absolute cherry on the cake of his discomfort and bad
judgement.

The thought was enough to distract Spencer somewhat as he swiftly pulled on clean breeches and absently unbuttoned his shirt. The cold air hit his skin,
making him wince as he shrugged the garment off
and hunted through his drawers for another. It was too
risky to call for his valet: the bell might wake Grace,
and he wanted more than anything to slip from the
chamber before she woke and felt the full force of the
embarrassment he hoped to save her. Shaving was out
of the question, but the thought barely crossed Spencer's mind as he found what he was looking for and
shook it out with a crisp snap, flapping like a white
flag of surrender.

A gasp made him look up sharply, pausing for a
moment in threading his arm into the safety of the
clean linen shirt.

Grace sat up in the rumpled splendour of his bed—
their bed, he reminded himself in reflexive disbelief—
her hair tumbling about her shoulders and her cheeks

flushed rosy with warmth and sleep. She looked like a startled angel, some ridiculously romantic part of him whispered, resplendent in her snowy nightgown and her curls framing her face like a golden halo of light.

You took too long, Spencer thought as he took in the strange expression on her face.

No wonder she looked so alarmed, waking to find her gruff husband dressing mere feet away, although the distress in her face struck him as unflattering to say the least.

'Ah. You're awake.'

She gave no answer. Instead she continued to stare at him in horrified concern, attention transfixed on his bare torso and her mouth opening in wordless shock that with a start of sudden dread told Spencer he had just made one grave mistake too many.

He slowly followed her gaze downwards to the mess of scars scattered across his skin. They covered him from breastbone to hip, a haphazard constellation of knots and ridges placed randomly as though an artist had flicked a paintbrush of pain across the canvas of his body. Two years had passed to fade them from the angry red they had once been, but they still stood proud against smooth muscle and beneath the coarse dark hair on his chest, permanent reminders of the agony he had felt in both his body and his spirit on the day they had soaked his uniform in bright crimson.

When she managed to drag her eyes up to meet his Spencer saw a thousand unspoken questions in their grey depths, none of which he intended, he knew with a flicker of stubborn determination, to answer.

He quickly buttoned the shirt around his body with clumsy fingers, cursing his carelessness with every movement of his hands. How could he have let her see? He'd been too distracted by his thoughts to exercise his usual caution and now she had seen his secret: the one not even his mother had known.

'What in heaven's name *happened* to you? Oh, Spencer… I had no idea!'

The powerful concern in her voice struck him squarely in the vulnerable place within him reserved only for her. She sounded so worried, so genuinely appalled he had obviously suffered, and some part of him wanted to grasp hold of that distress and wonder what it might mean. The events of the night before, when she had not only accepted his kiss but *kissed him back*, were surely more evidence her feelings towards him had softened—and yet some instinctive warning held him in check.

Anybody with an ounce of decency would be moved by his scars and wonder how he had earned them. If Grace was affected, that was only a sign of her soft heart, the concern in her stormy eyes of a kind she might turn on anyone. It would be yet another mistake to read anything further into it than that and a risky move towards accepting the shadowy desire within him that *wanted* her compassion. He should never hope she might have the barest glimmer of the same feelings for him that Spencer was forced every day to deny; wasn't her trust in men irrevocably shattered beyond repair by the cruelty of the one she had loved before and who might still—*damn him*—hold captive her heart? As for his own need to avoid another assault on his soul…it ran too deeply to be disturbed by one so wholly blind to her effect on him and there was nothing more to be said on the matter.

'Quatre Bras.'

Clipped and brisk, the two words were more of a statement than a real answer. He saw Grace waited for him to elaborate and felt his jaw clench in foreboding as her brows drew together and she peered at him in tangible dismay.

'The Battle of Quatre Bras, of course. But…forgive me, they look so *savage*. How is it you received such scars?'

He stood for a moment in silence, fingers still resting on the final button of his shirt and a hundred different thoughts whirling in an unceasing parade of wretchedness through his mind. It was such an obvious question—one anybody would be curious to know the answer to—and yet Grace's gaze held more than mere enquiry. There was another layer there, akin to a kind of wariness as if she already knew what had transpired that day—or at least had her suspicions.

She can't know, however.

Spencer swallowed down a sudden taste of bile that rose up in his throat.

I never told a soul what happened two years ago in that field across the sea.

In his mind's eye the scene played out once again, a series of lurid images that spilled out before he could stop them: Will running towards him, arms outstretched and such determination in his eyes Spencer had known exactly what his twin was about to do, before he even did it—and then nothing but mud and the sky above, and the sheer burning agony of hot metal on flesh that mingled with the iron tang of blood.

The familiar roar of guilt and anguish flared within him, attempting to squeeze him in its merciless grip. It took all his strength to turn away from it and the memories it conjured, and to answer Grace with a voice bordering on cold.

'As I said. Quatre Bras.'

It felt, as always, something of a betrayal to force his twin back into the deepest recesses of his mind, banishing him into the eternal darkness. There was nothing Spencer wouldn't have given to be able to think of him without the overpowering ache of regret and fear so vivid he could almost taste its bitterness on his tongue, but the happy moments they had shared were so eclipsed by that final terrible day Spencer knew it was hopeless. All he could do was *try* to focus instead on his current concern: the woman in his bed who looked for all the world as though she knew what secrets stalked him. It should be Grace who occupied his mind now; the events of the night before would have to be addressed, and the thought helped slightly to distract from the horror of his worst recollections.

She watched him in contemplative silence as he knotted a fresh cravat at his throat, although a swift flicker of alarm darted across her features when he approached the bed again and sat at the end to pull on his boots. It was so difficult to tell what was going on in her sharp mind when she sat with her face so serene and impassive.

So much better when her expressions betray her and I can get some idea of what she's thinking, Spencer mused with a touch of grim amusement. *If there was any doubt I alarmed her with my behaviour last night, her face when I came closer has just given her away.*

Once both boots were firmly in place there was nothing to delay the moment Spencer had been dreading any longer.

'I wanted to talk to you about last night.'

He saw at once how she stiffened, eyes dropping away from his to fix on her slim hands. The golden band he had slipped on to her finger only a few hours before gleamed in the pale daylight, a reminder to them both of what had happened to muddy the already confused waters between them.

'Yes?'

'I shouldn't have allowed you to see me in that state,' he began, his voice gruff with discomfort. 'I would like to apologise and ask forgiveness for anything I said or did that might have made you feel ill at ease.'

A small nod of the downturned blonde head was at first the only reply and he felt his heart sink at her silence. Could it be she barely wished even to speak to him now? Her face remained shielded from him by a cascade of curls, until she brushed them aside to reveal a flush of colour across her cheeks that only made her look, Spencer saw with a jolt of dismay, even more beautiful.

'Is that everything you wanted to say? Nothing more?'

Spencer hesitated for a moment. In truth, there was another question he would have liked to have asked: *Why did you kiss me back?* And another: *What does this mean?*

But he knew in the very same instant that neither would pass his lips. His memories of the previous night were tinged with port-induced blurriness, perhaps putting a slant on events that wasn't entirely accurate. Perhaps what he recalled as a dangerously romantic moment had been nothing more to Grace than a drunken embarrassment on his part, one her good manners and gentle breeding would rather she forget?

The more he thought about it, the more convinced he became that his traitorous enjoyment of their kiss had been one-sided and the notion made him wince.

I can never allow myself to behave in such a manner again.

He couldn't be trusted to ignore his secret desires while in his cups. What if next time he were to actually *tell* Grace of the strange reaction she conjured inside him, rather than just kiss her? The idea of laying himself bare to her inevitable rejection stung; she would be gracious, but her determination to guard her heart from the malice of men, combined with any lingering preference for Henry and the indifference she must surely feel for a sullen wretch such as himself, meant there could be no other outcome. It would be infinitely safer to continue to fight against the agitation she provoked in his mind and soul, and with that knowledge held tightly he made up his mind.

'Only that I promise you this: the drinking will stop. Today.'

Grace glanced at him sideways, stretching the vulnerable curve of her neck that drew Spencer's gaze quite unconsciously. 'Is that so?'

'It is. I've relied on a bottle for solace for too long. Time for another approach, although what I don't yet know.'

A ghost of a smile curved the corners of Grace's lips, a shy thing that eased the tension Spencer had formerly seen there and set his heart beating faster. 'Perhaps we can find another way together. I'm so glad you changed your mind.'

The short shrug he gave was churlish, he knew, but the sudden skittering of his heartbeat made it difficult to find a reply. He'd made her happy in some small way, and the knowledge made his insides feel…suspiciously warm. He shouldn't seek to please her like a child, yet that hesitant smile *did something* to him that surely a grown man, and a decorated Army captain no less, should be impervious to. Apparently, however, he was not and so it was rather swiftly that he stood up from the bed and threw a short bow in his wife's general direction.

'I imagine you're eager to rise. I'll have your maid sent to you at once.'

'Oh, yes.' Grace gave a tiny start of recollection and gathered the bedclothes around her a little more tightly as if to preserve her modesty. 'Thank you.'

Spencer inclined his head, feeling a slight ache beginning to grow somewhere behind his eyes.

It's just as well you're giving up liquor. You've never had much luck with the after-effects anyway.

'I have to return to my lawyers' office this morning, but I expect to be back in time to dine with you at luncheon. If you wish me to, of course.'

The little smile increased the smallest fraction, having a corresponding effect on Spencer's pulse.

'Of course. Shall we say one o'clock?'

'Very well. I'll see you this afternoon.'

He turned for the door, reaching for the handle just as Grace's voice from behind came soft and low to send a shiver beneath his skin.

'Before you go…about the ring. It's beautiful, but it's the thought behind it I value the most. Thank you for listening to my worries and trying so hard to ease them.'

She spun the gold band on her slender finger. In the morning light she looked more angelic than ever and

Spencer felt his throat constrict on the impulse to tell her just that.

Instead he bit back a smile of his own, keeping his voice as level as he could despite the distracting whirl of thoughts ricocheting around his head. 'You're more than welcome. It's the least you deserve for putting up with me.'

He opened the door and stepped through it to escape into the corridor beyond, supremely conscious as he did so of a fine pair of grey eyes following him as he disappeared from their sight—with barely contained unease at his own growing weakness for their approval.

Perched on the parlour window seat, Grace tried her hardest to make the most of the cold February sunlight to better see her embroidery, although it was apparently nigh on impossible to focus on anything other than the events that had unfolded behind the closed door of her formerly lonely bedroom. Every time she picked up her needle some image would flit in front of her, catching her off guard, and even a glance down at her hands showed the wedding band glinting on one finger, a constant reminder of the husband she couldn't get out of her mind. It was the strangest thing to see it gleaming there, slid on by the unlikeliest of men, and alarming proof that her vow to hold herself apart was in serious danger of weakening.

On a drawn-out sigh Grace set her embroidery hoop aside, driving her needle into the middle of the pattern that refused to hold her interest. With too many thoughts squashed into one brain it was no wonder her head had begun to ache, and Grace closed her eyes for a moment as the unstoppable barrage clamoured at her from all sides.

There was just *so much* to figure out, so much to try to understand. The ring, the kiss, the curious words he had murmured just before falling asleep... What did it all *mean*?

Not a syllable about any of it had passed his lips before he left that morning, other than so indirectly she couldn't be *certain* of what he'd meant. Had he been so deep in drink that he couldn't remember everything that had passed between them, or perhaps for him it had all meant so little it was hardly worth mentioning? For Grace, of course, the strange feeling of another's lips on hers had been completely unknown until a mere twelve hours ago, the sensation of a stubbled jaw against her skin and the breathtaking delight of being held by a set of strong arms even now setting her ablaze once more. That she had fallen asleep beside him was something she didn't dare spend even a moment considering—it was a mercy he had left the bed before she awoke, or else who knew how she would have coped with that handsome face as the first thing she'd seen on opening her eyes. She might have reached for him unthinkingly, still groggy from sleep, and then there would have been no hiding from him how much she desired to feel him beneath her hands once again.

Despite the shawl tucked firmly round her shoulders Grace shivered at the recollection of what had lurked unseen beneath the shirt her fingers had so wonderingly explored as she lay in Spencer's arms. She'd had no clue, no inkling whatsoever of the wounds covered by expensive linen, and the frozen dismay of her husband's face when he'd realised she had seen them was something she would never forget.

For a moment she stared down unseeingly at her neat stitches while the tumult of emotions that leapt inside her writhed ever faster. Her mind felt too full of unanswered questions, fear for the future and feelings for her husband she could neither name nor explain. It was so pointless to acknowledge the disturbance he had brought to her previously calm rationality, causing her spirits to rise up and then plunge downwards again with the power of a single word, look—or kiss. There was too much to work through, too many new desires to understand, and in her quiet solitude Grace suddenly felt lonelier than she had ever felt before.

I wonder if this is how poor Papa feels—cast into a situation he would never have dreamed possible, trying to make sense of it all and keep his head above water.

The thought of her father did nothing to raise Grace's spirits, the familiar ache at the memory of his beloved face squeezing her in its cruel grip. She'd long since ceased counting the days since she had last seen him, the growing tally only increasing her despair.

If only things had been different. If only Papa was still here...and as for Spencer...

A swift glance out of the window made her start as the very man in question, as though summoned by her thoughts, appeared at the end of the street, striding with his usual purpose in the direction of Nevin Place. Even from a distance there was no mistaking him: his tall stature cut an effortless swathe through a small cluster of people blocking the pavement and that impressive width of shoulder could hardly be attributed to anybody else. Grace had no choice but to watch in helpless fascination as he moved closer, self-assured as ever and leaving those he passed by peering after him in obvious curiosity that he completely ignored. More than one stared with distaste, turning to their walking companions to mutter who knew what libels beneath scandalised breaths, but Grace saw no more as she hurriedly turned her own gaze back to her hastily snatched-up embroidery, only looking up again when the parlour door opened and Spencer announced his arrival with something sweet-smelling held out, almost cautiously, towards her.

'I forgot to give you these last night.'

Grace took the posy of violets with surprised delight, looking up just in time to see a glimmer of something suspiciously close to satisfaction flit across Spencer's features at her reaction. She buried her nose in their petals to take in their heady scent, confused pleasure flooding in to replace the lonely unhappiness of moments before.

'Why, how sweet of you. Did you know that violets are some of my favourite flowers?'

'I didn't, but I'll certainly bear that in mind for the future.'

He seemed pleased, or as close to pleased as Spencer could get, and Grace inhaled the beautiful fragrance again as new bewilderment combined with her appreciation to make it difficult for her to find a reply. First a wedding ring, and now *flowers*? It was as though her sullen husband had finally decided to make some effort to bridge the gaping chasm between them and her heart leaped at the thought. Perhaps it was a foolish reaction, dangerous, even—but in honesty Grace knew that danger already circled, testing the strength of the boundaries she had once thought so stout. If Spencer was thawing, it could only mean a greater threat to her determination to ignore how he called to her, warmth creeping back into his soul again to match the attractions of his face.

Spencer stepped away to stoke up the hearth, holding his cold fingers to the blaze even as he glanced surreptitiously around the room as though searching for something. Grace watched him over the top of her bouquet for a moment, before realising with a clunk of dread what it was he looked for.

'After what you said this morning, I took the opportunity to have all the strong liquor removed from the house while you were in town.' She hesitated, aware of how his sharp profile glowed so handsomely in the orange firelight, tempting her to stare. 'I hope you're not too angry.'

For a split second she thought she saw something dark in his face when he turned to look at her and felt an unpleasant skitter of apprehension in her gut—before realising, with a sudden jolt, that it was a shadow of shame. It cloaked his features to enhance their contours, but likewise emphasised the sorrow in his eyes, making Grace's heart ache and her hands itch to reach for him.

'I can't pretend I'm happy about it, but I think it needed to be done.' He frowned down into the fire, what he saw in the curling flames Grace could only guess. 'Thank you.'

Thank you? That wasn't even close to the reaction I expected.

Grace held her posy up to her nose again, this time more to hide her face than to take in the delicate sweetness. No irritation, no rebuke, not even a sigh at her interference, only acceptance of her actions and the sad look in his eye that hinted how badly he needed someone to hold out a steadying hand.

That's what you should be occupying yourself with. None of those girlish fancies you allowed to cloud your mind.

All those thoughts of kissing and confusion, blushing and second-guessing Spencer's motives were a waste of the time she *ought* to be using to help him through his grief, as Dorothea had hoped. Trying to gauge his feelings for her—if he even had any—would do nothing to ease the suffering she saw in his face.

Spencer wielded the poker with a flourish, bringing to mind once again the soldier he had been as he thrust it into the fire. Grace could just picture him with a sword drawn, tall and proud in his fine red uniform. It was an altogether too-alluring image and she dismissed it as quickly as she could with sudden warmth flooding beneath her ribs.

He didn't stop stirring the charred wood, but Grace could have sworn she saw a new stiffness in the set of his shoulders and her heart gave a leap of powerful sympathy that sent ripples through to her core. There was such sorrow inside him, hidden away stubbornly behind a wall of stoicism he would not allow her to break down. Watching him in his lonely pain, she nodded to herself only once, but with grim determination. If he was going to stop relying on a decanter she would need to try harder to replace the bleak solace he had once thought drink provided.

Fortunately for Grace, she had an idea of where to start.

Chapter Eight

It took a firm push to shift the stubborn door of the glasshouse and when Spencer stepped inside he felt grit beneath his boots. One of the panes had broken, he saw as he looked about the little building set against one garden wall, but the rest were intact and sunlight streamed through them to warm his back despite the chill outside.

He hadn't set foot among the plants since Dorothea had died, although evidently somebody had continued to tend her collection. Green tendrils and waving leaves swayed gently as he moved past them, breathing in the pleasant scent of damp earth that lingered in the air like incense. With sunshine bathing the space and the call of birds in the bare trees outside it might almost have been spring, although Spencer's spirits hardly lifted.

Getting through each day without the aid of a bottle had been more difficult than he had anticipated—surely a sign Grace's intervention had been sorely needed. With nothing to replace its dubious comfort he found himself left with too much time in which to think, only increasing the hours spent at the mercy of his dark memories and the thoughts of his wife that would *not* leave him in peace. They chased each other through his mind until in desperation he had strode into the garden, hoping for a moment's respite.

He passed a hand across his face. *I'm so tired of this.* Would there ever be a time he wasn't tossed about on a relentless sea of feelings he had to deny? It was exhausting, the constant battle to keep himself in check, even if his past mistakes made it an absolute necessity.

'There you are! I was wondering where you'd disappeared to.'

Grace's voice made him turn, its soft cadence as always dropping a lit match into the pit of his stomach.

'I'm surprised to find you in here. I didn't imagine you to have green fingers!'

She stood framed in the doorway, head tilted in the appealing way she had when curious. Held to her chest was a book of some kind and a small wooden box, a welcome distraction from the quizzical turn of her countenance and a lifeline Spencer seized at once. He could hardly tell her the truth of why he was practically hiding in such an unlikely place.

I needed to get away from my thoughts of you. I can scarcely think of anything else.

Perhaps not.

'I just wanted to take some air. What are you holding?'

The hesitant look that stole over her face should have given Spencer reason for suspicion as Grace slowly unfolded her arms to show him more clearly what she held in each hand.

His brows twitched together as he took in the sketchbook and set of fine pencils. Evidently they belonged to

Grace, her initials embossed on both in gilt lettering, although why she held them out to him so expectantly was less clear. Before he could open his mouth, however, she spoke with swift caution that finally made him see the trap she had set.

'Now, before you say anything, let me explain.' Grace peered up at him earnestly, eyes wide with innocent entreaty that made Spencer pause in his automatic refusal. 'I know time has been hanging heavy on you since you changed your habits. I thought perhaps you might take up one of your old pastimes again, see if it brings you new amusement? Dorothea told me once how you used to love to sketch and showed great promise.'

Spencer raised an eyebrow, although his insides drew into a tight knot of dismay. What else had his mother told Grace of the secret sorrows he kept so determinedly inside? She'd known full well he hadn't so much as blown the dust off his own sketchpad since Will had died, taking Spencer's enjoyment of most things with him. The idea of revisiting the past sent the same old twist of pain through Spencer's gut and he shook his head firmly, dismissing the suggestion at once.

'I don't think so. The thought is appreciated, but I'd rather not.'

'Are you quite sure you won't even try? You might surprise yourself.'

Spencer pressed his lips into a tight line. Some part of him—an unexpectedly large part, he realised in surprise—actually *wanted* to take the book Grace offered, to try to recapture some shadow of the passion he had once been able to feel. The warmth in her gaze was so encouraging, tempting him back to shore from the shipwreck of his emotions…

Could it be that his suffering might be helped? It was a possibility that made him pause. Sketching had taken up so much of his time in years gone by, often distracting him from even remembering to eat. Surely such a thing was a far healthier route to oblivion than the decanter and one Grace evidently approved.

Damn it all.

With a heavy sigh Spencer took the sketchpad and pencils from her, trying to avoid an upward twitch of his lips at her beam of delight.

You weakling. Self-imposed denial for two years gone in a matter of seconds to please a pretty woman.

'Sit down, then.' He nodded towards a chair set in a corner of the glasshouse, despite himself taking note of the composition of plants around it and the way sunlight fell to illuminate it against the lush green. It was as good a backdrop as any for a portrait and the prospect sent a faint ripple of interest through Spencer's nerves; something he hadn't felt in years.

When Grace didn't move Spencer looked round at her as she hovered a few steps away, brow creased in a small frown.

'I can't draw you if you won't sit down.'

She reached up to tuck a non-existent lock of hair behind her ear. 'I didn't mean for you to sketch *me*. Surely you'd prefer to take one of these plants as your subject? This fern here is very beautiful…'

Her voice tailed off as Spencer shook his head. 'I've never cared for nature studies. Portraits are much more engaging, but if you'd rather not—?'

The question hung in the air between them. Spencer felt Grace's reluctance, a flicker of disappointment rising within him to meet it as he waited for her reply. Watching her as she stood among the scented leaves, hesitant and with her face lit by the sun streaming in from above, suddenly there was nothing he wanted more than to capture her for ever in pencil, to commit her loveliness to paper where it might never disappear. It was a startling feeling, but one he couldn't have denied even if he'd wanted to—which was just as well, for it settled inside his ribs with an insistence that wouldn't be ignored.

'Very well. If it'll please you.'

Spencer's heart gave a small leap as Grace settled on to the chair and elegantly arranged herself against its cushions. Her posture was quite correct, shoulders back and chin up in the very image of a graceful young lady, but her fixed smile radiated self-consciousness and a faint blush crossed her cheeks.

'Will this do?'

A wooden stool stood beneath one of the potting tables and Spencer retrieved it, seating himself before eyeing Grace with professional interest. 'You're a little stiff. It might help to think of something pleasant—you'll relax, and your smile will look much more natural.'

'I'll try.' A glimmer of doubt showed Grace didn't think much of his advice, but she gave herself a small shake and took a deep breath, before visibly loosening the rigid set of her body, her lips lifting into a gentle curve that this time added a touch of life to her eyes where before they had been clouded with unease.

Spencer watched her for a moment, taking in the new softness of her expression with something close to awe. There were so many facets to her: shy yet bold, unhappy yet cheerful… She was like a chameleon, always shifting between versions of the same woman according to the situation. He had yet to see her thrust into a storm she couldn't weather, her gentle exterior hiding a core of pure steel he wondered if she was even aware she possessed. How was he to reduce her to one image caught on a flat sheet of paper when the changing tide of her expression showed him a fresh angle each time he looked?

'Perfect. Try to stay just like that.'

Attempting to push the unanswerable question out of his mind, Spencer took up one of the pencils, feeling the familiar contours he grasped with practised ease. He could almost have smiled at the way his hand acted of its own accord, testing the point against a corner of his page in a way he hadn't done in more than two years. His fingers itched to begin, firm around the pencil as he looked up at his quiet model and felt a sense of peace begin to wash over him he barely remembered.

Hardly believing what he was doing, Spencer began, his hand sweeping across the page in long strokes as he sketched a basic outline. The details would build gradually, coming to life bit by bit until Grace looked up at him from the page, he hoped as realistically as possible.

Not that I'll be able to completely capture the intelligent glint in her eye, or the shy sweetness of that smile.

As the sun glanced off her golden curls and her clear skin gleamed in the wintry February light she seemed more striking than ever and Spencer found it increasingly difficult to stem the urge to lay down his pencil and stare.

Instead he carried on sketching, the strange sensation of peacefulness that had begun to stir inside him growing until with a start he realised the usual scowl had left his brow and the habitual weight in his chest had eased a little, still there but somehow more manageable than before. It was uncanny, the effect such a simple distraction had on his emotions; combined with Grace's calming stillness he might almost have felt a shadow of bizarre happiness, unexpected but more welcome than he ever would have believed.

Grace watched as Spencer's dark eyes flicked towards her and then down again, his clever fingers skating over the page. Each time he glanced up it sent a curious thrill right through her, the concentration on his face only making his features more attractive—if such a thing were possible.

Just keep smiling. He'll never know.

Think of something pleasant, he'd said, to make the turn of her lips more natural and her posture less rigor mortis. He probably hadn't expected her to return to the moment he had presented her with the wedding ring that now gleamed on her finger, or the little vase of violets that stood beside their bed to fill the room with perfume. Those were two of the most delightful memories she had tucked away in the back of her mind and bringing them out made her smile more genuine than anything else could.

It was still unnerving to feel his sharp eyes study her so closely and her heart fluttered against her bodice. She'd never had her portrait sketched before; it was strangely uncomfortable to sit beneath his silent scrutiny and possibly not an experience she'd be in a hurry to repeat.

But that's not the point. This was to take Spencer's mind off his troubles, nothing else.

She hitched the smile back into place and tried to drown out the rogue whisper threatening to take the edge off her triumph. Her scheme certainly seemed to be working: Spencer was absorbed in his task, too focused to even wear his usual frown. His face was set, but more attentive than brooding, the hint of some startling animation *just* visible in his intense gaze.

I should have thought of this sooner, she mused, hardly able to credit the change. *Perhaps we could have avoided some of the difficulties we've had. Then again...*

Surely it was *because* of those clashes and awkward moments that they had arrived at such a pass? Spencer had needed to come to accept her help himself. He would never have allowed her to intervene before he had kissed her, influenced by his drinking. It was strange to think how their relationship had progressed and the memory of that night made Grace's skin burn with unladylike heat. The feel of his lips pressed to hers, his strong arms around her and his weight bearing down on her with delicious friction... She felt herself drift off to replay that moment in her mind, as always feeling her breath catch when she recalled how her husband's fingers had skimmed the sensitive curve of her ear—

'Are you still comfortable sitting like that? I'm almost finished.'

Grace gave a start as Spencer's voice dragged her from her scandalous thoughts, the blood in her already flushed cheeks rising again in traitorous warmth. How long had she sat there with such *unsuitable* images darting through her mind? Evidently longer than she realised and hopefully with no trace of her musings showing in her face as the man in question broke her trance.

'Already? You're a very brisk artist.' She watched as his hand swept again with a confident flair, not able to see the page from her chair, but her imagination running wild. What would the portrait look like? Would he have been able to render her as skilfully as Dorothea had suggested?

'Drawing is like falling off a log once you've learned how. The technique came flooding back at once, even though I hadn't lifted a pencil since—'

Spencer bit off the end of his own sentence. He glanced up at her, the quickest of lightning looks, but his lips had clamped together in the stubborn line Grace knew only too well and she realised he had spoken without thinking.

When the suddenly tense silence between them stretched out Grace flexed her fingers held still in her lap, wondering if she dared voice the question that murmured in her ear. There might never be a better time to ask, Spencer having already opened the door to her query—but he had slammed it shut a split second after, the straight press of his mouth a clear indication he wouldn't appreciate her involvement.

She flicked her eyes to his face, seeing the new rigidity in it where before there had been dawning pleasure, and gathered all the courage she could spare.

Do it for Dorothea. It's what you promised, after all.

'Not since William died? Is that what you were going to say?'

Nobody could have missed the immediate ripple of

muscle as Spencer clenched his jaw, tendons flexing painfully with the harsh movement. He kept his focus firmly on the sketchbook balanced on his knee, but the atmosphere had changed to one of palpable wariness, crackling like an electric current in the air. The progress of his pencil didn't cease, the careful strokes belying the frantic activity Grace knew must be whirling inside his mind. There was no denial, though, of her hesitant words—and so with her breathing starting to quicken Grace pushed on.

'I thought it might have been. Dorothea told me you lost interest in most of your previous amusements after his loss…and that you never told her what happened the day he died. Are the memories truly so painful?'

As soon as the question left her lips Grace knew it was stupid, the answer blindingly obvious—but it might invite Spencer to share some of what he kept locked tightly inside, so she pushed aside the frustration at her own clumsiness to wait with burning cheeks for his reply.

Spencer's hand paused for a moment before continuing to move, although he still didn't look up from the page.

'We all have regrets and things we'd prefer not to talk about. My brother is that thing for me—I suspect Mr Earls would be yours.'

Grace swallowed, her throat suddenly dry. With his head bent over his work Spencer's face was hidden from her by the black curtain of his hair, but the carefully controlled flatness of his tone was enough to tell her she was in danger of straying too far.

'You suspect correctly. That's something I'd rather not dwell on any more than I have to.'

Henry was quite possibly the *last* person Grace wanted to recall at that moment. He was no longer welcome in her thoughts and never would be again, his humiliating treatment even now sending a wave of shame to crash over her.

'I'm sorry. Perhaps I shouldn't have said anything.'

For a moment Spencer said nothing, the sound of lead against fine paper the only sound within glass walls. When he finally raised his eyes to hers she saw something in them she struggled to name: not anger, but a gleam like warning in their cocoa depths.

'As you said so eloquently: my last day with Will is something I'd rather not dwell on. I'd be grateful if you didn't ask again.'

Grace swallowed, all too aware of the dryness of her mouth. That Spencer hadn't been frankly offended was nothing short of a miracle, and surely a sign their strange marriage was slowly growing warmer? It was a thought too tantalising to consider, although it lingered in the back of Grace's mind to make her wonder...

As if reading her mind Spencer fixed her with a knowing look, one dark eyebrow raised. 'I will not be laying bare my soul to you, Grace. Not now, not in ten years or more.' Another shadow of that warning edged each word, flatly resolute. 'So you may put that from your mind.'

'If that's your wish, but—'

'It is. Now. Are you ready to see your portrait?'

Even Grace knew when she was beaten, although the smallest flicker of determination remained. Spencer might have won this battle, but she had promised Dorothea she would win the war—and she would not be surrendering without a fight.

But this wasn't the moment for that siege. Instead Grace nodded, suddenly shy as she took the sketchpad Spencer handed to her with an ironic flourish.

She looked at the pencil likeness in quiet amazement, silent as she took in the skill of Spencer's hand.

The face peeping up at her wore a half-smile, full lips curving to drop a dimple in one cheek. A pair of intelligent eyes framed by long lashes seemed to sparkle with real light and the elegant line of the bone structure only added to the impression of serenity in the young face, timelessly pretty and gazing calmly out at the world as though she knew its secrets. He had even captured the slight taper of her chin, although his rendering was far softer than the point Grace had so often despaired of in various mirrors. In all it was a thing of wonder, Spencer's talent shining through despite the flattering liberties Grace felt sure he had taken with his clever strokes.

'I hardly know what to say. It's wonderful!' She couldn't take her eyes off it, each glance showing new detail picked out in curving graphite. 'The way you've caught the play of light and shadow…it's just so lifelike, if a little complimentary to the sitter.'

Spencer stepped round to stand behind her chair, looking over her shoulder at the sketchbook in her hands. He was close enough for her to feel the tickle of his breath on her neck and she had to check an instinctive shiver as sensation glittered across her nape.

'Complimentary?'

'Just a little.' Grace gave a shaky laugh, although her throat had tightened at Spencer's sudden proximity. 'You've drawn me a good deal prettier than I am in the flesh, although I appreciate you being so kind.'

There was a short pause—a few seconds when no sound came from behind her chair. It took her right back to the stormy day he had marched her to this house and set the ball rolling on their strange relationship, when he had stood at her back and glared down at her as though she was an intruder he longed to be rid of. Now when he answered it was in a voice quite unlike that terse tone of only a short time before, the difference so startling it took a moment for Grace to realise what he said.

'I disagree. To my eye it's entirely accurate.'

Any hope of reply vanished as Grace stared fixedly at the drawing in her hand, suddenly blind to what was before her. Nothing could have compelled her to turn and look into Spencer's face as a flood of molten gold worked its way down to her toes, seeping through every nerve to dazzle her with its lustre. She sat frozen to the spot, Spencer's delicious words echoing in her ears until they rang so loudly she could scarcely hear herself think.

This is how he sees me? He truly thinks I'm this handsome?

The picture was a million miles from the perception of herself she'd held ever since she could remember. Solemn and pale, her looks had never felt like much of an asset—certainly they hadn't been enough to hold Henry's attention after her fortune had disappeared without trace. Spencer had seen something in her she hadn't thought existed, her confidence in her value so shattered by her former fiancé's rejection it seemed hard to believe what she was seeing.

But there could be no denying what was before her very eyes. It was the frank truth and Grace could only blink in dazed wonder that it was her reluctant husband, of all people, who should have sent such shy pleasure stealing through her bones. If Henry had ever said such a thing, she would know now the compliment was born of manipulation, of trying to worm his way in to profit from their intimacy. Spencer, however... She knew him well enough to see the complete lack of artifice in him, his honesty so glaringly different from the false charm that had dropped from Henry's lying lips. If Spencer said the luminous woman who gazed at her from the page was a true likeness, he meant every word.

Grace ran a fingertip over the lines of her sketched cheekbones, tracing the contours rendered so skilfully. She still hardly knew what to say, but with Spencer at her back and her skin tingling at the sense of his closeness she had to summon up *something*.

'It's wonderful. I'll treasure it always.'

Her mind was too full of a buzz of amazement, pleasure and confusion to hear much of Spencer's reply, although the dim part of her not consumed by bewilderment thought he sounded pleased. The success of her plan should have made Grace satisfied likewise, for a short while at least distracting Spencer from his thoughts, but it was difficult to think of anything other than the chaos exploding behind her ribs.

'To my eye it is entirely accurate.' That's what he said.

Something between them had changed. There was surely no other explanation for his uncharacteristic praise of her where once there had been only tolerance, or her desire to cling to his words, defying the caution she had thought to keep so steadfast. Both she and Spencer seemed to be creeping carefully towards raising their heads above the parapets of their defences, to regard each other across the gulf between them in a wary truce that would once have been unthinkable— although only time would tell whether it was a development they would come to regret.

Chapter Nine

Standing before the green-painted front door, Spencer reached up once again to adjust the position of his cravat in an unthinking tic of apprehension. At his side Grace slid him a look that bordered on amused and he whipped his hand away at once, affecting not to have noticed.

'If I didn't know better I'd think you were nervous.'

'Of course I'm not. I just don't relish the prospect of having to socialise.'

That's partly the truth, he thought as he fought the upward twitch of his hand once again.

He hadn't seen the Linwoods since the death of his mother and his clandestine marriage, Grace carrying out her visits alone with the excuse of his being in mourning. Even while Dorothea was still alive he'd excused himself after a stiff greeting whenever they called, unwilling to force an hour of awkward small talk that might stray too close to revisiting the past… But that had been before something changed in the way Grace looked at him, before the distance between them seemed somehow less vast, and now he found himself more eager to make a good impression on her family than he wanted to admit. Vague memories of the house he now stood outside danced before him, of visits he had made while his own family was still intact and all but himself hadn't lain quiet in their graves, hopefully finding each other in the afterlife while he made his way without them.

He felt Grace's eye upon him again, another gleam of that knowing look, but she was given no chance to reply as the door to Number Four Regent Square was flung open and a veritable flood of females came spilling out in a storm of muslin and delighted chatter.

'Grace! How good it is to have you here again!'

'How we have missed you!'

'Are you well? You look so pale! And upon my word—what *is* that bonnet you're wearing?'

Taking a step backwards away from the fray, Spencer watched for a moment as Grace was embraced by her sisters and then her beaming mama, who held her so tightly he almost thought he heard bones crack, a sight that sent an unexpected skewer of pain right through him. He would never be embraced by his own mother ever again, he remembered with a dart of sudden sadness, but then Mrs Linwood's eye settled on him and with a flurry of unease Spencer dropped the most dignified bow he could muster.

'Spencer! How truly wonderful to have you here!' Mrs Linwood bustled towards him and seized both of his hands before Spencer had time to blink. 'I can't tell you how much we have all looked forward to seeing you. You must come inside out of the cold at once!'

For such a small woman Grace's mother had a very firm grip and Spencer felt himself propelled into the

house with no little force. He only had time to shoot
Grace one alarmed glance over her mother's head before he was placed firmly into a fine chair before a
roaring fire, to experience the uncanny sensation of
being fixed with four pairs of good-natured eyes.

'Ring the bell for tea, Cecily, and Peg—do pull that
curtain a fraction. The sun is in dear Spencer's face,
I'm quite sure.'

Mrs Linwood settled herself in another chair next to
his own, Grace arranging herself neatly on a plush sofa
at his other side, her quiet presence reassuring beneath
more scrutiny than Spencer had endured in months.

'That's better. We want our guest to be as comfortable as possible, don't we, girls?'

The three Miss Linwoods beamed across at him
from their perches on various seats the other side of
the fire, each a slightly distorted version of Grace as
though challenging him to spot the difference. Margaret, a girl of about eleven by Spencer's estimation,
seemed to smile the brightest, although with a hint of
shyness that immediately reminded him of that he had
often seen in Grace's expression. Her younger sister's
face was more round in contrast to Grace's oval, but the
fair hair was the same and the voice when she spoke a
similar well-mannered murmur.

'Are we to call you brother now, Spencer?' She
looked at him eagerly, her childish face alight. 'I have
often thought it would be so nice to have one.'

Something deep inside him twisted sharply, sending
a cold shard through to his chest. Margaret's innocent
words mirrored the lament he had muttered to himself
too many times to count, often with a glass clenched in
one tight fist. She had no way of knowing, of course,

what images she had conjured, although the subtle turn of Grace's head in his direction as though sensing his pain gave him reason for pause.

His wife's little hand lay on the arm of the sofa, mere inches from his own, and the urge to reach for it gripped him with instinctive force. Instead, however, he laced his fingers together on the broad spread of his own lap and regarded her sister with his best attempt at polite interest—not his strongest suit.

'Indeed? For my part, you know I have never had a sister.' A glance at Grace, a little tense beside him, prompted him to continue, the idea of pleasing her with his reply exasperatingly strong. The memory of her face that day in the glasshouse as she looked down at his drawing with such a shy, sweet smile rose up again and he suddenly wanted nothing more than to see it again. How it was her happiness had come to be so important to him he hardly knew, but it was a fact he found himself less and less inclined to fight. 'How fortunate for me I am now blessed with so many.'

It was a trite reply, the kind any nervous young man might use to sweet-talk his darling's family, but the sight of Grace's surprise, her face now free of the wary shadow that had followed her into the house, was all the reward Spencer could have wanted for his uncomfortably earnest words. Mrs Linwood looked perfectly satisfied at his praise of her daughters and the girls themselves seemed only too pleased with their new brother's candour—so much so that nobody seemed to notice he had avoided Margaret's question, or remember after a maid appeared with a heavily laden tray.

There was still a touch of surprise lingering on Grace's face as she handed him a cup and more than a touch in her voice when she leaned closer, beneath the fluttering distraction of tea being served, to murmur into his ear. The sensation of her breath on his skin sent a jolt of pure energy flooding through his every nerve and it was difficult to focus on the words she spoke in low disbelief.

'I had no idea you could be so charming. My mother seems quite enamoured already.'

'Well.' He shrugged, trying to ignore the damnable jitter her whisper sent through him. 'Even *I* know there are some it would be churlish to show disregard.'

'Is that so? I wonder if I ought to be offended it's only my mama and sisters who receive such treatment.' She withdrew before he could reply, but a small upward curve played about her lips and Spencer felt gripped with the sudden desire to watch the tentative smile grow.

When everybody was in possession of a steaming teacup and reseated daintily in their places Mrs Linwood turned slowly to Spencer, her previous cheer replaced by a look of such gentle sorrow that a flash of concern darted through his mind, momentarily distracting him from his secretive study of Grace's mouth.

'I'm so very glad you decided to join us here today. You've been so often in our thoughts since the loss of Dorothea.' The older woman's voice was soft in the quiet that settled in the room like a cloak of silence, the Miss Linwoods averting their eyes in well-bred sympathy. 'She was a true friend to us when we were most in need and we are more grateful than you will ever know for her kindness towards Grace especially.'

She patted Spencer's hand in a movement so filled with feeling he found himself unable to immediately respond, only capable of watching as the trio of blonde heads seated across from him bobbed in unison. Out of the corner of his eye he saw Grace's fingers twitch in his direction and wondered—with a flicker of anticipation—if she was going to brush his own; but she must have thought the better of it and Spencer pushed aside his absurd disappointment to reply.

'Thank you, ma'am. I know she was only sorry she couldn't do more.'

Mrs Linwood shook her head, still regarding him with compassion that could not be faked. 'By taking Grace in she allowed us to keep our home—what more could anyone ask? We've had to economise, it's true, but with my little savings and the sale of some trifles we have enough now to weather the storm. Without Dorothea we would have nothing…and without you Grace would not have the prospect of a future.'

For a moment nobody spoke, the soft collapse of charred logs in the fireplace the only sound. Spencer stared into the flames, seeing nothing of their orange tongues as he turned Mrs Linwood's words over inside his head, a chill sliding upwards towards his chest as the picture of his mother's serene, lifeless face returned to haunt him. It took its place beside those of his father and Will, terrible reminders of all he had lost…

It was uncanny how easily Grace was sometimes able to read his thoughts. Her fingers once again wavered in the direction of his chair and this time Spencer felt all the air leave his lungs as her hand settled on his forearm in a gesture of consolation she had no way of knowing made every nerve in his body stand to attention. She didn't even look at him, but two spots of bright colour appeared on her cheeks her pallor had no hope of hiding.

If Mrs Linwood noticed the suddenly fixed set of Spencer's expression she gave no sign, although he could have sworn he saw little Margaret's eyes grow round with fascination as Grace's hand moved slowly back and forth along his sleeve, each touch sending ripples of delight through to his innards. All rationality seemed to have deserted him as he focused on the feeling of those slender fingers' steady progress up and down his arm.

'I'm sure we can all learn from Dorothea's kindness and try to be a little more like her.'

A sad pause threatened to fall over the party, each person within the cosy sitting room reflecting on the sorrows of a life taken too soon. Only the gentle retraction of Grace's hand back to her own lap broke the spell on Spencer's attention, so transfixed had he been by her touch, and he ended the heavy silence with a forced cough.

'It would have been a pleasure to meet Mr Linwood again, had circumstances allowed. Do you receive word from him often?'

'A letter came only this morning.' Cecily, a slight girl of about seventeen, answered with the same sweet voice Grace shared with Margaret. Some of the animation had crept back into her face, evidently pleased to have heard from her beloved papa. 'He writes as often as he is able and we take it in turns to reply. It is the highlight of our week when we see his handwriting on the envelope.'

'As it ought to be, for it is the only trace of Papa we *get* to see.' Lucy, the most like Grace of all the sisters save for the dusting of freckles across her nose, carefully avoided meeting anybody's eye as she stirred her tea. 'If Mama allowed us to visit him, of course, we wouldn't have to rely solely on his letters.'

Spencer felt Grace shift a little on her blue-striped sofa, although her face when he glanced at her was determinedly blank. Her younger sisters, however, clearly had yet to develop her control, for their mouths turned down and Margaret sighed audibly into her teacup.

It was evidently a sore subject, Spencer realised at once. Mrs Linwood never faltered for a moment, but the stiffening of Grace's posture, imperceptible to all but the most interested audience—as Spencer had to admit he was—gave the game away.

'Come now, girls—don't let us be melancholy. Spencer will think twice about visiting us again if he thinks he will be met with long faces!' Grace's mother reached out to stroke Margaret's cheek, prompting a slow smile. 'We mustn't scare him away so soon!'

Spencer shook his head, alarm kindling inside him. The last thing he wanted was to be the kind of tiresome guest people dreaded seeing, the knowledge of his reputation for unfriendliness never far from his mind. 'Don't let me be a consideration in—'

'Oh, nonsense.' His charming hostess beamed at him. 'You are as much a *consideration* as anybody else in this room and I won't hear a syllable otherwise!'

Cecily leaned towards him, one eyebrow raised in a direct mirror of the arch look he had seen so many times from Grace. 'That's quite true, you know. Mama never will hear anything she doesn't wish to and you may as well get used to it now. Indeed, it will make your life much simpler if you do!'

The room rang with laughter, the tension of moments before artfully diffused. Even Mrs Linwood chuckled at her daughter's wit and turned to Spencer with her hands spread in mock indignation.

'Do you see how I am treated? I'm sure the only person who shows me any respect is you!'

She addressed him with such easy openness Spencer felt a dart of unnameable warmth within his chest, fluttering softly around his heart. It was strangely familiar and as he looked around at the five faces smiling back at him he tried to puzzle out what the odd stirring could possibly mean.

I know I've felt it before. But when?

Perhaps it was foolish on his part, but he found himself seized by the sudden—and startling—realisation that he knew *exactly* what the uncanny feeling was. It was one he hadn't experienced in more than eight years, hidden beneath grief and guilt and wishing the clock could be turned back…

Family. It feels like being part of a family again—as it did before Father died and sorrow robbed us of each other one by one.

Being welcomed by the Linwoods as one of their own was more touching than he ever would have thought. To be part of a family again, to feel wanted and treated as though he belonged, fled to the deepest, darkest recesses of his soul and lit a spark there to smoulder, small at first, but to grow with a vigour that surprised him. It was Grace he had to thank for this, he thought in wonder—she had given her word that she would help him in his grief and, in dragging him into the embrace of her kindly family despite how little he deserved their warmth, she had gone above and beyond her promise.

The knowledge struck him like a hammer blow, rendering him silent for much of the remaining time he and Grace spent within that happy sitting room before the morning fire. He ventured a few words here and there, but for the most part the strange feelings that swirled around the former emptiness of his heart stole any words from his mouth, and it was something of a relief when they finally stood up to leave.

Grace's sisters lined up beside the front door as Mrs Linwood helped Grace on with her cloak, tying the black ribbons of the sombre bonnet to frame her daughter's pale face. Each of the girls pressed Spencer's hands with real fondness and their mother gave his fingers an especially firm squeeze.

'It's been wonderful to see you. Please do feel as though you're welcome here any time, any time at all.'

Spencer's bow was deeper and more heartfelt than it had been when he had first set foot on the front steps with his brow creased in apprehension. 'Thank you for your kind hospitality, ma'am.' Some flicker prompted him to voice some of the emotion that nagged at him, unexpected yet refusing to be dismissed. 'I've rarely felt more welcome anywhere and I hope you feel at liberty to call at Nevin Place again whenever you choose.'

He almost felt the surprised flick of Grace's grey gaze towards him, mingled with a curious pleasure he could not have named. She said nothing, however, as she kissed her sisters and mother goodbye, turning to wave at them from the end of the gravelled path until the green door closed and Spencer found himself alone once more with the wife who tried to hide the gleam of sadness that crossed her countenance.

'Are you well?'

'Oh, yes. I've just never been very good at partings.'

Of course she would rather stay with her family, he acknowledged ruefully as they turned away from the house. The Linwood home was filled with laughter and light, whereas Nevin Place was quiet, shrouded in a gloomy atmosphere even on the sunniest of days. It was obvious which habitat suited Grace best; like a hot-house flower, she bloomed beneath the warmth of her family's kindness and merriment—without that, how long would it take for her vivacity to wither and die?

Determination to wipe the glimmer of unhappiness from Grace's face helped Spencer to make up his mind. She had tried so hard to bring him in from the cold of his self-imposed banishment.

Now it's my turn to lift her spirits, or at least attempt to.

Ignoring the nagging voice in the back of his mind that warned him against it, Spencer took Grace's gloved hand and threaded it firmly into the crook of his arm. His heart leapt within him at the contact, but he made himself disregard it in favour of drawing Grace away from where his carriage waited to whisk them away.

'Where are we going? Are you not eager to return home?'

'Not yet. It's a fine day, despite the cold; I thought you might like to walk into town, perhaps visit the bookseller's shop. You seemed very interested in the *Evelina* Margaret spoke of.'

Grace's cheeks flushed a little, a combination of surprise and shy pleasure that struck Spencer as very pretty indeed. The tip of her nose was pink with cold and her breath escaped in small white clouds, but her body was warm as she drew a fraction closer to Spencer and they moved down the frost-scattered street.

'I hadn't realised you were listening. You seemed so distracted by something, I feared you did not enjoy yourself.'

Spencer shook his head. 'Nothing could be further from the truth. I was merely thinking, that's all.'

'Of anything with which I might help?'

He glanced down at her hopeful face, luminous beneath the shadowy brim of her austere bonnet. How he longed to see her in glorious colour once again, he realised suddenly—she should be decked in emerald greens and periwinkle blues to complement the gold of her hair and bring light back to the clever gleam of her grey eyes. Black bombazine offset the flawless pallor of her skin, it was true, but it seemed *unnatural* to conceal Grace's verve beneath the sober gloom of mourning dress.

The look of uncertainty that crept over her face told him he'd been staring and he averted his gaze at once. He wouldn't be sharing his thoughts with her. It was one thing to feel the stirrings of life fighting to return within the sorrowful mire of his inner self; quite another to allow anybody to know of them.

Inscrutable as a cat. As usual.

Grace suppressed the pang of mild disappointment Spencer's lack of a reply inspired. Really she shouldn't have expected him to tell her what he had been thinking when he seemed so far away, present in her mother's tasteful sitting room but simultaneously miles away.

Some of the tension between them had dissipated, it was true, but her husband evidently still kept a tight grip on his secrets.

Still, there was definitely *something* altered in the way Spencer guided her on the chilly walk into town, her hand resting snugly on the rich fabric of his coat sleeve. He had placed it there himself, on his own initiative, so opposite to the first time he had escorted her through these streets, when he had fairly marched her along with a face like thunder and his hand like an unforgiving vice on her elbow.

That was before any of this happened. Before he knew of my pain and I discovered some fragments of his.

'Have you really not been to visit your father in the Fleet?'

Spencer's question shook her from her reflections with something of a jolt and she sighed before answering, a sad, deep breath that spoke volumes without words.

Poor Papa. How he would have enjoyed this morning—for once he wouldn't have been the only man in the house.

'Mama did not think it fitting for a group of young ladies to visit. The kinds of people Papa is imprisoned with are not particularly desirable. Neither my mother nor father would wish us to be exposed, or think it appropriate we went without a man to escort us.'

'Would you have liked to visit?'

'More than anything in the world, but we had nobody to step into Papa's place as our protector. He has been ill, according to his letters, but knowing him he has exaggerated his recovery so as not to worry us. To see him would have set my mind at ease.'

A well-dressed couple drew near to them, walking the opposite way on the cobbles. Their faces seemed familiar and Grace offered a polite smile—only for them to stare at her and then Spencer with naked fascination as though they were two creatures in a zoo, not returning her greeting with anything more than a look of burning interest that segued into whispers as soon as they had passed.

I ought to be used to that by now, Grace thought, a hot flush of embarrassment warming her despite the winter chill. *But somehow one never seems to grow accustomed to being notorious.*

She risked a swift cut of her eyes towards Spencer, worried what his reaction to their impudence could be and readying herself to calm him—but his sharp profile was still turned forward, his attention fixed on the street ahead and he took no more notice of the muttering than he would have a fly.

He truly doesn't seem to care, she thought wonderingly.

He appeared so unfazed by the speculating looks in a way Grace could hardly understand, her own wish not to provoke curiosity running so deep it felt unescapable. Spencer's uninterest was almost admirable, in a perverse sort of way, but it was easier to try to banish that strange thought as she stepped up into the bookseller's, the ping of the bell above the door announcing their entrance.

The elderly owner looked up from his perch behind the counter, peering over the top of the book held mere inches away from his nose. 'Good afternoon, ma'am. Do come in, come in!'

She stepped fully inside the little shop, Spencer following close behind. He had to stoop to fit through the door, she saw with vague amusement; for the first time his broad stature became a disadvantage as he stood among laden shelves, the width of his shoulders almost spanning the narrow space between the cases. The glorious smell of paper and leather assailed her and she breathed it in as deeply as one might expensive perfume.

The bookseller placed his book down carefully on the counter and squinted at her through round spectacles. 'Is there anything I might assist with?'

'Thank you, yes. My sister recommended I procure a copy of *Evelina*. Would you have one?'

The owner's eyes twinkled with the admiration of a much younger man. 'Your sister has fine taste. I shall search my storeroom, at once, ma'am… I feel sure I had a copy, if I could only remember where I put it…'

He slid down from his high stool and shuffled through a small doorway behind the counter, muttering to himself beneath his breath as he went. Spencer watched him go, raising an eyebrow as the man disappeared from sight.

'I think we might be here for some time. That gentleman must be a hundred and twelve if he's a day.'

'Are you in a hurry to return to Nevin Place?'

'Not particularly, although I would have liked to see it again before I turned forty.'

Before Grace could answer she heard the sharp ting of the shop's bell as some unseen customer entered, concealed behind Spencer's broad back. It was only when the newcomers edged round to the far side of the room Grace caught a glimpse of them: a fashionable couple about her age, watching her with looks of undisguised scorn that they swiftly redirected towards the nearest bookshelf the moment she caught their eye.

Beneath her cloak and sombre black gown Grace's heart began to skip a little more quickly. Surely she'd seen them somewhere before—weren't they acquaintances of Henry and George? Now she considered it, she *just* recalled meeting them at a card party months before, their names now having escaped her, but their association with the Earls' family enough to make her throat tighten in dismay.

Another quick glance up showed they had concealed themselves behind a set of shelves, for which Grace offered up a silent prayer of thanks, but they still lurked unseen and she found herself suddenly wishing she had refused Spencer's unexpected offer and gone straight home.

His look was a combination of mild concern and suspicion as he took in her frozen unease. 'What's the matter?'

'Nothing.'

'You are an appalling liar. Tell me.'

Grace shook her head stubbornly, attention fixed on the stack of books in front of her even as the sound of two whispered voices reached her straining ear, not wanting to listen yet at the same time intent on every sound.

'So George was correct, it seems—she *did* snare that Dauntsey. Upon my word, I can't imagine how she managed it.'

'Nor I. No fortune, precious little beauty and her papa locked up in the Fleet. What on earth can have persuaded the man to take her on? Her family is still

quite disgraced. Think what a fortunate escape poor
Henry had in calling off their engagement!'

There came muffled laughter, more like the cackling of two malicious old hens to send a dart through
to Grace's pounding heart.

'Mind you, the more I think about it the more I'm
convinced she and Dauntsey are a good match. *His* reputation is just as infamous as hers, after all. You must
have heard he was seen brawling in the Black Swan
tavern soon after his return? He claimed it was self-
defence, but what was a man of his standing doing in
such a low establishment in the first place?'

'If you ask me, they're each as scandalous as the
other. Quite the pair of miscreants—how well-suited!'

One glance up into Spencer's face told Grace he
had heard every word, but this time there was no blank
uninterest. Real anger lit the darkness of his eyes and
a scorching flood of mortification made Grace's skin
burn beneath her black gown. He looked ready to
stride the length of the shop and haul the male half
of the spiteful couple out from behind the shelf and
sharp alarm shrilled to mix with the nauseous churn
of Grace's stomach at the thought.

'Don't.' She laid a cold hand on his arm, feeling the
strength in it with a vague appreciation she dismissed
at once. There had never been a worse time for her
unconscious weakness for her husband to manifest itself—while he glared over her head in the direction of
the suddenly silent whisperers with such intensity it
was a wonder their bookcase didn't burst into flames.

'Please. Say nothing. Just take me home.'

Without pausing to hear his reply Grace gathered
her skirts and swept towards the exit, pushing past

Spencer's rigid frame. He merely stood, apparently deciding whether or not to obey, and she could only hope he would follow her as she flung open the door, careless of anything but escaping the cruel words that echoed in her mind.

Precious little beauty... Disgraced... A pair of miscreants...

Her lungs felt as though they might burst as she slipped down the front steps and into the street, before stopping uncertainly, unsure where to flee. In her distress she couldn't think where they had left the carriage and it was a relief to feel the sudden sensation of Spencer's hand tightening around her numb fingers, turning her about so he could look down into her face.

'Why wouldn't you allow me to confront them? The bile they were spitting deserved to be challenged!'

Grace's throat was dry and she tried to swallow, a tidal wave of shame rising to engulf her as unstoppably as the sea against rock. Spencer's expression was still angry, but edged with a puzzlement she could barely credit. How could it be that he still didn't grasp their situation? Must she truly spell it out to him in terms a child could understand?

'Surely you can see that would only have made things worse. If you'd stormed over to argue back, it would have caused an even uglier scene and given society even more reason to point fingers when I dare step outside my own door.'

'But why would it have been *you* who bore the brunt of it?' A frown pinched black eyebrows together in a stern line. 'Why do you suppose it would be you who was shamed? It would have been *I* who lost my temper and with good reason. I don't care for people upsetting my wife, saying whatever they please about her and especially not in my hearing.'

Grace blinked, the reply she'd thought to make mysteriously vanishing with Spencer's unexpected candour. She'd assumed his ire was the result of his hurt pride; not concern for her, a protective gesture that caught her off guard.

Surprise unravelled slowly in the pit of her stomach where before there had been only humiliation, travelling upwards to lick at her spine as she savoured his words.

He dislikes the whispers about me that much? I'd thought him so unmoved.

She peered up at him, unsure now how to respond. He had intended to defend her against the cruel slights of Henry's friends, a stark difference to how Henry himself had exposed her to ridicule, and the knowledge found the young girl that still lived inside her to make her flush.

Spencer Dauntsey, caring about my feelings above his own? Thirteen-year-old Grace would be beside herself.

But they weren't children any more, she a blushing girl and Spencer a handsome lad not yet grown. They were adults now and the thought that she had somehow, against all the odds, stumbled into a union with a man who not only made her heart race but seemed to care more for her with each passing day was surely too good to be true.

Unless it is true. Unless Spencer has proven, without even knowing it, that not all men see a woman's value in terms of her connections and fortune.

He evidently waited for her to speak and the seriousness of his comely face forced her to grope for a suitable answer.

'I appreciate the sentiment, but really, if you didn't want any further scandal heaped on my name, you would have gone entirely the wrong way about it. You and I are a pair now in the eyes of the world: whatever either of us does is reflected on the other, for better or for worse. I'm sure you can understand that.'

There was a pause. A slight action of Spencer's jaw caught Grace's eye as the muscle tensed and when he spoke she heard the note of displeasure there with a flit of dismay.

'I fear you might be right. I think I finally understand how the actions of one can so affect the other.'

The dark head turned away from her then, the complex expression that flared across chiselled features hidden from her as he moved. When he offered her his arm she took it, but the new dismay flared brighter at the silence with which he guided her back to the carriage and handed her inside, deep thought written in every line—although of what she could only guess.

Winter sunlight still shone merrily as they jolted in the direction of Nevin Place, although all the lightheartedness of a mere half hour before had been sucked out of the carriage as if by some dark enchantment. Spencer sat gazing fixedly out of the window like a marble statue, stiff and immovable with whatever grim thoughts spun inside him. Echoes of the spite Henry's friends had so gleefully spat still repeated themselves to jeer inside Grace's mind alongside the heavy weight of Spencer's discontentment, joining with the creak of the carriage and the sharp beat of the horses' hooves to make a cacophony that made her head ache.

How is it he seems so dissatisfied now? He was angry before, but now his mood seems darker than ever. What lesson did he take from my words?

Too distracted by her own thoughts, Grace didn't notice Spencer's eye upon her, or expect it when she heard his voice finally slice through the silence between them.

'I'd like to go with you.'

She looked up from her lap. At her clear lack of understanding Spencer leaned closer, the gap between them shrinking to no distance at all as his knee came into contact with the black fabric of her cloak and a sharp unmaidenly thrill shot straight to Grace's core at the touch of his leg against hers.

'To see your father. I'll escort you to visit the Fleet.'

Grace blinked mutely, unable to be sure she'd heard correctly.

From where did that decision spring?

'You'll—what?'

Dawning wonder crept up on her as Spencer watched with something akin to a shadow of a smile. She wouldn't go as far as to call it a real one—his lips were hardly curved out of their usual brooding line—but a faint glimmer of *something* lurked in his expression, increasing his already handsome features immeasurably.

'You suffered the impertinence of those halfwits with admirable dignity, although you shouldn't have had to. I thought perhaps a visit to your father might cheer you and make your situation a little easier to bear?'

Grace drew in a soft breath. 'Nothing would be more able!'

'Then we'll go. I have some business to attend to until Thursday week, but after that you can name the day.'

Surprise, delight and bewilderment came together in an overwhelming rush of emotion that stole all words from Grace's mouth. She would see Papa? After all these months, she would finally see Papa? She might as well have been a child again for the disbelieving excitement that welled within her, warmth spreading from her chest to light every nerve.

All thoughts of the unpleasant words that had taunted her only minutes before were forgotten, all clouds gone in the blink of an eye to be replaced by pure sunlight. That Spencer had offered her the most precious gift she could have wished for made her so suddenly giddy that she could have taken leave of her senses; so it was that without thinking, without pausing to consider the wisdom of her actions, Grace reached out across the narrow gap between her seat and his, drew Spencer's face to hers—and kissed him.

It was the softest brush of her lips over his—the feather-light touch of the gentlest breeze stirring among blossoms—lasting mere seconds; yet the fire of yearning that one chaste touch sparked in Grace's soul blazed at once with a flame nothing could have extinguished. It lasted only a moment and, as soon as she moved her hands from his cheeks to snatch them back to the safety of her own lap, she knew herself to have acted rashly, perhaps brazenly—yet the most defiant part of her spirit raised its head to boldly declare itself unrepentant. Her cheeks might burn with fierce heat and her heart leap within her like a deer through long grass, but the sensation of Spencer's lips on hers was something she had ached to feel again ever since she had first tasted them, the night he had shown her some humanity still remained hidden deep down inside him that she longed to bring out into the light. Nothing could make her regret giving in to that temptation, or restrain her from showing the depth of gratitude Spencer had no way of knowing flowed through her as a bottomless sea.

'Thank you, Spencer. Truly—thank you. You don't know what that means to me!'

He looked a little stunned as he sat back in his seat, although not—Grace saw with a kick of shy pleasure— displeased by her lapse of control. If anything, she thought she spied a glint of the same self-satisfaction any young man might show when praised by a pretty woman, although a moment later she wondered if she'd been mistaken. Spencer was above such petty charms, surely, and not likely to be moved by something so insignificant as a peck on the lips—but that did nothing to quell the conflagration that smouldered inside Grace, or to still the hands she gripped together tightly beneath the cover of her cloak to hide how they trembled with the urge to once again reach for the man who had so delighted her with the power of one simple promise. If her kiss had meant little to him, it had no bearing on her own confused delight; nor did it cause her to frown as she turned her face to the window so Spencer might not see the glow of her smile, cautiously questioning whether his feelings for her might not be as straightforward as she had once believed.

Chapter Ten

The sound of crunching beneath his boots followed Spencer all the way home from his accountant's office, a pleasing accompaniment to the dazzling sight of all Lyme Regis covered in a blanket of early March snow. Each step was muffled by soft drifts not yet trodden down to dirty mush by too many feet and a curious kind of otherworldly quiet stretched out across the empty streets—nobody else was in sight besides Spencer as he turned in at the path to Nevin Place, a black shape outlined starkly against a backdrop of glittering white.

I wonder if Grace will still be abed. It may be past eleven, but I wouldn't blame her if she didn't put a nose outside of the covers on a day like this.

She'd slept on, nestled among her pillows like a hibernating animal when he had slipped away some hours earlier. As ever, he had taken great pains not to accidentally brush the intriguing shape of her curled under thin linen. They might only share for appearances, but that seemed harder than ever for Spencer to remember these days and he could only hope she remained oblivious to the desires which gripped him night after night as he lay waking beside her, burning with the longing to reach out and touch.

Rivers and Thorne stepped forward to relieve him of his hat and coat, but nothing was able to drown out the whispers that now nagged at the back of his mind. It had been a mistake to allow himself to dwell on the thought of Grace occupying his bed, but the thought was one too damnably tempting to be easily dismissed.

Never before had a woman rendered him so helpless with so little effort. He'd been with women before, of course, in the years before he had so determinedly turned his heart to stone: merry, laughing girls who tumbled after him with smiles on their lips and hadn't expected—or wanted—anything more from him. But Grace—Grace was another creature altogether. She might surrender to him out of duty if he asked it of her, playing on her desire to fulfil her obligations as a wife, but the idea of her surrendering against her own inclination was abhorrent.

After her treatment by that idiot Earls when he had her heart—*how galling to envy such an obvious simpleton*—it was no wonder she still wished to hold part of herself in reserve, to keep back something Spencer would not be able to take and potentially destroy. There was still such sadness sometimes in the grey depths of her beautiful eyes, sadness he feared was tied to longing for the man she had loved before…so he would continue to wait, for hours in the inky darkness of night, listening to her gentle breathing with an ache in his chest and a yearning that could not be satisfied.

He frowned at his reflection in the entrance-hall mirror as he straightened his black cravat. It was pointless to focus on such unhelpful thoughts. All they did was stir feelings within him about which he felt only confusion, each day that passed making them stronger until their power could no longer be denied—even to himself. The walls he had built around himself for so long were in grave danger of crumbling altogether, their foundations already threatened by the twin assaults of Grace's good nature and a face that grew more lovely to him each time he saw it. If he had ever been at real risk of abandoning his restraint it was now, with an attachment to his unlikely wife that blossomed against all odds, like a flower in an arid desert that refused to wither and die.

Rivers hovered at his elbow, an obliging wraith Dorothea had scooped up out of some unpromising start in life to take on as a maid. She'd woven black laces into the frilled edges of her cap, he noticed for the first time; a little mark of respect for her late mistress that was unexpectedly touching.

'Is Mrs Dauntsey still above stairs?'

'No, sir. She rose some time ago and has been in the gardens for no little while.'

Spencer frowned. 'In the gardens? What can she be doing? It's cold enough to freeze Hephaestus's forge out there!'

A strange look crossed the maid's face. She was far too respectful to smile at the question, but evidently *something* had diverted her. 'In honesty, sir, I'd struggle to describe what the mistress is occupied with. It might be as well to see for yourself.'

Curiosity unfurled in Spencer's mind like smoke rising from a chimney.

What are you about now, Grace?

'Is that so? In that case I'd better have my coat back.'

Rivers fetched it again from the hall armoire, the fabric still warm as Spencer threaded his arms into the sleeves. Venturing back out into the cold wasn't a prospect that delighted him, but his interest in what could possibly make Grace venture forth likewise was too strong to ignore.

A brief scan of the garden didn't immediately offer any sightings of his elusive wife, although any one of the numerous well-kept hedges and trees could be concealing her. Closer inspection of the snowy ground revealed a set of neat boot prints leading from the door to skirt the glasshouse, disappearing behind an evergreen topiary peacock spreading its impressive tail against the red brick of the left boundary wall.

Following the telltale tracks with rapt attention, a strange scrunching met his reddening ears, mixed with the unmistakable sound of an unseen someone's slightly laboured breathing. The peacock loomed larger, its beak pointing accusingly at him as Spencer crept closer and peered round icy leaves—to finally discover what mysterious task took Grace from the snug comfort of her bed out into the merciless cold.

'What on earth are you doing?'

Grace started, the tall mass of snow she was busily patting into a column wobbling ominously.

'You startled me!' She looked up from her low crouch, not moving away from whatever it was she saw in the shapeless heap. 'I could have knocked my snowman over and had to start again!'

He watched for a moment as Grace resumed her meticulous patting and smoothing, concentrating on her task. The pile wasn't as formless as he had first thought, he realised now. Two rudimentary arms were held either side of a rather portly torso, although the figure seemed to blend into the ground at the thick base rather than stand on discernible legs.

'You've some skill at this.'

'It isn't my first time. As soon as I saw the snow this morning I knew I couldn't rest until I'd been out to build in it!'

The unlikely contrast between Grace's proper manners and this unexpected folly was so great Spencer could only shake his head in bemusement.

'Is that not a little childish?'

If she hadn't been so well bred he might have suspected Grace of being on the cusp of rolling her eyes. 'There's a good deal of difference between childish and young at heart, you know. My sisters and I would make one of these every time the snow fell—sometimes even Papa would help and nobody could ever accuse him of childish behaviour!'

Spencer spread his hands in defeat. 'I stand corrected. Building snowmen is evidently a very worthwhile and commendable undertaking.'

Grace's smile was all the reward he ever could have needed for his grudging acceptance. 'Quite so. I'm glad you've seen reason.'

She retreated a couple of crunchy steps to admire her work, little white clouds of breath coming slightly faster with exertion. With gloved hands on hips she surveyed her work with narrowed eyes, which widened as she turned them on Spencer with a look of enquiry.

'Come along, then.'

'I beg your pardon?'

'I said, come along. If we're to have this gentleman

finished by luncheon, you'll have to do more than stand around staring at him!'

It took a moment for him to realise she was being sincere. 'You want me to help? You want me to join you in…*this*?'

The expectant smile flickered a little. 'I thought perhaps you might. As I said, it's something I always used to do with my sisters and possibly Papa; with none of them here I admit it's not quite the same.'

A disagreeable sensation flared in the region of his chest at the note of sadness in Grace's voice, valiantly concealed, but present none the less.

Building snowmen, of all things?

It was the kind of silliness he hadn't taken part in since—well, he hardly knew when. Only children and the simpleminded would enjoy such a thing, surely— and yet the hopeful turn of Grace's countenance gripped him firmly by the heart and would not let go.

You know she's had precious little to smile about of late.

The memory of the enraging scene in the bookshop surfaced to stir Spencer's ire once again, her pale face as she had fled something he knew he would never forget.

What would it cost you to humour your wife in her sadness?

'Very well,' he muttered, gruff as any crotchety old man caught out in uncharacteristic sentiment. 'I'll help. What am I to do?'

'Oh! Truly?' She brightened again at once. 'You can gather some snow for his head, please, while I build up his shoulders. A few big handfuls should do.'

Still not entirely convinced he hadn't run mad, Spencer dutifully went about his task.

If Mother could see me now she would either faint with shock or fall over laughing.

Either reaction was as likely as the other, he thought as he scooped great piles of snow up between his hands and watched as delicate flakes clung to his gloved fingers, shining in the wintry sunlight like tiny jewels.

'Is this enough?'

'Plenty. Now, if you just shape it a little so it's more of a ball—'

Grace nodded encouragingly as Spencer squashed the icy whiteness into a rough approximation of a sphere, or a rather misshapen head.

'—and perch it on his shoulders.'

Spencer placed the lump on top of the leaning tower and eyed it doubtfully. 'Like that?'

'Exactly like that!'

Grace's grey eyes sparkled with new pleasure as he watched her carefully pat down the flaking pile of snow, her face alight and so animated for a moment she looked the most captivating woman he had ever seen. Standing in the bleached fairyland of his sunlit garden with her nose pink and her cheeks flushed with innocent happiness, to Spencer there was no other in all the world who would ever eclipse her.

I wish this moment would never end. If only we could be like this for ever.

It was the first time he had allowed his feelings to declare themselves so boldly and he found himself rocked by the realisation it was the truth. Somehow, somewhere along the twisting and turning road of their journey together Spencer's resistance to Grace's straightforward charms had begun to falter, until he arrived at the pass he had come to so gradually it had hardly felt like he'd been moving at all. Each day had chipped away at his studied indifference and now he was helpless in the face of the knowledge that shook him: that he was slowly but surely falling in love with the one woman who ever could have managed to melt the ice in his soul.

Grace's eager voice broke Spencer's trance.

'All we need now is some eyes and he'll be complete!'

She bent and ferreted two smooth pebbles from beneath the snow, holding them out to him triumphantly. 'Would you like the honour of the finishing touch?'

'I'm sure I'd be delighted.'

Conscious of Grace's eyes upon him, Spencer took his time in carefully positioning the stones in the figure's rough-hewn face.

'Very handsome!' Grace's beam of satisfaction warmed Spencer right down to his toes. 'I think, if I may, I'd like to name him Robert, for my papa, who thanks to you we shall see very soon.'

She gently touched the snowman's cold cheek as though it belonged to his flesh-and-blood namesake, her smile softening into a small, wistful thing that made her look so vulnerable Spencer ached with the desire to catch her up and hold her close to him, to shield her from anything that might dare make her seem so sweetly sad.

What I wouldn't give to be able to do such a thing. What I wouldn't give to allow myself that freedom and for her to want me in that kind of way.

Grace retreated a small distance away, probably to

survey her work from another angle, and Spencer likewise turned his attention to the substitute father-in-law who gleamed on his frosted lawn.

'What happens now?'

'Well…at home, something always followed to officially mark the completion of the snowman.'

'And what was that?'

Still admiring their creation, Spencer didn't turn around—so it was something of a surprise when a missile of powdery snow exploded gently against the back of his head, making him wheel about in disbelief to see Grace's mischievous smile, all traces of sadness gone.

'Why—a snowball fight, of course.'

For one heart-stopping moment Grace feared she had finally done it, finally pushed her serious, solitary husband past the point of his endurance.

What can you have been thinking of? What possessed you?

He stared down at her and she stared up at him, her smile slipping in dawning dread; but nothing could match the amazement that shocked Grace to the core as for the first time in all the long weeks of their renewed acquaintance Spencer's mouth opened, his lips curved up—and he laughed.

He actually *laughed*, a deep thing that echoed through the snowy garden and stole all the breath from Grace's body. It was a sound so unexpected and yet so utterly *wonderful* there was nothing she could do but stand transfixed, gazing at the man in front of her with half-melted snow slipping from his hair on to his shoulders and the most breathtaking smile she had ever seen lighting the sharp angles of his face.

Every last trace of the gravity usually so ingrained on his features was wiped away by the upward curve of his mouth, lines appearing at his eyes so suddenly alive in a way Grace had almost forgotten was possible.

He looks like he did when we were younger, she realised, still unable to tear herself away from this new creature's face. *He looks happier, so full of life...just as he did all those years ago.*

Spencer looked nearly as surprised as she was by his reaction, although his face was swiftly hidden by the sweep of his hair as he bent to scoop up a handful of snow.

'I think it might be prudent for you to run now, Mrs Dauntsey.'

Grace didn't need telling twice.

She turned and fled, ducking as a flurry of snow sailed past her ear to spatter softly against the peacock's outstretched wing. Behind her came the sound of boots crunching closer, but she didn't stop to peer over her shoulder as she waded through the deep drifts as quickly as she could, snow grabbing at her ankles to soak through her stockings. Another projectile narrowly missed her other ear, and this time she allowed herself the fleetest of glances backwards to taunt her hunter.

'Your aim is *far* worse than I would have expected!'

'Is that so? Then allow me to practise!'

Bareheaded and rosy-cheeked, Spencer looked the very image of the lad she had once known as he advanced ominously towards her, another snowball cupped in his hand. Grace backed away, feeling behind her with numb fingertips until, with a thrill of delicious horror, she felt the spiky sensation of a hedge block her path of escape and there was nowhere to run from the handsome man who sauntered closer with something almost a smirk playing about his lips.

'How unfortunate. You appear to be at a disadvantage.'

He watched as Grace's wide eyes tracked from side to side, searching for an escape, and then fixed on the missile he flicked up and caught again with repeated casual menace.

'I'm not sure this is fair!'

'No? You didn't seem particularly bothered about fairness when you attacked me, without warning, from behind. Am I to understand it's one rule for you and another for me?'

'You would not throw that at a defenceless woman!' She held up her empty hands. 'See? I am unarmed!'

'Of course not. That would be most ungentlemanly.'

The snowball fell to the ground, released from Spencer's hand as he instead reached up and with a grin of heart-stoppingly handsome triumph pinged the snow-laden branches of a tree overhanging Grace's hedge, sending a sparkling avalanche squarely down on to her head.

'Oh!' Grace squeaked as the snow cascaded over her, invading the collar of her cloak to slip horridly down her chest and back in freezing streams. 'You cheat!'

Icy water trickling down her neck captured most of her attention, although there was still some to spare for the fresh laugh that met her accusation—shorter than before, but filled with the same unfamiliar vitality that set her spirits soaring.

Spencer offered a mock bow, a wicked glint in his

brown eyes just playful enough to make Grace's breath catch at the sight. 'So gracious in defeat. May I in turn be a magnanimous victor and escort you inside, if you've finished your adventures for the morning? All that cold water you're swimming in can't be pleasant.'

He extended an elbow and Grace took it, grateful for a crutch as they retraced their precarious footsteps back to the house. Before pulling open the kitchen door Spencer turned to her with a rough snort of amusement.

'You're still absolutely covered. Here. Allow me.'

She stood obligingly still while he brushed off her powdered shoulders, staring fixedly ahead as he picked a stray cluster from the mound of curls pinned to the crown of her head. A few of them had come loose to wave softly in the March air and Grace felt every sinew in her body stand to sudden attention as Spencer smoothed one behind her ear, his fingertips grazing the cold skin of her face so gently it made her shudder.

Her heart had already quickened from their race through the snow, but it skipped faster still as she waited breathlessly to see if those fingers would again skim over her sensitive cheek, flushed now with both activity and anticipation.

Something deep down inside her had broken free at the sound of his unrestrained laughter—it spoke to her, offering undeniable proof that a carefree young man still lived within Spencer's troubled soul, and a sense of tentative hope rose to meet it. Perhaps there might be some way to find happiness together as Dorothea had wished. And perhaps…

I might be the one to help him see it?

It was a dangerous thought and one that flickered just out of Grace's reach, although whether she would have fanned its flames or doused them with a shower of ice she hardly knew. All she could do was stand and stare up at her husband as the possibility of a real connection, something based on more than mere convenience, filled her with hope and terror she well understood. To give in to these stirrings for Spencer that only grew in strength with each day that passed was achingly tempting, but terrifying in equal measure. Hadn't Henry shown her the consequences of entrusting one's heart to another? Hadn't Spencer likewise shown her his desire to withdraw from the world, despite the growing accord she could swear blossomed between them unless she had gravely misjudged their tentative friendship?

But that laugh...

As if carried along by some otherworldly force Grace felt herself rise on to her tiptoes and press a kiss to Spencer's cold cheek, the urge grasping hold of her without warning to bend her to its will. It was all too much: the wonder of Spencer's rediscovered smile; the concentration on his face as he had collected the snow; how carefully he had brushed off her hair. There were just so many moments that delighted her, the desire to allow herself to treasure them so strong surely no woman could have resisted. He was the most confusing, dangerous, enthralling man in the world to her at that moment as he stood among the frosted trees, strange and somehow so *other*—a threat and a promise all at the same time.

Almost as soon as her lips brushed the dark bristles of his cheek she felt his hand at her waist, anchoring her against him with gentle insistence that made her shiver, but she dropped back again with her eyes averted and cheeks burning hot enough to melt the snow around her. That ungovernable urge to feel him beneath her lips once more argued to be able to continue, to escalate the kiss by finding Spencer's curving mouth, but Grace steeled herself against its siren call. The last time they had tasted each other had been so bewildering, stirring up such confusion between them; a soft press of her lips on his cheek was as far as she should allow her desires to go, the morning already throwing up more questions than answers as to how their relationship had flourished.

'Thank you for humouring me this morning. I think perhaps now I'd like to go inside.'

The fire in his study's grate crackled merrily, casting Grace's shadow across the floor as she knelt before it and patted water from her hair with a warm towel. Spencer watched in comfortable silence, enjoying the way the damp ringlets shone in the firelight as they dried from dark to burnished gold. A small damp patch at the back of Grace's gown drew his eye, framing that tender nape he so often caught himself thinking of… It would be a fine thing to be able to touch it, to reach out and stroke its pale length and see if the skin there was as soft as it looked—

'For the life of me I can't get my hands warm.'

Grace held her fingers towards the blaze, wincing a little as they no doubt tingled painfully at the tips. 'The rest of me is defrosting nicely, but for some reason my hands always take an age to thaw.'

Spencer inspected his own palms, their usual healthy pink in sharp contrast to Grace's blue-white. 'Perhaps next time you ought to borrow a pair of my gloves instead of your flimsy things when we venture out.'

'Next time? Are you suggesting there might be a repeat of this morning's activities?' There was an impish gleam in Grace's smile that tempted Spencer to return it. 'I knew you enjoyed yourself after all!'

He hid the matching upturn of his own lips behind his coffee cup. 'I'll admit your childish pursuits weren't entirely tedious.' It was the stoutest of understatements, but it somehow seemed unwise to let Grace know exactly how much he had liked their snowy games. He would have to admit to being surprised at how easily she had drawn him in—and at how good it had felt to abandon, for an hour at least, the usual darkness that tried to swallow him whole.

How was it she had managed it so effortlessly? One bold request, one unhappy look and he had run to do her bidding like a puppy with no other thought but to please its mistress.

I'm not sure I've ever been so obliging to anybody in my life.

There was something about Grace that managed, time and again, to pull him down from the tower he had built around himself, to force him back out into the world and to face all the feelings he had never wanted to acknowledge ever again. Happiness, confusion, even *laughter*—Grace had inspired them all with the witchcraft Spencer knew he was powerless to guard against. Certainly the feel of her soft lips against his rough cheek had unmanned him, unexpected and yet a greater reward for his folly than he ever could have dreamed.

It was only when the unwitting sorceress in question gave another shudder that he was roused from his complicated thoughts.

'Your hands can't still be cold, surely?'

'I swear they are. I'll have to put them actually into the fire at this rate, or my fingers might very well fall off!'

Spencer cocked an eyebrow. 'You have an impressive flair for the dramatic. Let me see.'

Leaning forward in his chair, he motioned Grace closer and ran an eye over her mottled skin. 'Hmm. They do still look a little blue.'

Before he'd truly thought what he was doing he took her freezing fingers within both of his hands and chafed them, too intent on his task to notice the wondering look on her face—although the tiny gasp that escaped her when he brought them up to his lips and gently breathed on them, covering them with the secret warmth from his own body, could not be ignored.

She was close enough for him to kiss her—properly this time, not just the lightest brush across a cold cheek. That was the only thought that repeated itself over and over as Spencer looked into her upturned face, her eyes wide and her pretty lips slightly parted. It would be so easy to bend his head to touch them with his own, just as Grace had brushed his in the jolting comfort of his carriage mere days before, sending a wave of yearning through him so powerful it had robbed him of all speech. She'd done it of her own volition, he remembered, just as she had only that morning—out of gratitude, certainly, but possibly…also out of desire? Could it be that some of the spark that glittered beneath his skin also crackled inside Grace, mirroring the feelings that taunted him whenever she was near? It was the most shamefully exciting thought that Grace might feel the same secret flicker of heat she inspired in him, the notion of such a thing disturbing her quiet soul too rousing to even consider.

There's always the chance she still feels the sting of that fool Henry's rejection, of course, or that a part of her still misses him. I wonder if he knows how enviable such a thing might be to any sensible man.

The unpleasant thought muscled its way to the forefront of his mind, a spark of irrepressible jealousy stemming the tide of his rising hope. Grace had stated quite plainly she had no desire to risk her heart again, a resolution he understood only too well. It was the same worry that nagged at Spencer, muttering to him whenever he caught himself staring at Grace as she sat reading or drew his eye as she walked across a room.

Both of us so damaged and so afraid.

'Is that better?'

'Much. Thank you.' Grace's reply was little more than a whisper, so quiet it was almost lost in the rustling of her dress as she got to her feet and withdrew her slender hands from his, leaving them suddenly bereft. In the beat of silence that followed she hesitated before gesturing towards the bell by the door. 'Shall I ring for more coffee?'

'If you'd like.'

He watched her cross the room, moving noiselessly as any young lady taught from an early age. With her head up and her face impassive anybody else might have thought her mind occupied by nothing but her task, but...

You could have kissed her then.

Spencer cursed himself as he rubbed the shadow on his chin.

She was right there and you lost your nerve, you coward.

She had stared up at him, her stormy gaze locked dreamily on to his, but he had allowed his doubts to overcome him and now she looked…almost disappointed that he had not?

Perhaps he was imagining things. Perhaps she had no such thoughts. But it was always better to err on the side of caution, he resolved, in a vain attempt to brush off the regret that circled in the pit of his stomach at that wasted chance. It would be a long journey to London tomorrow morning, jolting along pitted roads to reach the grim Fleet. The last thing Grace would need on such a day was an increase in the air of confusing tension between them surely she felt, too—that whispered they were not quite just *friends*, but equally not quite arrived at something *more*.

Chapter Eleven

Apprehension swooped in Grace's stomach as she stepped from the coach into the bustle of Farringdon Street to take her first look at her father's new residence. Fleet prison loomed high above her to stare menacingly back with its windows like flashing eyes, a hulking brick shape set against an ill-tempered winter sky. She'd been so eager for this day to come, so filled with childlike excitement to finally see Papa again, but the long journey to London had given her too much time to second-guess what she might find and now her throat tightened with nerves as she moved towards the arched entrance and felt the prison's cold shadow envelop her.

'Stay close at all times, Grace. You're not to stir a step inside this place without me at your side.'

At any other time Spencer's wary command might have been met with a raised brow in reply, but Grace only nodded and increased her grip on his arm as he led her up a flight of dingy steps to tap on what a brass plaque named the warden's rooms.

'Yes?'

Spencer pushed open the door to reveal the owner of a rather hoarse voice sitting behind a messy desk. Grace's eye immediately flew to the half-full bottle of something close to the warden's hand, followed by a swift glance at the multiple days' worth of stubble coarsening his already heavy features, set in an expression of surly uninterest. He looked for all the world as though he should be in a cell himself rather than in charge of anybody else's and Grace's chest gave a nasty lurch at the thought of her gentle father at the mercy of such an unfriendly looking brute.

If Spencer noticed the unpleasant aroma of alcohol and unopened windows in the room he gave no sign as he stood firm in the doorway, his tone civil enough, but not for one moment relaxing his grasp on Grace's cold fingers.

'My name is Captain Dauntsey. I wrote to you some days ago stating my intention to come with my wife to visit her father—Mr Robert Linwood. Can you tell us where we'd find him?'

The warden squinted at them for a moment, one hand rubbing the sparse remnants of his unkempt hair. 'Linwood, you say? Linwood... Oh. Yes.' An ugly smile spread across his face and he peered at Grace more closely, sending a crawling sensation of revulsion down her spine. 'The *innocent* Robert Linwood. You'll find your father in the right wing, madam, just up those stairs there—in the Common side, of course. You're welcome to go up to see him, although do be sure to watch your step.'

His sarcasm made Grace's lip want to curl, but instead she lifted her chin and looked pointedly at the bottle he hadn't the good manners to hide, before dropping into the most elegant curtsy she could manage in the small and cluttered room.

'Thank you. Your kind concern is much appreciated.'

They were almost at the grimy staircase he had gestured to when Grace heard the raspy voice issue again from behind her, making her turn in reluctant enquiry.

'Beg pardon, sir?'

'I said—if there's anything you might be wanting, do let me know. For a small fee most things can be arranged: little comforts, some taste of home perhaps. Lice-free bedding and decent food can make a wondrous difference to a prisoner and at only a modest price.'

Grace narrowed her eyes at the slovenly warden lounging in his chair. 'Does my father not already have lice-free bedding and decent food? Why should there be a need to pay extra for such basic human dignities?'

An unpleasant look crossed the reclining man's already unpleasant face, but a swift glance up at Spencer's granite countenance seemed to make him change his mind about whatever he had been about to say. Instead he shrugged and reached to yank the cork from his bottle with an audible pop.

'As I said. If there's anything you want me to arrange, just tell me. Good afternoon.'

Grace's heart, already heavy with dread, had fairly fallen into her boots by the time she and Spencer reached the top of the gloomy stairs leading to the first floor of the Fleet. Each upward step took her nearer to a growing din of voices, footsteps, coughing and rough laughter that came from overhead, mingled with a horrible smell of tobacco and unwashed bod-

ies that struck her with its acrid scent to make her unconsciously wrinkle her nose. It was like nothing she
had experienced before and as she gingerly set foot on
the first landing Grace became aware she was holding her breath.

She stood for a moment, still riveted to Spencer's
side as she gazed around her with eyes wide and staring. It took time for her to make any sense of what she
saw and the hand that held Spencer's arm tightened in
instinctive horror.

*Thank heavens he is here with me. I can see now
why Mama was so insistent we didn't come to visit.*

How had her kind, generous, gentle papa ended up
in a place like this? Hardly any light filtered through
grimy windows to illuminate a narrow corridor with
rooms set either side, throwing the clusters of people
ranged about into shadow. Some of the doors to the
rooms were closed, but others stood ajar to allow feeble candlelight to spill out and touch the thin faces that
turned towards where Grace stood, some curious, but
others blank with the indifference of suffering.

With a sharp pang of surprise Grace saw there
were women there, not just the men she had expected,
and with another jolt she recognised several of them
clutched babies in their skinny arms or held little hands
as toddlers tottered to and fro. Many of them were
dressed in scarcely more than rags and the sounds of
thin cries combined with the rest in a terrible sym-
phony of wretchedness that wrung every ounce of compassion from Grace's aching chest.

'Do you need to sit down for a moment?'

She hardly heard Spencer's murmur, so occupied
was she with the squalor that surrounded them on every

side. Even if she had wanted a seat there was nothing more than the floor to sink on to, so filthy it was impossible to tell what colour it might have originally been.

'No. I am quite well.'

Grace took a deep breath to calm herself, immediately regretting it as she took in a great lungful of the awful mix of sweat and stale beer that permeated the air. Her head swam a little with shock and dismay, the truth of her father's plight never more plain than at that moment.

Oh, Papa. Why didn't you tell us?

'Grace? Come with me. Let's find your father.'

Somehow Spencer's arm freed itself from her vice-like grip to be replaced by his palm, comfortingly warm against her thin glove. By another mystery their fingers unconsciously intertwined, so it was hand in hand Grace blindly followed Spencer as he carefully pushed through the sullen crowds. There were some whispers, a few vulgar words hissed at Grace's back, but one ferocious look from Spencer was enough to silence them—as Grace would have seen, had she been able to raise her eyes fixed on the dirty floorboards in fright and a terrible dismay that tore at her leaping heart.

Hazily she heard Spencer speak to a man standing by one of the doors, just catching his word of thanks as the prisoner pointed silently towards the last room at the end of the passage. There were fewer people down there and Grace took a moment to steady herself in the relative quiet, still holding tightly to Spencer's hand. Under other circumstances she might have pulled away, worried he would see how much she enjoyed his touch, but with only an ill-hung door standing between her and whatever sorry fate had befallen poor Papa she felt nothing but grateful relief for the comfort of Spencer's firm grasp.

She sensed his gaze upon her and looked up to see a troubled shadow in his warm brown eyes.

'Are you sure you're ready? I confess I hadn't expected this place to be quite so grim. Perhaps it would have been better if I hadn't brought you—I see how distressed you are already and I fear seeing your father and the state he could be in might only add to it.'

Grace shook her head. 'Don't say that. Escorting me here is one of the kindest things anybody has ever done for me and besides…' she attempted a small smile despite the rigidity of her jaw '…if you think for one moment I have got this close to seeing Papa only to turn and leave now, you've another think coming.'

The shadow segued into a glimmer of admiration that sent a faint thrill through Grace's nerves and Spencer raised his free hand to rap smartly at the peeling door. 'Very good, Mrs Dauntsey. I'd a suspicion that would be your response.'

At first there was no reply to their knock—only the muffled sound of coughing followed by silence in which Grace and Spencer exchanged swift looks of concern. The second tap, however, warranted an explosion of hacking and wheezing followed by a weak 'yes?' that sent Grace striding into the room as though propelled from a cannon, Spencer following close behind and scarcely less concerned than his wife at the feebleness of that wavering voice.

Grace lurched to a halt so abrupt Spencer almost careered into her, only just in time able to sidestep where she stood just inside the door and rooted to the spot with an expression of vivid, open-mouthed horror. He followed her appalled gaze to an untidy heap in one corner that might have once been a serviceable bed, but now sagged to the ground beneath a scattering of blankets Spencer could smell from across the room. Half submerged under the greying material was a thatch of thinning silver hair atop a face so white it could have been carved from the snow outside, if two feverish red spots hadn't burned brightly on the sunken cheeks. At their sudden entrance to the room the figure in the bed rose up stiffly on one elbow to peer in their direction, his face anxious in the dim light fighting its way through one grubby window.

His eyes grew round behind his spectacles as they fixed on Grace's stunned face, disbelieving as he sat up sharply.

'Grace? It can't be—I must be feverish again. My Gracie? Is it truly you, or am I dreaming?'

Mr Linwood pushed his blankets aside with hands that even at a distance Spencer saw trembled with either shock or illness. There wasn't any time for him to wonder which it was, however, before Grace stumbled forward, reaching out for her father with equally faltering fingers.

'You're not dreaming, Papa. I'm here, truly!'

She was in his arms before he had managed to move a single pace from his bed, her face pressed into his chest with her bonnet askew and her shoulders moving beneath her gown in such a way Spencer knew at once she was crying.

Her father stroked her back in mute amazement, holding her close to him as though to convince himself she was real. Looking over the top of her head, he peered in Spencer's direction, still seeming to doubt what was in front of his eyes and even teetering on the brink of fainting away in astonishment.

Spencer stepped forward and gently laid a hand on Grace's shaking shoulder to feel delicate bone beneath black silk. 'Let's sit down. You and your father have both had a shock and need time to collect yourselves.'

Grace drew back a little, wiping her eyes with the back of her black-gloved hand. Her tears reflected the grey light from the window like tiny diamonds of emotion, the sight of them pricking Spencer in the vulnerable place inside him only his unhappy wife was able to invade.

'You're right. Come, Papa. Won't you sit and tell me—oh, *everything* you thought you had to hide?'

She guided him back down on to the bed and perched beside him, making the rickety frame creak ominously. A broken-backed chair stood by the empty hearth and Spencer hooked it towards him with one foot to carefully settle on to its worn seat, leaning forward to hear what Mr Linwood might croak through chapped lips.

Grace's papa shook his head in quiet wonder as he took in his daughter's face, drinking in the sight of her like a thirsting man given a glass of cool water. 'I can't believe you're here. I hadn't thought to see any of my beautiful girls for a long time. I thought I must be losing my mind when you burst through my door, yet here you are!'

A frown briefly creased Grace's brow. 'Did the warden not tell you we had sought permission to visit? I would have written to you directly, but I thought he would pass the message on.'

'He did not. I'm afraid I rather think he would find it amusing for me to be surprised and dismayed by your coming.'

Grace blinked at her father, a flicker of pain slicing though her expression that made Spencer's insides twist sharply. 'Why would you be dismayed? Are you not happy to see me?'

Mr Linwood took up her hand and held it tightly, looking firmly into her eyes as though she should understand his next words very clearly. 'There is nothing in the world that could ever make me happier than seeing your face and I'm moved beyond words that you came to find me—but I would not have chosen for you to come here. Upon my word, I never wanted you to see me in this state or have your innocence tainted by such an evil place.' He lifted his spectacles to rub at his tired, bloodshot eyes. 'Your mother and I vowed we would protect you and your sisters from the reality, although I must confess even your mama wasn't aware of the full truth of my life here. I'll have to beg forgiveness for the deception…my only excuse is a misguided desire to save you from worries you should never have had to bear.'

'Oh.' Fresh tears sparkled in Grace's eyes to once again claw at Spencer's insides, but she forced them back with the determination he had long since admired. 'You should have told us your living conditions were so bad and that your health had so clearly not recovered. There must have been something we could do!'

'No, Gracie. To make his time in the Fleet tolerable a man needs a deal of money to pay for luxuries, money that you would not have been able to spare. I feared you would go without yourselves to make me more comfortable, when I am the cause of our troubles and deserve no such kindness. If I'd only seen those villains Fisher and Armand for what they were, none of this would have happened.'

With a sigh he turned to look across at Spencer properly for the first time, eyes behind his round glasses the same colour as Grace's own and a shadow of his daughter's tentative smile visible beneath a greying beard. 'But enough talk of my folly. Please forgive my lapse of manners. I should have greeted you when you first arrived, but I was hardly able to think straight.'

Spencer gave the best bow he could manage while sitting down and extended his hand. 'Mr Linwood. It's a pleasure to meet you again after all these years.'

The older man took the proffered hand with real enthusiasm, tempered slightly by the weakness of his cold fingers. 'I would have known you at once, sir. I am vastly pleased to see you and overjoyed to shake your hand. I don't mind admitting I was grieved when I was told Grace was no longer engaged to Mr Earls, but on balance I feel she has ended up with a far superior husband given the glowing reports I hear from my wife and daughters—and, of course, from Grace herself.'

'Papa...'

Grace flashed her father a look that made Spencer's lips twitch with surprised amusement. *Glowing reports from Grace, indeed?* The idea was so absurdly pleasing he felt the urge to preen, only increased by the hint of colour that bloomed in his wife's cheek. He would have to investigate what exactly this praise involved if he ever had a moment alone with his father-in-law, the temptation to find out what Grace said about him in private too intriguing to ignore.

Far superior to Henry Earls, am I?

He could only hope Grace herself thought some-thing similar, confirming the triumph over his rival that crowed inside him at her father's honesty.

I like the sound of that. Perhaps I ought to ask Mr Linwood to put in a few good words on my behalf.

Before he had a chance to continue along what she evidently deemed a dangerous path, however, Grace shook Mr Linwood's arm. 'You were saying there was nothing we could have done and that you didn't deserve our help. Do you not think it was our right to decide whether that was true? We would never have allowed you to be living like…*this.*' She gestured around the dingy room in obvious distress. 'And your health is so much poorer than you let us believe!'

'Ach, it's not so bad. Most of the time I barely—' An untimely bout of coughing seized her papa in its unforgiving grip, squeezing until his face flared red and tears ran from his eyes. It was so reminiscent of the way Dorothea had gasped for breath Spencer felt himself tense in instinctive concern, new worry ris-ing inside him as Mr Linwood wheezed into silence.

One look at Grace's white face was enough to con-firm her mind ran with the same deadly comparison, sharp fear tightening the set of her jaw. She rubbed her father's back consolingly, but nothing could wipe away the alarm Spencer saw flit across her features and bring tension to the slight frame he longed to draw into a comforting embrace.

He watched for a moment, taking in the unhappy scene unfolding in the cold, bleak room with the stirrings of a plan flickering at the back of his mind. Quite possibly it would meet with opposition from his kindly father-in-law, but that was nothing when measured against the terrible prospect of Grace having another reason to wear black—which she most certainly would, unless something was done and fast.

'Mr Linwood. Please allow me to insist upon paying for you to be moved to better quarters and be seen by a physician. This room isn't fit to be borne a single day longer and certainly was never meant for a gentleman such as yourself.'

With his attention turned to her father Spencer only saw the snap of Grace's head in his direction out of the corner of his eye, but even that glimpse showed how her lips parted and eyes widened in sudden hope so vivid it knocked some of the breath from his lungs. A flick of his eyes towards her was met with the most precious reward he ever could have wished for: a beam of wondering gratitude that spread across her face to light what had previously been shrouded in terror, almost identical to the secret smile of months before that had captured his heart without him even knowing it.

But Mr Linwood was shaking his head and some of the buoyancy left Grace's expression.

'I couldn't agree to that, Captain Dauntsey. It's a very kind offer, but the price for my mistakes must be paid by myself and myself alone. As I said, my family's suffering is a direct result of my stupidity and I hold myself accountable.'

Spencer inclined his head, but the firm set of his chin should have told Grace's papa his objections were futile. 'With the greatest respect, sir, I am resolute. I have already had to endure the loss of my parents and would keep Grace from such an event for as long as possible. Even if you wouldn't accept for yourself, please think again for the sake of your wife and daughters.'

'Do listen.' Grace leapt in immediately. 'We all admire your principles, but they are like to do more harm than good. Surely you can see that? In any case—' she broke off for a second to give a wry half-smile '—there's precious little point in arguing with Spencer. If he's made up his mind to help you, you may as well reconcile yourself to being helped whether you like it or not.'

Mr Linwood opened his mouth to speak, but hesitated before any words could come. 'Are you—are you quite sure, sir? I confess it would be a blessing to be moved from this room, but—' The same look of regret that sometimes crossed Grace's features showed in those of her father and he stared down at his hands in something like shame. 'I don't know that I could repay you. I'm not sure how much Grace has told you of the circumstances surrounding my being here, but thanks to my business partners I am officially bankrupt and a debtor. There isn't likely to be any way of returning your money.'

'I don't expect to be repaid. It would be a gift and one I give gladly.'

There was a tiny intake of breath from Grace's direction, but Spencer kept his eyes firmly on his father in-law, who rubbed his forehead in a combination of amazement and dawning wonder.

'Your generosity is astounding. If you truly mean it, I'd be so grateful to accept your offer with the sincerest of thanks.'

Spencer gave a brisk nod, allowing a small smile

to lift the corners of his usually straight-set lips as he rose to his feet and turned for the door. 'For my part I'm happy you accepted. I'll go and speak to the warden without delay.'

There was just enough time to register the vivid relief in Grace's sigh before he stepped out into the corridor to be enveloped once again by the noise and smell of the wider prison. Angry shouts echoed from the floor above and Spencer shook his head in disgust as he pulled the door closed behind him.

To think they keep a decent man in conditions like these.

The thoroughly honest and civil Mr Linwood he had once known would never have committed any offence, he was certain—the honesty and lack of artifice in Grace had evidently been inherited from her papa and the seed of another idea began to slowly take root in the back of Spencer's mind.

What was it he said his partners' names were? Fisher and Armand? I wonder...perhaps there might be some way...

He'd barely managed ten steps when he heard the door creak behind him again, followed by rapid footsteps at his back. Turning showed Grace standing behind him, cheeks flushed and a look on her face that would have melted Spencer's heart all over again had it not already thawed to be given into her unwitting keeping.

Spencer frowned, her sudden reappearance momentarily distracting him from the plan unfurling itself in his thoughts. 'Grace? Is something amiss?'

She shook her head, fingers working together in a movement of uncontrollable emotion. 'No. Quite the opposite. I just had to tell you…you don't know what this means to me. This kindness to my poor papa is the most wonderful thing. Thank you, thank you—a hundred times, thank you!'

She was in his arms before he could blink, the soft warm shape of her held closely against the column of his body just as he had longed for more times than he could count. The beat of her heart next to his own called to something inside him that responded in turn and before he knew what he was about he had leaned down to kiss her—and she had kissed him back.

It was a different kind of kiss to the one she had given him in the snowy garden, or even the carriage when he had promised her this very visit. That had been brief, a chaste brush of her lips on his like a butterfly settling on a flower that still managed to heat his blood like a furnace. This time when their mouths met it was with a burst of fire that shook every sinew in Spencer's body and made him need *more,* a primal desire that roared up inside him to howl that to merely kiss her wasn't nearly enough—he wanted to hold her, pull her to him and explore the dips and curves until now only hinted at by the thin fabric of her nightgown that tortured him night after night.

Still Grace didn't pull away as his hands dropped to her waist and seized her firmly, only breaking the contact of their lips to suck in a harsh breath that made Spencer's knees almost buckle with longing. Her own hands fled to his back and traced the muscles she would have felt there, wandering over the places scars marred his skin as though she could heal them with her touch. Perhaps she could, he thought distractedly as he felt her tremble with something he wished he could bottle.

She'd repaired the battered remnants of his soul easily enough despite every obstacle he had thrown in her way, determinedly drawing him out until he was vulnerable as a child at her feet. It was impossible, incredible—and yet Grace had broken through the barriers he had hidden behind for so long and as his nerves sang and his blood boiled he knew he never wanted to release her from where he pressed her against him with a desire that was almost frightening.

The sound of rough cheers sliced through the breathless moment like a knife, sending both Spencer and Grace starting apart like a pair of wild deer to look about themselves in confusion. A small group of onlookers had gathered at the other end of the passage and were watching them with interest, grinning in encouragement.

'Don't stop on our account, lad—you were doing well!'

Grace gave a gasp of horror as mortification brought the blood rushing to her face, although she said nothing as Spencer replied with a few choice words of his own that sent their cackling audience sloping away. Once sure they had gone he turned his attention back to his blushing wife, only inches away but frozen with uncertainty that had apparently robbed her of the ability to move.

He ached to run his thumb over her just-kissed lips, to feel the gentle warmth of her breath as it came harder against his skin. She looked up at him with the wide eyes of a startled fawn, so innocent he longed to throw off his hesitation and bend to kiss her again—but something unreadable flared in their grey depths to make him pause. It was still so difficult to know what she was thinking, what hopes or fears skipped through her busy mind; she could just as easily have accepted his advance out of mere gratitude as real desire, and the possibility of the former made regret writhe in his stomach.

Damn it all. Why not just ask her? Why not just ask why she allows you these liberties: out of hunger for them or from polite compliance?

The question danced on the tip of his tongue, tempting him to ask it out loud. It was such a simple thing, he thought, still within touching distance of the woman who blinked up at him with slightly parted lips as though awaiting either more kisses or dismissal—and yet with a creep of shame he found he didn't dare. What if Grace confirmed his worst fears and told him in no uncertain words she felt nothing for him, her affections still held by the first love she had all but admitted would never be forgotten? What would happen then to the yearning for her he could only now admit to himself burned within him? He would be thrown back into the pit of despair his growing love for her had helped him to escape, Grace herself having leaned down into it to offer him a helping hand. If she rejected him now, he would be left with nothing and the idea of frightening away his only reason for living with a declaration of sentiment she might not want made his words turn to dust in his mouth.

'I ought to speak with the warden.' He stepped away from her, only a half pace backwards, but enough to break the dangerous spell of the warm, clean scent of her skin that whispered to him like a siren's song. 'The sooner we get your father moved and seen by a doctor the better.'

'Yes, of course. I won't keep you a moment longer.'
Grace nodded quickly, an attempt at a smile stretching the sudden stiffness of her mouth as she made as if to return to her papa's door—but even so Spencer remained all too aware of the feeling of her eyes on his back as he turned and walked away.

Chapter Twelve

Grace's breath misted the window as she peered down from her hiding place on the second floor, peeping round one velvet curtain at the street below. Black clouds on the moody horizon threatened thunder while heavy raindrops hurled themselves against the glass to form miniature rivers skating in front of Grace's curious eyes, but even the freezing downpour hadn't stopped Spencer from slipping out to speak to the stranger who loitered once again at the end of the path. It was the same small, shrewd-looking man with auburn hair who had appeared each evening for above a week, and she was yet to understand why he kept coming—or why Spencer attempted to conceal their multiple rendezvous behind a tall bush at the side of their gate.

What is he about that makes it necessary to be so furtive?

It was his secretive movements that had first caught Grace's attention the day after they had returned from visiting the Fleet, when Spencer had left the house early to stride purposefully in the direction of the town and returned a few hours later smelling of tobacco smoke and spirits. He had skilfully dodged Grace's enquires and shut himself up in his study for the rest of the afternoon with only the sound of pen on paper signalling his enigmatic presence, occasionally summoning a servant to convey a note to the post tray for delivery to who knew where. It was all very odd and Grace still couldn't make head nor tail of it as she hovered at the window and watched Spencer and his mysterious companion converse despite the deluge that must have been soaking them to the skin.

Although the combination of grey dusk and distance made it difficult Grace could *just* make out the intent set of Spencer's face as he listened to whatever the smaller man was telling him, before a sudden glance in the direction of the house sent her dodging smartly back behind her curtain. It wouldn't do for him to catch her looking. Whatever he was meeting the shifty-looking stranger for was evidently supposed to be a secret—and one he had little intention of sharing.

We've come so far together. I wonder why he thinks it necessary to conceal this—whatever it is—from me now?

There was no way of denying how her spirit soared in Spencer's company, the smiles he now offered the most delightful she had seen in her entire life. Her steadfast refusal to ever surrender to the ache of longing her husband inspired in her seemed so irrelevant now, like a relic from a past age with no place in the new life they were forging together. Henry still crossed her mind, of course, every now and again, to remind her how reckless the giving of a woman's heart into a man's keeping could be; but each day that passed showed how entirely different Spencer was to the man who had so cruelly rejected her and even the alarm bells that still tried to peal in her ears had grown muffled by the unlikely warmth she now knew hid behind Spencer's grim façade. His behaviour to her poor papa at the Fleet, which even now warmed her as she thought of her father's expression of dumbstruck gratitude, was the final nail in the coffin of her resolve not to give in to her feelings. That determination lay in tatters at her feet, ripped apart by the kindness her gruff husband was slowly allowing to come forth, bit by bit like ice melting in the first sun of spring.

There wasn't anywhere left to hide from the truth that declared itself so boldly Grace couldn't have denied it if she'd tried, every shadowy corner of her fearful heart illuminated by the knowledge that, yes, she loved her husband and now nothing would be the same again. Whether he returned those feelings was almost immaterial; they were a part of her now as fixed and permanent as her hands that itched to reach out for him or her eyes that searched his beloved face for some clue as to what he was thinking as he sat in his chair before the fire and stared into the flames. If he felt the same stirrings in the depths of his soul for her, her unlikely happiness would be complete—if not, there was precious little she could do to quell them, so brightly did the spark of tenderness for him burn inside Grace to scald her with its heat.

She reached the entrance hall just as the first crash of thunder sounded and Spencer stepped hurriedly through the front door, hair plastered flat to his forehead and the scant cover of his soaking coat clinging to every contour of his broad frame. It was a picture so reminiscent of the first time she had found herself in Nevin Place Grace had to blink back the vivid memories that assailed her—only a handful of months ago, but so different from the present day, when Spencer had worn a scowl instead of the suspiciously evasive smile he now aimed in her direction to make her heart flutter like fledglings in a nest.

'Good evening. Are you well tonight?'

'Yes, thank you, although I'm not sure the same will be said of you if you insist on walking out in a storm. Why, you're absolutely wet through!'

Spencer glanced down at his drenched clothes and the mud that hugged his long leather boots as another growl of thunder echoed through the hall. 'Would you look at that—you're absolutely right. I should go to change at once.'

If she hadn't already felt a gleam of powerful inquisitiveness as to what her husband had just been doing, the speed with which he strode away from her would surely have given her reason for pause. Grace could only watch as he retreated up the stairs she had just descended, following the progress of long legs and impressive shoulders with interest that was by now second nature. Once upon a time she might have blushed at the thrill that ran through her at the sight of Spencer's wet shirt emphasising his powerful build, made starker still by a sudden flare of lightning, but with her curiosity piqued by other things there was no time for such prissy thoughts—or for any attempts to drag her eyes away that she knew would not be successful.

What are you up to, Spencer? What is it you're trying to hide?

* * *

Sweat ran down Spencer's face to sting his eyes as another roar of gunfire came in a relentless barrage that made his ears ring and the ground tremble beneath his feet. A wild scan of the heaving, churned field showed more men stretched out in the mud, arms reaching as though for help that would never come and empty eyes staring as Spencer moved among them in a disoriented daze with hardly an idea of where he was going, knowing only that he *must* keep pushing forward. His horse was gone and the fine red of his jacket flecked with filth and blood he should have been grateful was not his own, but nothing in the shouts and screams and jostling of too many bodies could distract him from his purpose in forcing his way through the throng.

Where is he?

On his right a voice bellowed something in a language he only vaguely understood and Spencer turned to parry the sword that flashed towards him, bringing his own up in a powerful thrust that sent the other man crumpling to his knees. There was no time to stop and look down at the French soldier curled on the ground; Spencer turned mechanically away and continued his terrible progress among the clash of bayonets and whine of rifle fire that keened in his ear as he once again surveyed the horrors on every side,

And then he saw him.

He was wading through the mire towards Spencer as quickly as the gouged ground would let him, mud up to his knees and his arms outstretched, brown eyes glowing with desperate determination as they fixed on something over Spencer's shoulder. Spencer turned to look, knowing with sudden, sickening dread exactly what he would see—but then a deafening bellow roared out its fury and he was on the ground, shoved roughly aside by a familiar hand, and burning agony seized the front of his body and shook him like a terrier would a rat—

A man's shout rang in his ears, a guttural cry like that of a beast in such terrible pain it made Spencer's heart freeze in primal fear. He only realised it had come from his own lips when he opened his eyes to see somebody leaning over him, their face a white shape in the darkness that suddenly felt so oppressive he could scarcely breathe.

The cannons fired again, but more softly this time and he realised with a flare of sick understanding that there had never been any at all. The sound was nothing but the distant rumble of retreating thunder, intruding into his dreams to fool him into reliving the worst hour of his life—only this time was worse than the others, the noise of the storm outside dragging his memories out to haunt him even more vividly.

'Spencer? It's me, Grace. It's only me. You're safe, you're quite safe.'

The face swam into focus as a flickering candle appeared, illuminating Grace's frightened eyes and expression of such concern Spencer felt his tight throat give an involuntary swallow.

He tried to reply, but found no words would come to him as he lay on his back with every muscle tense and the horrors of his nightmare still holding him in their merciless grip. The vision of moments before circled before him—bodies, mud, pain, blood—and to his shame tears tried to fight their way past his lashes to run down the blanched skin of his cheeks.

Cold sweat crawled beneath his nightshirt as he pushed himself up to lean against the pillows—or where the pillows would have been had his fevered thrashing not hurled them to the floor. Grace watched him still in silent concern, her skin more luminous than ever in the candlelight in a way that was almost angelic.

'You were shouting… What were you dreaming about?'

He brought a hand up to wipe the sweat from his brow and felt another flicker of shame as he saw how it trembled. 'I don't—I don't remember.'

The lie lay heavy in his gut, but he rose from the bed and pulled on his dressing gown. All possibility of sleep had fled from him and Grace's worried gaze only made it more necessary for him to escape before he surrendered to its power and revealed more than he ever wanted about the secrets that still haunted him.

'Go back to sleep. I think I'll sit in my study a while.'

He turned to leave, almost missing the quiet murmur at his back that made him pause.

'Please, Spencer. After all that's passed between us, you needn't shut me out.'

His chest gave an especially painful squeeze as he threw a glance over one shoulder, the soft plea in Grace's voice piercing his heart. It would be so easy to unburden himself to her, to tell her exactly what had transpired on that terrible day and the weighty guilt that had crushed him ever since, but still he could not. The shame was too great, his weakness for Constance costing him so much he could have avoided had he behaved as Will had deserved.

'There's nothing to tell. Go back to sleep.'

Grace's lips twitched as though about to say something, but Spencer gave her no time to reply as he stumbled for the door, leaving her alone in the great bed with her anxious face lit by the single flame.

His own quiet footsteps and the distant murmurs of the dying storm were the only sounds as Spencer moved through the silent house, joined by a single creak of his study door as he entered. The darkness inside the room reached out to claim him, but was chased away by the fire he soon had dancing in the grate, determined to banish the terrors that particular night was so cruel as to conjure.

Spencer drew his chair as close to the flames as he could get, although its warmth did nothing to melt the agony that had turned his blood to ice, and dropped his head into his hands.

He rubbed his aching eyes, sore from both the flames and the effort of holding back the emotion he feared with sudden dread he might not this time be able to repress. Before Grace had come into his life he would have numbed this pain with a large measure of something from a bottle; now he had no such consolation left in the house and he wondered if, for the first time in two years, he ought to try to confront the spectres that still chased him whatever steps he took to escape them. Fleeing their merciless grasp meant he had spent the past years running, never able to rest or share his suffering with anyone… Could it finally, after all this time, be that he had arrived at having no other option left but to tackle his demons head-on and not shy away to hide behind some prop that only delayed the inevitable?

It was a thought that frightened him—and above

all Spencer hated being afraid. It felt too much like weakness, too similar to the helpless terror that had consumed him in that hellish field, unable to do anything but watch as the worst thing he could imagine unfolded before him, with nothing he could do to stop it. Being afraid tasted like the iron tang of blood and sounded like the cries of wounded men dying beneath a foreign sky, and that was something Spencer never wanted to experience ever again.

The worst image flared through Spencer's mind again like a flaming arrow, twisting his insides and sending him doubling over with pain so intense it took his breath away. He screwed his eyes shut, attempting to block the memory before it could rake him with its claws, but it didn't retreat, instead bringing forth cold nausea that made Spencer's head swim and his throat burn just as on the day he had stared at that familiar face with numb disbelief: a pair of warm brown eyes vacant and staring below black hair soaked with blood, the mouth open as though to implore him although no words would ever again pass the still-warm lips.

Spencer wasn't aware of the tears that streamed down his cheeks until a pair of soft hands framed his face and kissed them away, so impossibly gently it would have broken his heart were it not already lying in ruins within his heaving chest. Without opening his eyes he reached for Grace with hands that ached to touch her and she came to him without a murmur, settling in his lap and taking him in her arms as emotion racked Spencer's body in a relentless flood and forced him to speak before he could stop himself.

'He died for me, Grace. He pushed me out of the way even though I didn't deserve it and it's all my fault he never came home. My brother, my very best friend—I as good as killed him.'

She said nothing, merely stroking the hair back from his forehead and listening to the damning confession that sprang from his mouth. There was no recoil of horror or revolted gasp and the steady feeling of her fingers through his hair gave Spencer the courage, which he never knew, until that moment, he had lacked, to continue.

'We *should* have been fighting side by side at Quatre Bras and would have been if we hadn't argued the night before. It was the first time we'd ever let anything come between us, the first time we had ever really quarrelled, and all for a woman whose face I can now barely remember.' He drew in a ragged breath, fragments of Constance's chestnut hair and tilted nose gleaming dimly in his memory like pieces of shattered glass.

'Both of us fancied ourselves in love with her, although neither of us truly knew the meaning of it, I realise now. We argued so fiercely that we went our separate ways, only reuniting on the battlefield—when it was all too late. I'd only just seen Will when we came under fire from enemy grapeshot and he—he threw me out of the way to take the worst of the impact himself.'

It was the worst of sensations to hear himself spilling out his darkest secrets, his deepest shame with no hope of stopping himself. By some magic Grace loosened his tongue beyond his control, all without a single word, still silent as he damned himself for ever beneath her soft fingers.

'If we had been together from the start he wouldn't have had to stray so dangerously close to guns looking for me. We could have survived the battle and returned home together if only I hadn't been so selfish, so determined to be the victor of our competition for a woman's heart… We might never have argued and, if it wasn't for me, Will might still be alive, not turning to dust in some Belgian grave with nobody there to mourn him.'

A fresh storm threatened to spill from his burning eyes, but this time Grace wiped them away with fingertips that left a stream of fire in their wake. Belatedly Spencer realised the intimacy of their position, Grace curled in his lap like a cat and his face buried in the warm curve of her neck to breathe in the rich scent of her skin—it had happened so thoughtlessly, as though it was the most natural thing in the world for her to kiss away his tears, and any shame he felt at his naked emotion seemed suddenly misplaced in the world of compassion he saw in her eyes as he lifted his chin to look into her face.

'It was not your fault. None of it was. He loved you as you loved him and it was his choice to save you— just as you would have done for him, had your places been reversed.'

Spencer shook his head, although his grip on Grace's waist never faltered. 'I should have stopped him. I've replayed that moment over and over in my mind for two years, wondering what I could have done differently, but I can never get past the memory of his cheek pressed to the muddy ground, or how his fingers twitched for a moment before falling still—'

The words choked him, sticking in his throat as the horrors of his nightmare reached for him again to pull him back beneath their dark surface. He shouldn't be telling Grace any of this, he knew; and yet somehow she drew him out, the unceasing caress of her fingers on his brow soothing the turmoil that shook him to the bone.

'You hear the songs and the poems, see the grand paintings of the noble glory of war—but it's all a lie. It isn't glorious, or the pure fight of right against wrong. It's men dying slowly in the mud, terrified and alone, coughing out their last breaths knowing they'll never see their homes again. Those of us who return are the lucky ones, but even we who make it back alive leave pieces of ourselves behind, fragments of our humanity that we can never get back. I am only half a man now, Grace. I can't escape those memories and neither do I deserve the mercy of being able to forget—'

He broke off, blind to everything but the horrific pictures chasing each other through his mind as he unconsciously tightened his hold on Grace and pulled her warm body closer to his chest as though she could ward off the terrors. She in turn twined herself around him, encircling him within the quiet peace of her arms, and hesitantly—as if surprised by her own courage— sought his mouth and kissed him with such simple sweetness Spencer's heart soared in his chest.

'You're still whole, Spencer. You've just been in such pain these past years, keeping your secrets for so long you've come to believe your own fears.'

Spencer's pulse skipped ever faster as her lips again came down to his; a little more firmly this time, al- though still careful as he felt himself respond and al- lowed his fingers to stray from her waist round to her back to trace the column of her spine. She gave a little shiver, delightfully guileless, and drew back a fraction to look into his face.

Returning her gaze, he took in the petal-soft shape of her lips and the way she blinked, a little dazedly, as he reached up to wind one blonde tendril round his finger.

'You're as gentle as if I were a wounded creature.' He meant to make her smile, to break the rising tension between them that was rapidly building to something Spencer couldn't quite name, but instead Grace's expression changed into a look that made his mouth dry and the hairs stir at the back of his neck.

'But isn't that precisely what you are?'

Shyly, as though half expecting he might still her hand and hardly believing her own actions, Grace slowly unfastened the buttons of his nightshirt and gently pulled the front open to reveal his ugly mass of scars. Spencer held his breath as her eyes roamed the ruined flesh stretched across taut muscle and saw her throat contract in a dry swallow—and he couldn't help but utter a gasp as she leaned down to press her lips to the worst scar running a jagged line across his chest.

'So many of them. How they must have hurt—and how you must have suffered, keeping the truth inside for so long.'

Spencer shook his head slightly, helpless beneath her touch. 'Grace…' The rest of his hoarse sentence stuttered and died as she trailed light fingertips through the tangle of coarse hair to trace another silvery ridge, the sensation awakening the longing within him he had tried so hard to master. An electric current began to flow through his veins, crackling in every nerve to rob him of any rationality he might ever have possessed.

'You need never suffer alone again. All your confession made me feel was sorrow for you and regret I couldn't share your burden long ago.'

She peeped up at him, pupils huge in the dying light of the fire that made her hair shine like spun gold. There was nothing he could do to quell the temptation to reach out and bury his fingers in its softness, to feel its silk beneath his hand and gently cup the back of Grace's head to draw her into a kiss that made both of them breathless with desire. It was like a living flame passed between them, reducing everything in its way to ash as the conflagration Spencer had kept hidden for so long roared up to consume him and he held Grace to him to melt together in ferocious heat neither had ever experienced before.

A fine rug stretched out before the hearth and Spencer gathered Grace to carefully set her down on it. He joined her there, taking her back into his arms to feel her heartbeat racing next to his own and her breathing come hard and fast as this time it was his turn to explore her skin, one hand sliding cautiously at the neck of her nightgown to feel her pulse flutter at her throat. She let out a small sound, almost a sigh that hinted at more—so more Spencer ventured, gentle fingers seeking her delicate collarbone and lower until she gave a shudder and arched against his palm.

'I didn't think—I wasn't sure you wanted me.' Grace's words came out in a rush against his ear, her lips finding the lobe and closing around it to send a spike of longing through to Spencer's core.

He pulled back a fraction to look down into her heavy-lidded eyes, taking in her blushing lips and cheeks flushed with yearning that made him want to groan aloud.

'Have you run mad? It would be a man of stone who could have you in his bed night after night and not find himself wishing he could touch you. I told you once before I wasn't there to impose and I intended to keep to my word until told otherwise.'

His mouth lowered to her neck and he relished the gasp and shiver that sent her jolting in his hold. The power of his hunger for her was becoming overwhelming, yet he held himself back from allowing it to overcome him, aware in the fuzzy part of his mind not yet hijacked by want that Grace was an innocent; that fool Henry hadn't even kissed her, let alone counted the ribs that encased her pounding heart to feel her curve against his hand. The last thing he wanted was to go too far, too fast, and ruin the unexpected turn this unpredictable night had already taken.

As though reading his racing thoughts, Grace stilled and took his face between both hands, making Spencer pause in his blistering exploration of the forbidden paradise secreted beneath her gown.

'You needn't feel you should hold back now. I wouldn't feel you had—*imposed*.'

Spencer swallowed, the beat of need deep inside him echoing louder to drown out all other thought than that of how beautiful Grace looked in that moment, lying back with her hair fanned out like a golden halo and her grey eyes alive with the same feeling that flickered in Spencer's soul. She stared back, the smallest suggestion of a defiant smile at her own boldness curving the lips he leaned down to capture once again that trembled beneath his own.

'You've always known your own mind, Mrs Daunt-sey. It's one of the things I've always admired about you.'

He reached down to take the hem of her nightgown between his fingers, allowing them to trace the slender length of her leg as he sought it out and wanting to smile in turn at her quiver. With one fluid movement he drew it over her head and, as the long night crept towards dawn, by the light of the glowing embers, the Captain and his unlikely bride were as one at last.

Chapter Thirteen

Grace's dreams were interrupted by a startled gasp, filtering through her hazy unconsciousness to invade the deep sleep that fogged her mind and made her slow to open her eyes.

'I'm so sorry, sir, ma'am. Please forgive the intrusion. I'll just—I'll make up the other fires instead.'

Hasty footsteps made floorboards creak oddly close to Grace's head and she finally prised open an eye to see why her usually comfortable bed felt as though it was made of wood that morning and the mattress so strangely *furry*...

'That should put paid to any lingering rumours about whether we're truly married.'

Grace blinked as Spencer's familiar features hove into view, hardly lit by sunlight creeping beneath still-drawn curtains. He lay propped on one well-muscled arm, hair tousled and, judging by her excellent view of his ravaged torso, wearing nothing beneath the blanket that covered them—the same state of undress a swift glance down showed she shared. His eyes were warm and held a gleam of humour mixed with something else as he watched Grace's gaze flick from his chest to the bearskin rug they lay on to the empty hearth, understanding beginning to bloom on her face.

'We're—we're in your study, aren't we?'

Spencer nodded, the amusement in his look growing with the horror in Grace's own.

'And was that one of the maids? She came in and saw us—like this?'

Another nod, this time accompanied by light fingers tracing the ridge of her collarbone to make her mind stutter to a halt and her breath seize in her throat.

A small smile curved Spencer's lips, enhancing their already tempting contours and sending a flicker right through to Grace's centre. 'Don't look so mortified. I'm sure she's more embarrassed than you are, if that's possible.'

Any reply Grace might have made was stolen by the caress of those warm fingers across her skin, the unfamiliar sensation scattering stars through her nerves with each stroke. They visited the hollow of her throat to feel where her pulse fluttered before venturing upwards along her neck, skimming its length with such determined softness Grace had to grit her teeth on a sigh.

She was aware of every inch of her body as she lay next to Spencer and allowed him to explore the curve of her bare shoulder emerging from beneath the blanket. Every nerve, every fine hair at her nape felt alive and ready to welcome Spencer's gentle hands in their careful study, so different from the feverish movements of the night. In the darkness their hunger for each other had seized them in its grip and refused to let go until Grace had arched in Spencer's arms and come apart at the seams, leaving her breathless and dazed. Now they faced each other in grey daylight all impatience was stripped away to reveal the sweet truth of Spencer's fascination for the shape of Grace's knuckles as he stroked each one and she couldn't help the glow of cautious joy that warmed her at his intent face.

Is this what it's like? To be with a man who values more than just your name and fortune?

The thought bubbled up inside her to increase the already rapid flit of her heart, so novel and delightful she hardly dared allow it to cross her mind. If Spencer felt the same flood of happiness that coursed through Grace's veins, it would be the most wonderful thing, more than she had ever dreamed possible. All the hurt, all the painful education Henry had given with her as his unwilling student would be forgotten in the wake of new lessons: that she was worthy of real love and her feelings for Spencer were not a sign of bad judgement at all, rather of her ability to see the good in a man so determined there was none left for her to find.

The desire to follow that delicious train of thought whispered to her again with every pass of Spencer's fingers down her own as though he was memorising each detail to recall later, his dark brows slightly drawn in a pinch Grace longed to smooth away. It would be so tempting to give in and simply *ask* Spencer if he felt the same way, and yet…

Her eye fell once again on the complex mess of scars scattered across Spencer's chest, some hidden beneath the blanket, but others standing proud amid his thatch of dark hair.

There are other things to discuss first. The reason

we're in this situation in the first place is because of his distress last night.

Carefully, as slowly as she might have reached to calm a frightened animal, Grace placed her hand on Spencer's wounded chest and watched as his throat moved in a reflexive swallow of apprehension and help-less desire that made her shiver. His own hand stilled in its mission of capturing the slight dip of her inner elbow and moved to cover hers, hovering as if to be sure she didn't venture too far across the ruined skin.

She hesitated, trying hard to find the right words to begin. The knowledge of how close his body was to hers, both of them missing the nightclothes that lay in a tangle of linen a few feet away, made it difficult to think.

'Do you want to talk about it? What you told me last night?'

Spencer's sharp eyes dimmed for a moment. A ghost of the pain that had made Grace abandon her self-control the previous night returned to once again tear at her until Spencer dismissed the shadow with a small shake of his head.

'No. For now, it's enough that you know the worst of it—and didn't turn away.'

The temptation to reply was so strong for a moment Grace thought her lips might frame the words of their own volition, but she regained hold of her tongue and instead merely nodded. It was surely safe now, after the events of the night, to tell Spencer she had no inten-tion of turning from him for the rest of her life; but the final dregs of the fear Henry's rejection had instilled in her still circled, to murmur there was no harm in some attempt at restraint. They might have achieved the closest accord a man and a woman ever could, their bodies moving together in instinctive rhythm they had no need to choreograph, but the cruel roots of that pain had forced themselves deeply into Grace's heart, to twine around it and do their damnedest to halt how it leaped with fresh hope.

If Spencer's feelings mirrored her own, there would be time enough to explore them later, once she was *sure* her affections weren't again misplaced. The way he looked at her now, drinking in the unsure set of her mouth and the way her hair fanned across the rug like a pool of melted gold, was surely the image of a man in love—but she had been wrong before and there was nothing to be gained by rushing in only to have her heart shattered beneath the soles of another man's boots.

Belatedly Grace realised goosebumps prickled on her skin and she drew up the blanket—*taken from the armchair, I see*—to cover her bare shoulder. 'It's cold in here. Perhaps we should have let that poor maid make a fire before scaring her away.'

Spencer's dark chuckle stirred the glowing embers in Grace's stomach, stoking them brighter as he sat up and the cover slipped down to his waist to display his upper body in its full glory.

'Were you thinking of staying in here a little longer? I can easily warm you myself if that was your intention.'

Distracted by the fascinating and disconcertingly *close* show of masculinity mere inches away it took a moment for Grace to understand his meaning, but the sudden wicked gleam in his eye wiped away all traces of the sorrow of moments before and she could only gasp as he leaned down to steal the sound from her mouth.

Bracing himself on one strong hand, Spencer gathered her to him with the other, never breaking the heated contact of their lips as Grace reached to twine her arms around his neck. He pulled her closer as effortlessly as if she weighed nothing at all, warm fingers sliding beneath the blanket to curl round and glide down her spine, tongues of fire crackling in their wake. Grace arched her back to allow more room for those clever fingertips to explore, feeling almost faint when they retreated to wander lazily over her ribs and higher while the searing heat of Spencer's body touched her own and set her every sinew ablaze with want.

He trailed his lips from her mouth to her ear, dropping kisses as he went, the sensation of his breath on her lobe robbing her of all rational thought. She thought she felt him whisper something against her skin; something sweet, no doubt, but the singing in Grace's blood and the taste of him on her tongue rendered her insensible—until he drew back to turn his head quickly in the direction of the study door.

The creak of footsteps on floorboards came from the other side, accompanied by rapid whispers that sent Spencer rolling on to his back to exhale deeply through his nose.

'Damn. There won't be a moment's peace now the whole household's awake.'

Grace swallowed hard, blinking as the blood that had rushed to flood her cheeks made its way back to her brain and her senses began to return. Of course they shouldn't still be lying on the study floor, for heaven's sake—even if they hadn't been so embarrassingly discovered it was still *most* improper and a little of the blush remained as Grace clutched the scant cover to her with a shaking hand. Desire still raged inside her like a forest fire, wanting to consume everything in its path, but some rationality managed to force its way back in and it was with no little shyness she sat up, careful to maintain her precarious dignity.

'You're right. It isn't fair of us to disrupt the servants, either.'

Spencer's eyes followed her hungrily as she stretched to catch up their nightclothes, showing no intention of looking away when she held hers to her chest and peered down at him expectantly.

'Aren't you going to avert your gaze while I put this on?'

'No.'

One corner of his mouth twitched up as she flicked a sleeve at him and he sighed, shifting to face away from her with a roll of dark eyes.

'Is it not a little late for us to suddenly be so coy with each other?'

Grace didn't reply as she pulled the gown over her head with wary haste and primly tied the ribbons at the neck. There was precious little she could do to tame the interesting arrangement of her hair, she supposed, and even less point; by now all of the servants would know of the under-maid's shocking discovery, but Grace would be damned if she left the study looking like a—like a… She hardly knew what, although she *did* know she wasn't going to look like one.

A swish of material at her back suggested Spencer was likewise now decent and Grace turned to him with new hesitation pooling in her gut.

What happens now? Do I say something? Will we spend the day together now—and then the night?

It was uncanny how accurately Spencer sometimes seemed able to read her mind. Getting to his feet, he reached down to help her off the floor, taking the blanket and draping it around her shoulders like a fine cloak.

'There. Perfectly respectable once again.' He flashed her a glimpse of that heart-stopping smile, so long hidden and now more dear to Grace than she could ever explain. 'Although I fear you'll still need to change before we go into town today. You wouldn't want to give the bookseller a shock.'

'The bookseller?' A flicker of concern skittered through her before Grace could stop it, the memory of the last time she'd set foot in that shop unpleasantly vivid. 'Whatever for?'

'I still owe you a copy of *Evelina*, do I not? Besides, a trip out will mean you can avoid having to look the maids in the eye for a few hours more and I imagine *that* at least might tempt you.'

Quick heat rose in Grace's cheeks at the suggestion, although she would have to admit he had a point. She might be the undisputed mistress of Nevin Place, but being happened upon in such an undignified state was still more embarrassing than she would have liked... The recollection of her dismay on her previous visit to town returned to nip at her again, however, and some echo of her thoughts evidently showed in her face as Spencer raised a serious brow.

'I won't make a scene, but nobody will be allowed to make you feel as you did before. Please trust me, Grace.'

She looked up at him, unsmiling now with his jaw set so firmly it might have been made from stone. The dim sunlight struggling through the curtains lit one side of his face to illuminate the appealing irregularity of his broken nose that only enhanced his other features, his gaze direct and honest in a perfect mirror of his open words.

Do you know, I think I do. Surely this time I can't be wrong.

The gentle pressure of Grace's fingers on his arm was nowhere near enough to satisfy the ache in Spencer's chest that longed to snatch her to him, but there was nothing he could do as they walked the short distance into town.

Anybody looking at us would hardly believe it possible. I can scarce believe it myself.

Waking to find Grace lying beneath the same covers as himself was nothing new, but to realise she did so without her nightgown was a development he would never forget. With her eyes closed and blonde curls loose around her she had looked like a fallen angel and even now, restored to prim normality, the image caused Spencer's innards to flare with ready heat. He longed to slide a hand to her waist and cup the hidden swell of her hip as he had before the cold study fire, to hear Grace's breathy sigh and feel her warmth as she surrendered to his hold—

He bit the inside of his cheek to distract himself from that dangerous train of thought. Lingering on their night together was best left until he wasn't required to maintain a respectable public façade. There was enough to unpick already in Grace's reaction to his confession, making her bolder than he had thought her capable of, and now he would have to come to terms with the fact he had betrayed the secret he had vowed to take to his grave.

A little of the shame he had felt when Grace wiped his eyes returned to settle behind his breastbone. She had been so understanding, spoken to him so gently as though she truly believed her own soothing words—it was tempting to grasp hold of the assurances she had given him and allow himself to begin to let go of the guilt and fear he had run from for so long. Part of him still wished Grace hadn't seen his weakness—he would never forgive himself for letting her, or anybody, see him cry—or known the horrors that stalked him, but another fragment felt differently. That shard of his soul was curiously relieved to be deprived of its heavy burden, for the first time in years not pinned beneath the weight of regret that had made him turn to a bottle again and again. It was like a window had been opened, allowing fresh air and light into a dark room left shuttered for too long…

I feel clean. For the first time since Will died, I feel clean.

The realisation reverberated inside Spencer's mind, so sudden and surprising and yet the absolute truth. The pain of his brother's death still remained as permanent as the scars on Spencer's body, but the feeling of blame for what had happened across the stormy sea was receding, forced back by the powerful compassion of his determined wife.

'What are you thinking about?'

Spencer started at the voice at his side and looked down to see Grace peeping up at him from below the brim of her solemn bonnet, a trace of hesitation making him want to stroke her pale cheek.

'Nothing of any importance.'

That was a lie, he had to admit to himself as he took in the unconvinced flicker of one female eyebrow, but Grace didn't press him any further. Perhaps she'd learned it was more profitable to allow him to spill his secrets in his own time—which was fortunate, given there was one final truth he would need to gather all his courage before he revealed.

You may as well tell her your feelings now. It's likely she's guessed them already.

Grace was an intelligent woman, one of the reasons he could no longer deny she had made a home for herself in his heart. Surely she'd realised his growing vulnerability to her kindness, or seen how his lips now curved into a smile shown only to her. If nothing else had given her an inkling of the tenderness for her Spencer felt in his very bones, how reverently he had touched her skin and wondered at its smoothness, the night before should have told her all she needed to know. It had been nothing like the laughing tumbles beneath blankets he had experienced with women in the past—somewhere in the darkness before dawn Grace had shattered the last brick in the wall built around Spencer's soul and pulled him from the rubble, her rapt face and sweetly questing lips innocent of the power they wielded. They hadn't just joined physically; Spencer's pulse skipped faster as he recalled what he had whispered in her ear, lost in the scent of her hair and buried beneath the sigh Grace had uttered at the feel of his breath on the delicate shell.

I love you.

Those three little words had dropped from his tongue before he could stop them and as Spencer guided Grace towards the bookseller's shop he swallowed down the desire to repeat them. They might have escaped him as he held Grace close and at last made real the longing that had robbed him of sleep, but she had been too deep in sensation to hear them. The next time he told his unwitting wife he loved her would be planned, private and hopefully reciprocated—and if not, he would have to find a way to bear the rejection that would surely tear his newly whole spirit in two.

'Mrs Dauntsey?'

Spencer glanced down at the woman hovering close by them, a stout figure more than able to hold her own against the jostling of passers-by. Her face struck him as vaguely familiar, but it wasn't until Grace held out her hand that he remembered her name.

'Mrs Lake! How pleasant to see you.'

The older woman pressed her fingers and returned Grace's smile, casting a quick flicker in Spencer's direction. What she was looking for in his face he didn't know, but the sudden crackle of pain in his gut was one he understood only too well.

She was one of the midwives who laid out my mother. I think I'd rather not be reminded of that night.

No doubt she was a perfectly pleasant woman, but the sight of her brought to mind memories Spencer didn't want to relive. That strange night seemed like a dream now, or perhaps more like a nightmare with its bizarre twists and turns, and the shard of grief that wedged itself into his chest was something he could have done without.

'I'll be inside.'

He gestured towards the bookshop and caught Grace's answering nod, keen understanding mingled with a touch of shared sorrow plain in her expression before she turned back to her acquaintance.

The little bell above the door pinged cheerfully as Spencer entered, its greeting joined by the heady smell of leather and ink he remembered from his previous visit. This time, however, there were no unpleasant interruptions as the owner went in search of Spencer's prey, returning from his fusty storeroom with *Evelina* held triumphantly aloft. Expecting Grace to join them at any moment, Spencer was surprised when she didn't appear and a glance through the fogged windows showed the spot he had last seen her conspicuously empty and his wife now nowhere to be seen.

'Have you lost her?' The elderly gentleman wheezed his odd laugh that even Spencer couldn't help but like.

'It appears I have. Thank you for the book—I ought to go and find its eager new owner.'

The bookseller beamed benevolently from behind thick spectacles like an ancient, good-natured tortoise. 'Of course, of course. I do hope your wife will enjoy it.'

Reaching the street again, Spencer scanned the crowds that thronged it, looking this way and that for his elusive wife. How pleased she would be to have a new book to lose herself in, he thought as he craned his neck past a pair of horses pulling a swaying coach. The thought of Grace curled in her favourite chair, her face intent as she turned the pages brought a smile to Spencer's lips—which vanished abruptly as he finally caught sight of her across the busy street, her hand gripped firmly in the crook of Henry Earls's arm and her eyes never leaving his face.

Spencer's heart gave a sickening lurch and he stood rooted to the spot, unable to tear himself away from the sight of his wife gazing up at the man who had caused her so much pain. It *had* to be him: the similarity to George was striking, fair hair and a handsome face working hard to conceal the unpleasantness lurking beneath that charming surface.

Even from a distance Spencer could see how Henry commanded Grace's attention, her little hand resting snugly on the sleeve of his jacket drawing Spencer's eye like a magnet, but his muscles had frozen in cold disbelief and his legs refused to obey his order to cross the street and knock the simpering idiot into the middle of next week. He could only watch as Henry dropped his head a little to murmur into Grace's ear…the same ear Spencer had kissed mere hours before…and his fingers tightened around the book he held as a wave of incredulous anger crashed over him.

Is the man insane? Trying to speak to Grace after how he humiliated her?

Any second now she would pull away, Spencer thought with vicious certainty. She wouldn't want to give her former fiancé more than a moment of her time and there was no way she would tolerate him imposing on her for much longer. Grace would wrench her hand out from under his elbow and move away, not sparing a single look back as she crossed the street to her rightful place at Spencer's side—

But she didn't.

Instead she stood silent as Henry spoke to her, the rattle of passing carriages and the beat of hooves against cobbles ringing in Spencer's ears with no choice but to endure Grace's passive acceptance and the tide of anguish that swirled through his body. He willed her to break away, to treat the man with the contempt he deserved, but a cold stab lanced through him to turn his innards to ice.

She still cares for him, exactly as I always feared. What other explanation could there be for her to remain so close?

The question hit him hard, more painful than the punishing blow that had broken his nose many years before. *That* pain had been purely physical, but the raw agony that now swept over him was worse by far. It seized his heart in a fiery vice and wouldn't let go, wretched unhappiness squeezing until each beat was an ordeal.

The words she had spoken on the day he'd rescued her from George Earls's scorn, her eyes averted as she had walked by his side, rang in his ears again, burning themselves into his consciousness like a flaming brand.

I don't know if any woman would forget her first love, especially when her notoriety makes it so unlikely she will ever have another.

That had been her confession, the one he had envied for so long, and now it returned to taunt Spencer with cruelty he felt in his soul.

Could it be that she had been telling a half-truth? Perhaps she'd never expected to love again—but not because of her shame. Henry had been the first one to rouse her feelings, the first to make his mark on her gentle heart—for a woman as loyal and true as Grace, wasn't it possible she had no desire for another to take her former fiancé's place?

All the bustle and noise of the street fell away as Spencer watched Grace's beloved face flush with that ready pink he had come to know so well. He had been the last one to bring colour to her cheeks, marvelling at their softness with his lips, but now Henry's words were having the same effect and with a fresh drag of cruel claws through his insides Spencer couldn't *stand* it.

Why else wouldn't she pull away? There was no other explanation that made sense and above all things Grace could be relied on to be sensible. His worst fears *must* be correct—and terrible enough to bring Spencer to his knees.

Grace hadn't seen him yet. Her attention was too focused on whatever wheedling nonsense the other man was pouring into her ear—Spencer could just turn and walk away without her ever knowing he had seen the truth of where her affections lay, saving himself the humiliation of letting her see his pain. If he'd previously hoped she had guessed at his feelings, he now wished the exact opposite: that she was oblivious to his cursed weakness and would have no reason for guilt or pity at knowing she had crushed his dreams into dust. Her heart was far too kind to take any pleasure in such a thing, but the outcome would be the same nevertheless, so there was no other option but to blindly wrench himself away from the sight that had scorched itself into his brain, aware of nothing but the need to conceal his new suffering before anybody could see. If there was a tavern open, so much the better—a large glass of something strong might help him to forget that all his plans for the future now lay in ruins and that the heart of the woman he loved still clearly belonged to another so entirely unworthy of it. Grace might be his lawfully wedded wife, but what was the good of that if her feelings lay in the keeping of another? It was the entirety of her Spencer wanted, not the outer shell while her soul longed for escape.

A hand on his arm made him turn sharply, halting his mindless stride in a direction he was hardly aware of.

'Captain. I've some news you'll want to hear.'

Through the fog of his emotion Spencer took in the auburn hair and sly features of the man before him, who held out a grubby piece of paper and continuously glanced about himself as though expecting a nasty surprise.

'Harwell? What is it?'

Some of Spencer's misery was driven back by a surge of interest, bright against the grim backdrop of his distress. If his shady acquaintance had sought him out so boldly rather than wait for their usual secretive rendezvous he must have something important to impart—something Spencer realised with a startling upswing of optimism might be very important indeed.

'I found what you were looking for. Through my contacts in the less salubrious taverns I got a hint and now I have two addresses written on this very sheet.'

The man placed it in Spencer's hand with a flourish, standing back to grin at the disbelief spreading across his face.

Spencer unfolded the paper and ran his eye across the slanted writing inside. The growing boldness of moments before increased further, chasing down the bitter disappointment still circling in his stomach and fighting it with renewed valour.

'I can hardly credit it. I wasn't sure such a thing was possible!'

'Anything's possible if you know the right people, lad.'

He shook his head, still not quite able to believe what he was seeing. The war raging inside him, despair fighting with a silver glimmer of rising hope, tore at him with its teeth, but it no longer seemed like such a forlorn cause.

'For this you have my everlasting thanks. You'll have my additional thanks—and this coin—' he held out a guinea and placed it on top of the copy of *Evelina* in his hand '—if you deliver this book to that woman over there. Blonde hair, black cloak.'

He felt his jaw tense as he allowed himself one fleeting glance in Grace's direction, the temptation to stare calling to him so irresistibly he clenched his hand into a fist.

Don't look. You have a plan.

The smaller man's eyes lit up at the unexpected bounty and he took the proffered book and pocketed the coin with the same swift, practised movement.

'Any message?'

Spencer paused, thinking quickly. The ache in his chest was slowly ebbing away, giving ground to the determination he had always been so proud of. Fresh hope, tentative but holding its head high despite the rising odds, unfurled to stoke higher the flames of battle curling in his belly.

You won't be keeping my wife's heart without a fight, Earls. If I can help Grace see she has other paths to choose, you can be damned sure I will.

'No details. Just tell her I know now what I must do.'

Looking up into Henry's face Grace felt her lip long to curl, but she kept her expression carefully blank.

Every nerve screamed to yank herself free of his insistent grip and push him away, but that would draw stares from those passing by and with another horrible plunge of her stomach Grace realised Henry knew it. She was trapped: either cause an embarrassing scene in the middle of a busy street or endure the nausea that brought clammy coldness to her skin at Henry's touch.

When a hand had reached for hers she'd turned with a smile, her heart leaping at the prospect of Spencer's return—only to check in sudden horror at the all-too-familiar face of the man looking down at her, who had taken advantage of her stunned dismay to draw her into his grasp and guide her unfeeling feet across to the other side of the road.

'It's been far too long since I had the pleasure of seeing you. Be assured, it is a pleasure indeed.'

A shudder ran through Grace's body as she watched the shapely mouth moving and blue eyes twinkle with the undeniable charm she had been so vulnerable to only months before. How could she ever have thought herself in love with him? The handsome façade so many had thought her fortunate to have attracted hid nothing of worth below its surface, although by the way Henry pressed her hand so closely to his coat he evidently still believed in its power.

He gave her cold fingers a lingering squeeze, sending another dart of revulsion to make Grace flinch. Not so long ago she would have given almost anything to hear him speak those words, but now all she wanted was to be free of his unwanted presence and once again find comfort in the circle of Spencer's muscular arms.

The thought of her husband's unshakeable strength gave Grace courage. He had found the will within himself to confess his deepest shame to her the night before; if he could overcome his own demons, she could face hers.

'What is it you want, Henry?' The words came abruptly, pleasing her that their sharpness cut him off in mid-flow. 'I seem to remember at one time my company was not as agreeable to you as it appears to be now.'

A flicker of surprise crossed the comely face and his fair brows twitched together in a frown. 'Come along. That isn't true. We've always been good friends.'

'Good friends? Is that what you believe?' Grace's eyes widened incredulously, hardly able to believe his arrogance. She had always liked his confidence, so opposite to her own shy reserve, and wished some of it would rub off on her.

How obvious his shortcomings are now I know how a real man conducts himself.

His 'confidence' was nothing more than brash self-satisfaction, pathetic when compared with Spencer's cool capability.

'Of course. It's because of that friendship I wanted to speak with you. I have an offer that I think you'll see the benefits of—for both of us.'

Grace gave her arm another experimental tug, only for the crook of Henry's elbow to tighten on her wrist. There seemed little chance of fleeing until the slyly smiling man released her—or until Spencer came charging over to force the issue, a prospect so alarming Grace felt herself swallow hard.

Please stay inside, Spencer, she thought desperately.

Don't come out and make an exhibition, even if that's what Henry deserves.

'What kind of offer?'

Henry's smile spread a fraction wider. 'George told me of his meeting with your new husband. He wasn't much impressed with his manners, I'm afraid, finding them far beneath your own—which suggests to me you wed him for reasons other than his company. I understand his house is very fine and George *did* remark on the quality of his tailoring—both signs of a comfortable income, unless I'm much mistaken.'

He sounded approving, oblivious to the sudden stiffness of Grace's wary frame. 'I have a few schemes that require generous financial backing. If you were to persuade Dauntsey to invest, I could put in a few recommendations for you to the right people, see if you couldn't find yourself invited to the occasional ball. You'd have to come alone, of course—my influence doesn't stretch to cover violent thugs—but for the sake of our friendship I might be able to manage a favour to you.'

A beat of silence followed, filled by the chatter of people moving past where Grace stood immobile with amazement, staring up at the man in front of her with no words to break the pregnant pause.

When she didn't answer Henry bent to murmur into her ear, lips almost brushing her skin to make it crawl. 'Wouldn't you like that? Wouldn't you enjoy seeing all your old acquaintances again and perhaps even—me?' His voice was like silk, soft and persuasive—and the most repugnant thing Grace had ever heard.

He must have been so sure of his success to let his guard down. In his careless vanity, certain victory was in sight, it was suddenly easy for Grace to remove her hand from its unguarded snare and slowly, deliberately, wipe it against her black cloak as though cleaning dirt from her fingers.

'No, Henry. I would not enjoy that. In fact, spending another moment in their company or yours is something I never wish to endure ever again.'

The pure shock that spread across his face wiped away all traces of his good looks, leaving behind only incomprehension that turned to anger as though she had slapped him. He reached for her hand again, but Grace stepped smoothly away, his fingers closing on empty air.

'What do you mean, no? Did you understand what I said?'

'Perfectly.' Grace smiled politely, feeling the blood thrumming in her veins at her uncharacteristic bravery.

Spencer's influence. I almost wish he could see me now.

'I understood perfectly, but I'm afraid I will have to decline. I have no wish to enter into any kind of arrangement with you and there's absolutely no chance I will be petitioning my husband on your behalf. He may not be the most amiable, I'll admit, but he's a good man and I will allow nobody to take advantage of that.'

The colour of Henry's face had darkened and his blue eyes stared with the barely suppressed bad temper of a spoilt child. All charm had deserted him and when he spoke his voice was thick with displeasure, shadowed by an unmistakable edge of—

Jealousy?

Could that be right? It might stem from the dent to his swollen ego at Grace's rejection, but the possessive flicker made her fight back a sudden perverse desire to laugh.

'You don't actually like him, do you? Surely having had your standards set so high previously you can't care for one such as him!'

Another bubble of suppressed laughter prevented Grace from replying straight away, but when she was sure she had herself back under control all she could do was smile. The truth was right in front of her, so simple and so pure she could hardly believe she had ever fought against it. It was the path to the most sincere happiness she could imagine and all she needed to do was reach out and take hold of it with both hands.

'I don't merely like him, Henry. I respect him, I care about him—indeed, I love him.'

Henry's lower jaw seemed in grave danger of falling off as Grace turned neatly on her heel and began to walk away. Her parting curtsy was elegant, definitive: the final interaction she intended ever to have with the one who had never let her into his cold, selfish heart. There was only one man whose affections she now craved and the moment had come for her to throw caution to the wind and declare her truth to him—whatever the consequences.

She'd barely set one foot on the steps leading to the bookseller's shop when she sensed a presence at her side, a furtive shape at the very edge of her field of vision making her pause. Had Henry sent someone running after her? He would have thought himself far too important to pursue her himself, no doubt; she spun quickly, unaware of her look of suspicion that turned to powerful interest as she took in a vaguely familiar face.

'Beg pardon, ma'am, but I've a message for you. From the Captain.'

The shady figure she had seen lurking outside Nevin Place waiting for Spencer held a book out towards her, shaking it so insistently she took it without a word. 'I'm to give you this and to tell you he's had to leave immediately on urgent business.'

Grace felt herself sag as a heavy blow of intense disappointment thudded into her chest. Spencer had gone away? So unexpectedly, so suddenly, and just as she'd made up her mind to lay her feelings for him bare with nowhere left to hide?

'He has gone already? Are you quite sure?'

Harwell nodded. 'He left at once. He would have told you himself, I'm sure, but you were deep in conversation with another gentleman and I think he didn't want to interrupt.'

The gasp torn from Grace's lips was ragged, a sharp breath that emptied her lungs entirely.

Spencer saw me with Henry? But why did he not approach?

Surely he would have recognised Henry and attempted to free Grace from his clutches as he had with George? Her mouth dried with a sudden sinking feeling and her heart skipped one painful beat before railing against her ribcage with vicious speed.

'Did he leave any word for me? Any explanation at all?'

She watched the shake of his head with despairing eyes. 'The Captain said only that he knew what he must do. Make of that what you will.'

Grace's stomach turned over in a hideous flip as she digested Spencer's message, sure now her sinking suspicion was correct. To some the words might have been cryptic, but to her their meaning was abundantly clear.

He had abandoned her. He'd seen her with Henry and among the confusion and still-raw events of the night had used it as an excuse to bolt. There was no way, surely, Spencer could genuinely believe she still had any yearning for the wretch she had loved before; how could he, when Grace had shown her true feelings so plainly, giving her husband the only gift she had left to give? She'd *trusted* him, had allowed him to wear down her defences so gradually, and still he had run from her when she dared let herself draw close.

Telling the truth about Will must have been a step too far and now he has turned away from me again rather than let me in. Seeing me with Henry just gave him the pretext he needed to retreat.

Perhaps it was a leap to jump to such an awful conclusion, but the memory of his words that morning told her all she needed to know. He hadn't wanted to discuss what he'd told her the night before—hardly the action of a man comfortable with what he had done. Fresh regret *must* have burned inside Spencer at his lapse of control and now he was seeking to limit the damage the only way he knew how, regardless of Grace's dismay when she learned of his escape.

All the trust they had built between them, the connection she had been so sure they had forged as they lay breathless on the study floor must now be in tatters, with Spencer apparently unwilling to even look upon her face. There was no other explanation for his abrupt departure on some mysterious business never mentioned before and now Grace's whole being froze with sickening despair that made her want to cry out loud.

It was an effort to force her dry lips to move and when she managed to finally bend them to her will the words came out as a croak. 'Did he at least say when he would be back?'

'No, ma'am, he didn't. He said nothing of returning at all.'

Chapter Fourteen

Grace looked up sharply as Cecily entered the parlour with the morning post in her hand, only to drop her eyes to her book once again at her sister's regretful shake of her head.

'Still nothing from Spencer, I'm afraid. Did he truly give no clue when you might hear from him? No message at all?'

The same page of *Evelina* Grace had stared at for the past half hour swam before her eyes as she commanded ready tears not to fall and when she spoke it was with a throat tight with unhappiness.

'None whatsoever. I know only from his associate that he had to leave without delay.'

Her younger sister's face showed a world of sympathy, although Grace didn't raise her eyes to see it. With her gaze fixed on the printed words before her she allowed her mind to revisit the day on which she had received them, the book she held so tightly a precious—if painful—reminder of its giver.

It had been almost a week since Spencer had disappeared into thin air and with every day that passed Grace cursed herself more desperately for her stupidity in allowing Henry even a moment of her time. If she'd only stayed with Spencer, hadn't left him when his emotional scars were so vulnerable and raw... She *should* have shaken Henry off at the first touch of his hand on her arm, defying the deeply ingrained desire to avoid making a scandalous scene that had lived within her all her life. If she had, Spencer might not have fled, taking her hopes for the future with him to who knew where.

Grace clenched her jaw against the emotion that wanted to burst forth, a wordless cry of pain that clawed at her insides and would not leave her be. She turned her head to look beyond the parlour's fogged windows to survey the wet street, some naïve part of her still hoping to catch a glimpse of the man who had stolen her heart even as the rest of her knew it was useless. Nevin Place had seemed so empty without its master, the lonely bed in which Grace had curled into a ball of misery on the first night Spencer had not come home somewhere she couldn't bear to sleep again. Perhaps it had been childish to seek the comfort of her family, but the sight of Spencer's silent study—and the rug in front of the cold fireplace—had brought hot tears to Grace's eyes and she had alarmed her poor mama by falling into her arms as soon as the cab had set her down on the doorstep of Number Four Regent Square.

She felt her mother's gaze on her now, but refused to meet it, wretchedness still circling in her stomach to make it rail against the breakfast she had been forced to take an hour before. It was a horrid sensation, distress making her feel as hollow as if her insides had been scooped out.

'Don't fret. I'm sure there's a perfectly good reason

Spencer has been unable to write. When your father had to go away on business it was sometimes above two weeks between letters and there was never any cause for alarm.'

Grace nodded, still focused on the rainy world on the other side of the glass as her innards churned with unceasing sorrow and sweet memories sent daggers to lodge between her ribs.

If only it was that simple.

They had found something real between them, she had been so sure of it. The picture of Spencer's face in the light of the dying fire, his eyes ablaze with feelings he had no need to explain haunted her, appearing behind her eyelids when she closed them to sleep and even now never a hair's breadth from her thoughts. All the emotion of that one night could not have been faked by either of them; or at least she'd thought. If only he would come home she could tell him the truth: that he had nothing to fear from confiding in her and that if he would allow it she would help him through the darkness of his agonising memories and the spectres of his guilt.

But in order for that to happen he would have to return and Grace turned away from the window again with despair making each breath a raw gasp of fire.

She turned a page, pretending to read while affecting not to notice the worried glances between her mother and sisters as they busied themselves with their embroidery. There was no need for Grace to spell out her feelings any more clearly; they knew her well enough to see her sorrow and even the far-off sound of the front door opening and closing again didn't interrupt their quiet concern.

The housekeeper putting Peg's cat outside, I imagine. I wish I could escape my thoughts so easily.

She couldn't even glance at her own hands without catching the glint of her wedding ring and from between the pages of her book peeped the portrait Spencer had sketched of her that sunny afternoon in the glasshouse. It lay between the leaves like a secret treasure, his signature scribbled in one corner to make her heart ache each time she surrendered to temptation and snatched another look. The memory of that day and the delicious words Spencer had uttered taunted her, precious yet painful in equal measure.

Footsteps on the other side of the parlour door prompted Mrs Linwood to finally shift her attention from Grace and she sighed with quiet relief. It was such an effort to control the twitch of her lips as they fought to turn down, to keep her eyes dry despite the tears that ached to fall in a river down pale cheeks. Hopefully the footsteps signalled the maid bringing tea, although the clock perched next to Lucy's chair showed it was still surely too early for such a thing as the door handle turned slowly and a figure stepped into the room.

Mr Linwood looked around him, taking in the five faces that stared back in mute disbelief. For a long moment nobody moved, each frozen to the spot by paralyzing shock—and then in a flurry of whirling skirts and thrown needlework all five descended upon him, their shrieks rebounding about the room in a cacophony of unbridled amazement.

'Papa!'

'Papa, you're home! How is it you are home?'

'Robert! What is this? Why are you here?'

Even Grace's troubles were momentarily forgotten as she clung to her father, the only part of him she was able to reach through the cluster of bodies that surrounded him one of his damp-coated arms. It felt thinner than she had known it before the gates of the Fleet had closed behind him, but the glimpses of his face she caught between her mama's kisses showed it to be a much healthier colour than when she had last seen it and filled out a little with obviously better rations. The improved quarters and food Spencer had insisted on providing had evidently worked wonders and Grace felt a sharp upswing of gratitude for the absent husband she wished was here to share in their joy.

Hardly a single sensible word was uttered for some minutes as faces were blotted with handkerchiefs and tears wiped from astounded eyes. It was only when Mr Linwood looked to be flagging that his wife came to her senses and ushered him towards a chair, allowing no refusal in the same way Spencer had been given no option on his visit.

'How can it be that you are here, my love? What has happened for this to be possible?' Grace watched as her mother perched on the arm of Papa's chair, her hands gripping his tightly as though to make sure he didn't disappear. 'This is the most wonderful thing. Are you home for good?'

There was an intake of breath from around the room as Mr Linwood nodded, the smile that stretched the creases at his eyes only widening at their wordless delight.

'I am indeed. I have returned to live with you all again and, what is more, I come as a man whose innocence is finally beyond refute.'

Another gasp was torn from five mouths to ripple around the room in a wave of wonder.

'How, Papa? What happened?' Cecily knelt on the floor next to her father, gazing up at him as though she still couldn't quite believe her eyes. 'How was your innocence proven?'

'Fisher and Armand arrived at the Fleet and confessed their guilt. It seems they were hunted down by a predator who would not rest until he had tracked his prey and caught them, leaving me a free man and the true villains where they belonged.'

The low flicker of some dim suspicion began to kindle at the very back of Grace's mind before she dismissed it with a brief frown. It was so unlikely, surely so implausible—a silly fancy she'd be a fool to give a moment of consideration. And yet…

Kneeling at her father's other side, she couldn't help the stirrings of the idea from growing.

But surely he would have no cause to do such a thing. For what possible reason would he undertake such an enormous task and so secretly? Seeing Papa again so unexpectedly has surely confused me; that's all it can be.

'Who was this person?' Mrs Linwood blinked back fresh tears welling in her blue eyes. 'Tell me his name so I might kiss him myself!'

Her husband squeezed her hand with tender affection before turning to Grace, who returned his look with eyes wide with dawning understanding.

'You already have his name. It was Captain Spencer Dauntsey—the husband of that very daughter who sits at my side, looking as though she knew nothing about it!'

Grace's mouth fell open, her mind completely blank as her mother and sisters stared at her in frank astonishment.

'You never let slip a word! I had no idea you could be so sly!' Margaret gaped as though she'd never been more stunned, her amazement turning to confusion at Grace's frozen shock.

'I didn't know.' Her voice was quiet, scarcely more than a whisper that had to battle against the sudden roar of frenzied activity that swept through her dazed mind. Her consciousness swung from empty to buzzing with too much commotion in the blink of an eye and Grace raised a hand to her heated brow as if cool fingers could soothe how it now burned.

It was Spencer, after all? That's where he went when he ran from me?

It couldn't be true. Spencer was filled with regret at their moment of closeness, appalled at any fondness he might have unwillingly felt for his new wife—wasn't he?

A creeping hope began to steal through Grace's nerves, a tentative gleam of light where before there had been only darkness.

Surely if he wished to distance himself from me he would not have done such a wonderful thing. He had already helped Papa so much—why would he have ventured further?

'Upon my word, I had no idea what Spencer intended when he left. Are you quite certain it was him?'

'Well, of course. He escorted me home himself! We stopped at an inn last night so I could change and make myself presentable, then Spencer was good enough to let me have his carriage—*your* carriage, I suppose, Grace—to bring me straight here this morning.'

Grace's spirits soared up to the sky at her father's words, but she forced herself to temper their wild climb despite the heat beginning to gather in her stomach. She could feel the questioning eyes upon her, although the room had begun to blur with the excitement she felt pulse within her that she feared she might not be able to contain.

'But he is not with you?' The sudden notion he might be waiting outside the room or somewhere else unseen kicked Grace's already thumping heart up another notch, but her father shook his head.

'No. He thought we would want this moment for ourselves. I tried to persuade him to come with me, but he insisted on getting down from the carriage at the crossroads and walking the rest of the way back to Nevin Place so I could travel on immediately.' He smiled, admiration hiding behind the upward turn of his lips. 'You weren't lying when you said he was determined. I'm not sure there's anybody in the world who could alter any course he's made up his mind to pursue—except for you, of course.'

Mr Linwood regarded his eldest daughter for a long moment, some unreadable expression on his drawn face that made Grace pull up short in her hurtling zig-zag between joy and intense confusion.

'Me?'

'It's quite a journey from London, as you know—plenty of time for talking. I already had the idea that behind that serious exterior lay a good heart. Listening to his praise of my daughter only convinced me further that whatever beats within his chest is now entirely in your keeping.'

The rest of the world fell away to leave Grace bathed

in a burst of sunshine, illuminating every shadowy corner of her soul to sparkle in its light. Her doubts dimmed beneath its power, brushed aside like cobwebs covering a window, and a bright glow of optimism seeped in that took root and wouldn't be denied.

He loves me? Can it be true?

The tentative hope raised itself higher above the parapet of her former unhappiness, reaching out to seize her fears in its burning grip and turn them to ash. It was determined, courageous and gave Grace the push to rise from the floor.

Every eye was on her as she got to her feet, hardly knowing how she managed to stand on legs that felt like water and a head that swam with blind wonder. Hands reached out to steady her as she stood, swaying slightly beneath the weight of her amazement—but she needed no help, suddenly knowing without question what she needed to do.

'Would you excuse me, Papa? I'm happier than I can say that you are home, but I need to see my husband.' The thrum of her pulse in her ears was like the rush of a waterfall, powerful and terrible in its unstoppable force. Every inch of her skin tingled with new life, vigour returning where only a half hour before she had felt nothing but despair.

I have to see him. I have to see if this is more than a dream.

'I must go at once.'

She made for the door, placing one foot in front of the other as though in a trance. All around her were stunned faces, delighted and amazed in turn, but nobody spoke until Mrs Linwood checked her with a gentle hand on her arm.

'But the carriage will have left for Nevin Place again by now. You'll have to wait until Spencer sends it for you.'

Grace looked into her mother's earnest face, at the eyes still wet with happy tears.

I can only hope the next time I cry is with the joy dear Mama is feeling at this moment.

The alternative was something Grace didn't dare consider as she allowed the smile she had been holding back to unfurl across her cheeks with its full strength.

'I'll walk. It's only a mile or so and I would walk ten times that if it meant reaching Spencer as soon as may be.'

Mrs Linwood's brows rose in vivid surprise, but she gestured towards the window where a thousand droplets skated down the cold glass.

'But it's pouring with rain! You can't possibly walk in that.'

Grace laughed. As if that made a difference now, with all that was at stake. 'Then I'll run! I *must* see Spencer and it must be at once. I've already wasted enough time on things that don't matter. Let me go to attend to something that does!'

Scandalised gasps escaped from more than one sister and even Mr Linwood looked a little uncomfortable at the new abandon shown by his eldest daughter. Mrs Linwood blinked rapidly, concern clouding her open face, but the smile never left Grace's lips as the delightful whisper of something she had never felt before cheered her on. She had a purpose, now: determination to reach her husband and tell him in no uncertain terms how he had won her heart. Nothing would stop her and the sudden blissful freedom that coursed through her

veins made her blood sing in harmony with her racing thoughts.

'But, Grace, consider. Running about in the rain?
What will people think?'

It was the influence of the man she wanted nothing
more than to run *to* that gave Grace her answer. She
looked down at her mother, seeing the worry and love
in her eyes and appreciating both beyond measure—
but no longer willing to live by the rules she had been
taught, with the best of intentions, to obey.

'*You* consider, Mama. What people think, what people say—if they are so shallow as to judge us by such
trifles surely we don't care for their good opinions. As
a wiser woman than I once said: society busybodies
will always find something to talk about. We shouldn't
care three straws—and that's my final word!'

Spencer bent his head against the rain lashing into
his face and kept walking, shouldering past the people
he met with barely a thought. His mind was too full to
allow anything else to enter it, fixed on imagining the
scenario that might be unfolding even now in a blue-
papered parlour less than a mile away. If he was growing steadily wetter it hardly mattered—only Grace's
reaction to his surprising success was important and
whether she might slowly be realising there could be
another man worth taking into her heart. Even if he
hadn't been trying to prove his worth Spencer would
still have intervened for Mr Linwood, of course—but
could there be a chance his doing so might have shown
Grace she had more than one path to happiness after all?

I've done all I can now. The rest is up to her.

It was an uncomfortable thought and one he tried

not to dwell on as he pulled his hat down on to his head more firmly and felt how sodden the brim had become. Getting down from the carriage and allowing his father-in-law to proceed alone had seemed like such a good idea at the time, but now Spencer grew closer to Nevin Place he reflected how sweet it would have been to see Grace's beloved face light up at the first sight of her papa. Joy brought such animation to her features, enhancing the loveliness he had come to admire so much and chasing away any suggestion she might not be the most beautiful woman in the world. How she had managed to eventually overcome his defences Spencer would never know, but there was no denying she had conquered him so completely, and now all he could do was wait with his heart in his mouth for her to make his life complete—or crush his hopes within one perfect fist.

If Henry Earls still reigned supreme in her affections even after Spencer had spent the better part of a week visiting dubious tavern after dubious tavern, tracking his prey to the two addresses provided by Harwell, then he would have to accept it. It would be more painful than he could imagine to see how his wife pined for another, doubtless wishing for a fair-haired head on her pillow in place of Spencer's dark one; there was still the very real chance he had lost, that any fondness for him he thought Grace might have developed paled into insignificance compared to the man she could not have. If that was the case his misery would be fathomless, another agonising loss to add to his list of trials…

But you might be getting ahead of yourself.

He tried to suppress his darkening mood, although

despair attempted to creep beneath the shutters around his dreams to snuff them out between cruel fingers.

While there's still a chance you shouldn't abandon all hope. Grace has never let you down—you should have more faith.

The imposing frontage of Nevin Place hove into view through the murk and Spencer felt his pulse skip as he remembered the last time he had approached from that direction during such bad weather. On that occasion Grace had barely seemed to want to touch him, steeling herself against the feel of his hand at her elbow even as she hurried along beside him with her quick, quiet step.

I had no idea then how much my life would change from that day on. If nothing else, I have Grace to thank for saving me from the wreck I could so easily have become.

The memory of her standing so sad and alone on the windswept Cobb overcame him again, so powerful it was suddenly difficult for Spencer to breathe. She'd looked so fragile, so in need of a friend—he would never regret stopping to help her, even if that decision led to a lifetime of unrequited love from which he knew there would never be any escape.

With the rain beneath his boots and a stiff breeze keening in his ear, it took a moment for Spencer to hear the sounds coming from behind him, a combination of pattering feet and laboured breathing, but it was only the alarmed glance of a man walking towards him on the flooded pavement that made Spencer turn.

Grace's hair tumbled about her shoulders, great swathes of curls springing free from their pins to surround her with a halo of wet gold. Her cheeks were ruddy and her lips parted on snatched breaths, coming hard like a horse galloping flat out. With her head bare and her eyes shining with some unnamed emotion she looked like a wild creature, an untamed changeling left in place of the prim and proper Grace that Spencer had come to love—but this strange woman was just as lovely and he found he had no words as they stood in the pouring rain and stared at each other as though fixed to the spot by some mysterious force.

More than one passer-by looked Grace over with disapproval, some bordering on scorn at her dishevelled appearance so at odds with the usual decorum of a well-dressed young woman. Spencer thought he heard a few muttered words, some low murmurs of censure from the elegant people who stepped round them with lips thinned at Grace's heaving chest and skirts held up away from her muddy boots, although everything else in the world was a vague blur compared to the vivid picture of his wife's upturned face.

She was the one to break the silence, bridging the gap between them with words he only dimly heard drop from her pretty lips.

'You freed Papa.' Her eyes were wide with innocent wonder, glittering with happiness that touched Spencer's soul even as rain flecked her face and darkened the flax of her hair. 'I've never seen my mother and sisters more shocked than the moment he walked through the door—thank you, truly, from the very bottom of my heart.'

Spencer nodded distractedly, trying to listen above the furious pounding of his heart as he watched her lace her fingers together as though suddenly ill at ease. She wore no gloves, he noticed belatedly—had she actually *run* from her parents' house all the way across town, not even stopping to catch up a pair or even a bonnet? The idea gave him courage, lighting the taper of his hopes to begin to smoulder and wish they could burst into leaping flames.

'And you? Were you surprised to see him likewise?'

'More than you'll ever know. It was the most wonderful thing to speak with him again, to hear all he had to say...'

Grace's voice tailed off and she swallowed hard as if the sentence stuck in her throat. When she managed to continue it was in a voice tight with strain, carefully level but thrumming with repressed emotion that made Spencer's spirits fly upwards towards the stormy sky.

'There was one thing in particular my father told me that I wanted to speak with you about right away. He said you'd got down from the carriage to walk home so I came after you as quickly as I could.'

A smile tried to tug at Spencer's lips, but he held it in check with great effort. Surely Grace would not have come hurrying after him in this growing storm without a good reason? It was so unlike her to appear so ruffled, cheeks still flushed and her hair more abandoned than he had ever seen it before—aside from the morning he had woken beside her on his study floor and felt the tangled threads of his life finally knit together beneath her skilful fingers.

'It must have been something important to send you running without even a bonnet in this weather. You look quite fierce!'

It was true: she *did* look like a new woman, filled with confidence that took his breath away. Her back was straight and her head held high, and she met his eye without shrinking from the warmth she must have seen in the set of his helplessly admiring expression.

'He said...' She hesitated, grey gaze fixed immovably on his as if trying to read something in the darkness of his eyes before she took the plunge and committed herself to her fate. 'He said he thought your heart was in my keeping. Why would he say that?'

A powerful blast of winter air worried at Spencer's clothes, trying to wrench the hat from his head and the coat from his back, but he hardly felt a thing as he stared down at the wife who had changed his life beyond recognition. She stood firm, rapt attention on nothing but him despite the tutting of passers-by and the rain steadily seeping through her black cloak, chin up with bravery that dared him to return its challenge. It was the moment for honesty, even if the prospect of winning or losing Grace's good opinion for ever now rested on a knife-edge with no guarantee which way it would fall. There would be no better time to abandon himself to his destiny and so he surrendered to it, finally giving himself up to whatever future his wife held in one small hand.

Spencer took a deep breath, squared his shoulders—and leapt into the fray with all the courage he possessed.

'Because it's true. Everything that I have, everything that I am—it's yours, Grace, if you want it. Body and soul, I am yours.'

There was a beat of silence, only rain trickling into the gutter in limitless streams.

And then—

Grace was as light as a feather in his arms and Spencer almost groaned aloud at the relief of touching her again. Her warmth through her soaked gown, the fragility of her frame, even the damp scent of her hair bewitched him all over again and as he cradled his wife against the solid breadth of his chest Spencer felt the tension that had held his muscles taut and aching for so long vanish without trace. The desire to keep her there for ever as a prisoner in his embrace overwhelmed him in an unstoppable tide, but surely a *prisoner* would not have thrown themselves so willingly into the arms of their captor—Grace nestled against him by *choice*, his dumbfounded mind knew with growing wonder, and he couldn't restrain himself from cupping her cold face in both hands and leaning down to cover her curving mouth with his own.

He drank her in as though she was the most expensive wine, although he knew he would now have no need of any such oblivion ever again. With Grace at his side he would be able to deal with his pain, confront it head-on and never allow it to consume him with its cruelty. The bitter sea in which he had been drowning for the past two years would run dry now Grace had hold of his heart, keeping it safe from all harm until the day they would be parted only by death.

His saviour stretched up on her tiptoes to wind her arms about his neck and pull him closer, her sweet lips stealing all words from his mouth. There was nothing Spencer could do but submit to their gentle insistence as the rain fell unceasingly down upon their heads and scandalised glances mixed with offended whispers fluttered unnoticed around them, unable to force their way into the bubble of pure joy the Captain and his wife stood within, locked in each other's embrace.

Grace swayed in his arms like a reed in a breeze and Spencer dropped his hands to grip her waist as she drew back a fraction, looking into his face with such dazed elation he had to battle the urge to pull her lips back to his. Instead he cradled her carefully, his breath still coming fast as Grace placed her hands on his cheeks to bring his forehead to rest on hers.

Nose to nose they merely watched each other for a long moment, almost afraid of the new truth that passed unspoken between them until Spencer pecked a kiss on to the end of Grace's pink nose to make her giggle, a sound more delightful than any he had ever heard before.

'When I saw you with Henry Earls, I thought—'

She interrupted him with a swift kiss of her own, mischief and pride mingling in her eyes to make them sparkle.

'You thought wrong. Henry was most displeased when I told him I wanted nothing more to do with him, or to spend another moment in his company.'

'Is that so?' Pride kindled inside Spencer's chest and he felt his admiration for this strange, spirited creature grow.

'It is. I've never seen him more surprised than when I refused to approach you on his behalf with the idea of investing in some of his schemes. He seemed unable to grasp the thought that I might care for you and quite speechless when I told him—'

Grace hesitated for a moment, fresh colour lighting her cheeks to make Spencer adore their softness all over again.

'What? Told him what?'

'That I didn't merely care for you. In fact—that I love you.'

Spencer's entire existence ground to a halt as

Grace's voice echoed in his ears, his every last hope and most precious dream distilled into those three short words. They were everything he had ever wanted, without even knowing it, and now he had heard them he could scarcely believe the shining truth.

'Do you truly mean that?' His eyes searched Grace's face, suddenly earnest as he watched her confirm his wonder with one shy nod.

'I do. There's nobody in this world that will ever come close to you.'

She gave a little squeak as her feet left the ground, but her surprise turned to a laugh of radiant happiness as Spencer lifted her with effortless ease to hold her against his chest. Her little hands came to rest on his shoulders and she laughed again as he spun on the spot, her wet cloak flaring and skirts flying in the most undignified manner imaginable. An elderly couple hurried past them with eyes firmly averted and two well-dressed ladies huffed by with clearly audible mutters of 'unbecoming' and 'shameful', although nothing else seemed to matter one jot as the Captain and his unexpected bride clung together and knew, beyond any possible doubt, that their suffering was over. Never again would Grace feel unwanted and scorned, too afraid to trust in the love of another; Spencer could grieve his losses without the cold fingers of guilt and regret snaking their way down his spine. In each other they had found what they had always needed—and so in two souls a fire blazed that no power on earth could extinguish.

Suddenly aware of his impulsive actions, Spencer carefully set Grace back on her feet and looked down at her, a little shamefaced at his lack of control.

You'll be for it now.

Declaration of love or no declaration of love Grace still had her standards, and he had once again exposed her to the disapproving mumbles of the *ton*.

'Sorry. I couldn't help myself. I suppose we'll have our first argument now as a truly married couple.'

His wife smoothed down the damp silk of her gown and twisted a wet ringlet back into place, the very image of a fastidious, well-bred lady—until she shot Spencer a gleam of pure mischief that fled straight to his bounding heart. 'Do you know, I really don't mind. You can do that again if you wish.'

Spencer blinked, amused and surprised in equal measure even as he itched to catch up the little imp before him and hold her closer once more. 'I thought you didn't like scenes. What about society?'

'Hang society. What's that to us?'

Grace smiled at the shock in his face and reached up to kiss him again.

* * * * *

If you enjoyed this story,
check out this other great read
by Joanna Johnson

The Marriage Rescue